ARIA
FOR
MURDER

ARIA
FOR
MURDER

A Julia Kogan Opera Mystery

Erica Miner

LEVEL
BEST BOOKS

First published by Level Best Books 2022

This novel is entirely a work of fiction. The names, characters and incidents portrayed in it are the work of the author's imagination. Any resemblance to actual persons, living or dead, events or localities is entirely coincidental.

Author Photo Credit: Stephen Dorian Miner

First edition

ISBN: 978-1-68512-198-3

Cover art by Level Best Designs

This book was professionally typeset on Reedsy.
Find out more at reedsy.com

Praise for Aria for Murder

"Erica Miner, the Agatha Christie of the opera world, continues the genre with a wickedly wonderful, fast-paced updated version of the former 1st book in the series, Murder in the Pit. Her brand new thriller, Aria for Murder, delights in every way, as plot twists and turns left my heart racing through the suspenseful dénouement. Miner's 21 years as violinist with the Met Orchestra gives credence to her knowledge of the opera house, both in front of and behind the Gold Curtain. This is simply brilliant writing. *Bravissima!*"—Richard Stilwell, international opera star

"A ruthless and clever killer haunts the Metropolitan Opera and the hidden recesses of Lincoln Center. Violinist Julia Kogan, a rising star in the pit, must unmask the murderer or become a victim herself. Erica Miner's richly satisfying *Aria for Murder* delivers a compelling mystery, replete with devious characters, glorious music, and plenty of behind-the-scenes dirty laundry. A musical and dramatic triumph. Bis! Encore!"—James W. Ziskin, Anthony, Barry, and Macavity Award-winning author of the Ellie Stone Mysteries. Edgar®, Agatha, and Lefty Award finalist

"A brilliant murder mystery set in the grandeur of the Metropolitan Opera House in NYC. Filled with nonstop action and vibrant color, this story will whisk you away to another world where you'll fall for the characters and yearn for more. I really loved this book. The opera background just filled me with so much joy. your background and scenery all played so strong with me! All in all, a brilliant work. Highly recommended."—Aaron Paul Lazar, *USA Today* Bestselling Author

"An expert in the opera world, Miner strikes a major chord!"—Gerald Elias, Author of *Devil's Trill*

Introduction

When Erica Miner asked me to read *Aria for Murder* and consider writing a blurb, I leapt at the chance. I'd read her other opera-themed mysteries and gladly accepted. From the first page, I fell headfirst into the story. The elegant prose; the lush descriptions of the music, the inner workings of the Met; the cast of memorable characters; and the thrilling mystery at the center of the book all conspired to keep me turning the pages. You'll find my humble attempt at praise somewhere on the cover.

You've probably come to *Aria for Murder* because you love grand opera. Or perhaps you simply enjoy a clever mystery. In either case, you've chosen well. The novel you're about to read opens with the emotional debut performance of Julia Kogan, a brilliant young violinist at the Metropolitan Opera. It promises to be a magical night she will never forget. But before the final curtain falls on this performance of *Don Carlo*, murder will take center stage.

To my knowledge, opera is one of very few—perhaps two or three—live artistic endeavors in which most of the performers are hidden from the audience. The musicians inhabit an underworld just out of sight beneath the stage, Their home's very name, "orchestra pit," suggests an abyss of damned souls. So it is befitting that an opera should be the setting for a murder mystery, and—what's more—that the main players emerge from a darkened pit. Yes, an opera house is the ideal location for a murder. But beyond the majesty of Verdi's *Don Carlo* and the grandeur of the Met, the eerie backstage passages, and dark corners of Lincoln Center add spice and intrigue to an already compelling setting.

Told with meticulous detail only a true insider can hope to know, *Aria for Murder* offers up the history, traditions, superstitions, and secrets of a world-class opera company through the eyes of the neophyte violinist, who's also something of a lightning rod for trouble. Julia's charm and talent shine in this story, endearing her to most, but not all, of the cast of characters. In fact, her vulnerability attracts those who wish her ill and then some. The resulting counterpoint gives us a perfect duet and a spellbinding mystery.

And now they're dimming the lights. The curtain is about to go up. Enjoy this gripping, informative, and richly satisfying read.

—James W. Ziskin, author of the Anthony, Barry, and Macavity Award-winning Ellie Stone mysteries

Characters

- JULIA KOGAN, a young neophyte violinist in the Metropolitan Opera Orchestra
- SIDNEY RICHTER, her avuncular best friend in the orchestra
- KATIE MA, Julia's roommate, and violinist colleague
- MATT REYNOLDS, head stagehand at the Met, Julia's admirer
- ABEL TRUDEAU, conductor of the orchestra, Julia's mentor
- PATRICIA WELLS, General Manager of the Met
- CHARLES TREMAINE, Met tenor; another of Julia's admirers
- LARRY SOMERS, NYPD Detective, and opera aficionado
- TONY ROSSI, orchestra personnel manager and conductor wannabe

Prologue

Chi è morto, voi, o il vecchio?
Che domanda da bestia! Il vecchio.
Who's dead, you or the old man?
What an idiotic question! The old man.
—Mozart, *Don Giovanni*, Act I

Collateral damage. Sometimes it just can't be avoided.

That was what his partner had told him. When you're trying to kill someone, other people can get in the way. It's not planned. It just happens.

Though the Metropolitan Opera's orchestra pit was the largest in the world, when the orchestration of an opera was vast, as in Wagner or Strauss, things could get quite crowded for the one hundred or so musicians squeezed together there. Tonight's Verdi was no exception. Grand opera at its loftiest, with plenty of brass, extra strings, and the like. He would do his best to hit his target precisely. But it wasn't an exact science. And if, under pressure, he was slightly off, well…

Tanto peggio, as they say in French.

He chortled to himself. Everyone in the Met knew *"tanto peggio"* was Italian, not French.

He salivated with anticipation as he lovingly cleaned his VAL Russian sniper rifle with its special bronze-bristled brush, and oiled and lubricated the ammunition chamber with the fine-spray One Shot gun cleaner and a cotton swab. He picked up the last tiny fragments of powder residue with an alcohol patch threaded through a needle attached to the brush. Then he polished the entire instrument with one of his special-order McAlister microfiber gun cleaning cloths.

If you look after your firearm, when the time comes, it will look after you.

A vintage model, no longer available, the VAL was precious, but not because of its monetary or historic value. It was his own personal Stradivarius: a thing of beauty, a state-of-the-art example of genius in design at its time, and still as reliable as ever. He knew that the cartridge of this rifle, with the immense power contained within its barrel, was capable of forcing a bullet to explode at a higher speed than a mere handgun: the kind of velocity he needed to accomplish his goal.

Lord knows I need something dependable—and powerful.

No one knew he kept the VAL right inside the opera house, practically under everyone's noses. To head off the possibility that they might install metal detectors at the Met—which everyone seemed to be doing these days—he had found the perfect hiding place for his beloved firearm, in a far-off corner away from prying eyes. It remained there, at the ready, just in case he needed it. No one was aware of its existence, let alone its hidden location.

Except me. And my partner.

And what better time for an assassination than opening night at the Met?

My partner is a brilliant planner. I will do my part. Justice will be served. Finally.

With a sigh, he wrapped his instrument in its plush chamois cloth and painstakingly laid it in its temporary resting place beside its smaller sibling, the Beretta.

It won't be long now, my trusted friend. It won't be long.

Chapter One

Quanto hai penato, anima mia!
How you have suffered, oh my soul!
—Puccini, *Tosca*, Act II

Julia threaded her way through the waiting crowds of patrons in front of the Metropolitan Opera House, her violin case strapped to her shoulder. She stopped for a moment to gaze wide-eyed at the parade of celebrities being disgorged from their limos onto Lincoln Plaza, and the paparazzi jostling each other to capture the ultimate photograph.

I can't believe I'm here.

As she approached the front entrance of the Met, Julia glimpsed the street violinist in his usual location, giving a passionate rendition of the fiendish showpiece, *Zigeunerweisen*. Despite his brilliant playing, he was ignored by the throng. He deserved something for his efforts.

She watched for a moment. Then she opened her violin case, extracted her violin and bow, and started to accompany him. Passersby began to stop and listen and toss bills into the violinist's open case. Julia and the violinist exchanged smiles. Then she packed up her violin and moved on.

How lucky am I to have a real job with a weekly paycheck?

This evening, the night of her first performance as a violinist with the Met Orchestra, Julia was seized by the desire to enter the opera house through the front doors on Lincoln Center Plaza rather than the stage door artists' entrance toward the rear of the theater. The revolving glass doors overlooking the plaza afforded a much more elegant entrance, and she desperately wanted to be among the opening night glitterati.

No stage door tonight. I go in with the paying customers.

Julia gently squeezed past a chic older patron in a fox stole and diamond necklace and inhaled the woman's heady perfume. From her position in front of the giant glass windows that revealed activity inside the Met lobby, Julia could see the distinguished cavalcade sweeping through the doors and up the circular Italian marble staircases, past the red velvet-flocked walls, and underneath the famed Austrian lead-crystal chandeliers.

She took a moment to admire the immense, towering forty-foot Chagall murals, the signature of the Met's façade that distinguished the Metropolitan Opera House from all others. Their brilliant colors displayed the French-Russian painter's genius to New York's Lincoln Center and to the world. Much as the Eiffel Tower represented the genius of late nineteenth-century French engineering, these exquisite paintings stood as a monument to music: inspiring admiration, and awe.

A pair of life-sized, glass-enclosed posters standing guard in front of the Met's massive glass doors heralded the evening's performance: "Metropolitan Opera, Gala opening night performance: Verdi's *Don Carlo*, Abel Trudeau, Conductor—Sold Out."

Something tells me things will never again be the same after this night.

Julia checked her reflection in the glass. The early autumn sun gave an extra gleam to her shoulder length chestnut brown hair and a sparkle to her deep brown eyes. She smoothed out a wrinkle in her V-neck black georgette blouse and was pleased to see that the cut of her black velvet pants made her petite frame look even slenderer than usual and a bit taller. She had always wished she could have added some extra height to her five feet-four inches, but her lack thereof didn't affect her violin playing, so she resigned herself to her petiteness.

As she gazed at the *Don Carlo* posters, Julia contemplated how she had overcome every possible obstacle to be there among the *crème de la crème* of New York musicians. But she knew in her heart that she owed her career to the great maestro: Abel Trudeau.

As her mentor, Abel had nurtured Julia's musical gifts since she was a child. Because of his unwavering attention, she had developed a single-minded confidence in her ability to function under pressure in auditions and performances, which gave her an edge over her fellow Juilliard students. Most of them resented her talent, not to mention her beauty. Her looks inspired jealous glances from female colleagues wherever she went. But Julia decided early on that making Abel proud far outranked the social acceptance of her peers.

Her mind wandered back to the day when Abel had witnessed her dazzling display of violin mastery in the Juilliard School's production of Britten's opera *The Rape of Lucretia*. He had praised her unstintingly and unbeknownst to Julia had placed her on the list of auditionees for an opening in the Met's first violin section. He then proceeded to coach her on her audition repertoire. Most of it, she could perform with ease. But a fiendish passage from Verdi's *Luisa Miller* Overture eluded her.

"I'll never get it right, Abel."

"As far as I'm concerned, you've got it right. You're ready for the Met."

"If I am, it's only because of you."

"No. It's because you have the gift of an artist's soul."

"The gift of an artist's soul."

She was so overjoyed at Abel's praise, she almost hugged him. She didn't, of course. She wasn't capable of physical contact with anyone. Not since the wrenching loss of her father twelve years ago.

But Abel looked after her and remained closer to her than any other person. Julia sensed that since he had no family of his own, perhaps she was his daughter substitute. If so, it was a role she was happy to play. Not even her perennial sadness at her father's passing could keep her from focusing on her goal: to please Abel and to be a part of his prestigious orchestra.

"Remember, Julia, never let anyone undermine your confidence in your abilities. And always think *beyond* the notes. Be true to the music, and to yourself."

Abel also taught Julia about letter designations of certain notes changing from language to language. Her favorite example was the note "B natural" in English, the equivalent of "H" in German. But Julia felt sure that his wise advice about notes referred to something else, something subtler. She was touched to the core that Abel had considered her worthy of sharing such precious information.

Maybe I'll understand better when I'm older and more sophisticated.

As Abel had predicted, Julia had been ready. She blew away her competition at the grueling round of auditions and won almost unanimous praise from the judges. At age twenty-two, she became the youngest member of the Met Orchestra.

I'll be in Abel's debt forever. There's nothing I wouldn't do for him.

* * *

Julia knew the evening ahead was going to be a long one, full of excitement. But a sudden yearning for her father replaced Julia's anticipation with intense pain. She deeply felt the lack of his presence that night, to see her fulfill her dream.

It just isn't fair.

A tear escaped her eye and clung to her cheek, glistening in the bright lights of Lincoln Plaza, and melding into the cascading jets of its famed fountain.

Chapter Two

O dolce notte, scendere/ Tu puoi gemmata a festa
O sweet night, descend/ Starlit on our celebration
—Verdi, *Un Ballo in Maschera,* Act I

As she disappeared through the revolving doors and into the Met lobby, Julia gave one last wistful glance at the patrons ascending the elegant staircase and headed toward the stairway that led to the lower level and the alley where the stage door was located.

The servants' entrance.

Life at the opera house appeared glamorous to the patrons and public at large, but Julia knew that she and her overworked cohorts in the Met Orchestra were just the hired help. The true megastars of this exhilarating world were the contemporary equivalents of Domingo and Pavarotti. Musicians were underlings, and no one was better at putting them in their place than Patricia Wells, the Met's formidable general manager whom Julia had dubbed "a barracuda in high heels."

Julia held a grudging respect for Patricia's running the Met like a well-oiled machine, but she had no love for Patricia's personality or for her spiteful attitude toward musicians. Most of the Met musicians had been honing their craft since early childhood, and without an orchestra, as Mozart had demonstrated in the movie *Amadeus,* there was no opera.

The orchestra was the lynchpin of the opera house, but high-and-mighty Patricia did not appreciate the magnitude of their contribution. She disdained the musicians as low-class drudges who were ungrateful to the

5

organization responsible for putting bread on their tables.

While Julia admired Patricia's *chutzpah* as a woman who had clawed her way to the top of her field, she could not abide the attitude of someone who had docked her own pay to attend her own father's funeral. Julia thought this behavior a perfect example of Patricia's lack of sensitivity.

She's barely a warm-blooded mammal.

Julia had grown up without parents most of her life, yet still maintained a commitment to compassion. Since losing her father, Sol, so suddenly and violently, she had never allowed herself to demonstrate physical affection. Her father's hand was the last she had ever clasped.

Putting such musings out of her mind, Julia entered the stage door and approached the security guard's station. She was not surprised when she noticed numbers of extra guards patrolling the area. Between the assemblage of stars onstage and bigwigs like New York's mayor rumored to be in the audience that evening, security was super tight.

Julia had heard that before the September 11 attacks, the guards were friendly and affable and even kibitzed with the personnel. Now, checking people out as they passed through was serious business, and the guards, sequestered in a bunker-like contraption high off the floor, no longer smiled. To enter, everyone was required to tap their ID card on a device that brought up all their info on a screen for the security guard to check and make sure they were who they claimed to be.

Julia had been a mere toddler when the horrific terrorist incidents had occurred, but the thought of this change in procedure and mindset still saddened her. She totally believed her older colleagues when they told her life in New York City, and at Lincoln Center, had never been the same since 2001.

Julia fished for her Met ID in her pocketbook, extracted it, and tapped it on the magnetic device. At that exact moment, Sidney Richter squeezed past her, waving his ID in haste, jostling her, and hurrying off without so much as an apology.

Julia was miffed. "Where are your manners, Sid?"

A jaded first violin section veteran in his late forties, Sid was Julia's frequent stand partner, and her best friend in the orchestra. Julia found his distinctive wire-rimmed glasses and curly, graying "wild man" hair oddly appealing, but she could not fathom how he managed to bypass the security procedure required of "normal" personnel. And he complained constantly.

"The pay is too low. The hours are too long. And why did Abel have to add the extra forty-five minutes of music to *Don Carlo*? Christ, it's already long enough."

Don Carlo was Julia's favorite Verdi opera. She inwardly agreed it was too long but still defended Abel. "You know he's a stickler for doing operas uncut, Sid."

Sidney had reason to object. Sitting through the longer operas irritated his diverticulitis, causing him to get up and rush to the men's room. From his seat toward the back of the pit, he was able to slip out without being seen from the audience. The other musicians griped, but as Sid was consistently protective toward Julia, she felt sympathetic toward him. Nonetheless, she frowned at the guard with mock bravado.

"How come he gets in with a wave but not me?"

Sidney flashed her a quick smile. "You're just a newbie. Give it a couple decades."

Julia rolled her eyes at Sid and pivoted back to the guard. "Is that fair?"

But when she turned back, the older violinist had already dashed through the gate and disappeared down the stairway toward Pit Level. Julia scurried to catch up with him.

Oh, Mister Rabbit...

* * *

As she headed downstairs, Julia stopped to watch from the wings as Patricia calmed the nerves of the evening's lead tenor, Giuseppe Masini, while the harried wardrobe mistress fussed with his costume. Julia couldn't help but notice that Patricia's elegant turquoise couture gown set off her slim stature, steel-blue eyes, and perfectly coiffed blond hair to maximum effect. She had often observed the way Patricia masterfully stroked Giuseppe's and other opera stars' egos.

"The Maestro will be watching you like a hawk, Giuseppe. Don't worry. *Non preoccuparti.*"

"*Grazie*, Patrizia, you are *Regina*, a queen among general managers."

"Ah, you are too generous, Giuseppe."

It was a scenario of dramatic proportions rivaling the operatic performance itself and a familiar drill at the Met. Opera, after all, was the epitome of drama. To her left, Julia spotted Charles Tremaine, whom she knew as Giuseppe's perennial understudy, glowering at the star tenor. Seeing Charles, Patricia shot him a burning glance. He turned and stalked off.

Patricia corralled head stagehand Matt Reynolds. "Tell Charles not to stare at Giuseppe, Matt. He's already jumpy."

"I'm not sure my union allows the general manager to order around the head stagehand, Patricia."

"Oh, it does. When my lead tenor's sanity is at stake. "

Matt frowned. "Anything else, Patricia? A glass of Chianti Classico for Giuseppe? Maybe something stronger for you?"

Patricia's nostrils flared. Matt escaped quickly.

Julia reluctantly tore herself away from this spellbinding tableau, descended the dimly lit stairway, and passed through the noisy, fluorescent-lit area one level below the stage. Alternately called A-Level, Pit Level, or Orchestra Level, this was the orchestra's hub located just a few steps from the pit entrance. Musicians signed in on a list posted near the men's locker room entrance and milled about during pre-performance frenzy and intermissions. The women's locker room was discreetly separated from the men's by a long hallway.

The conductor's dressing room was close by, so the musicians also could observe whoever visited the maestro. Patricia was seen there frequently, as were nervous solo singers, management types, and others who felt welcome in the conductor's inner sanctum.

The pit also was accessible from the opposite side via a low-ceilinged tunnel strategically situated near the company cafeteria. The café was one of the few places in the opera house where musicians mixed with people from Stage Level: choristers, stagehands, ballet dancers, and solo singers. Even illustrious tenor Juan Diego Flórez had made appearances there.

Julia had confided her excitement to Sidney the first time she saw the star up close. "He smiled at me, I'm sure of it."

"Those Latin types can smell a young, inexperienced chick a mile away."

Julia bristled at the word "inexperienced" but decided to let it pass.

Most of the time, however, orchestra members stayed sequestered in their own little world, a planet apart from the real guts of the opera house, in Julia's opinion.

Julia glanced at the date at the top of the sign-in sheet.

September 29. One I'll always remember.

Julia scanned the sheet for Sid's name and glanced around. He was nowhere to be seen, but she was embarrassed to find a small "heart" symbol scrawled next to her name. Looking to her right, she spied cute head stagehand Matt Reynolds smiling at her from the opposite side of the hallway. She was wondering how to react when a familiar, scolding voice interrupted her.

"Haven't I told you not to let him deface the sign-in sheet with his little love notes? People are beginning to notice."

Tony Rossi, the orchestra's personnel manager, was glaring at her. A wannabe conductor, he walked around waving a baton, with which he tried to corral the musicians.

"It's not my fault, Tony. Why don't *you* tell him?"

"Is that any way to talk to your boss on your first night?"

"Should I wait until my *second* night?"

He didn't laugh. "I don't have time for this." Tony flapped the baton in her direction. "Just tell your boyfriend to cease and desist."

"He's not my boyfriend."

Julia turned around. Matt had disappeared. Realizing she couldn't afford to anger her boss so early in the game, she decided to suppress any further protest.

"Miserable stagehand," Tony grumbled to himself loud enough for Julia to hear. "Just because he played clarinet as a kid, he thinks the Met owes him a living."

As she tried to escape in the opposite direction, Julia slipped on the well-polished floor and felt her feet go out from under her. She clutched her violin protectively. As suddenly as he had vanished, Matt reappeared at her side and grabbed her around the waist as she went down.

"Are you okay?"

"Me? I've been taking care of myself most of my life." Blushing, Julia gently pulled away and tried to regain her composure. "It's just opening night jitters."

Matt lowered his voice. "You should be more careful. An opera house can be a dangerous place. You'll find out after you've got a few more years' experience."

There it was again, that word. "Experience."

Someday I'll show all these guys I can hold my own with any "veteran."

Julia took off before she could do any further damage to herself or her violin.

* * *

After convincing Giuseppe he was a twenty-first century Caruso, Patricia made her way to Abel's dressing room and peeked in the door.

"I just wanted to wish you *'merde'* for tonight, Maestro."

Wishing someone *"merde"* was the operatic equivalent of saying, "break a leg."

"One moment, Patricia. I just wanted to make sure you received that interoffice mail I sent up this afternoon."

She stepped inside. "Oh? I didn't see anything cross my desk from you."

A shadow fell over Abel's face. "You're certain?"

"Quite certain. Now, if you'll excuse me, I have a baritone to appease."

Patricia withdrew, closing the door behind her. The moment she was gone, Abel hurried over to the piano, picked up a piece of music, and started to scribble on it.

Chapter Three

Non esser, gioia mia, con me crudele:
lasciati almen veder, mio bell'amore
Don't be cruel, my treasure:
I beg for one glance, my beloved.
—Mozart, *Don Giovanni*, Act II

O n her way to the women's locker room, Julia stopped in front of Abel's dressing room. She glimpsed the *"Maestro Trudeau - Do Not Disturb"* sign posted on the door and felt a little flutter of excitement as she glanced at her watch.

Half an hour, and he'll give the downbeat for my first performance.

Even with the door closed, she easily could distinguish the raised voices from behind it as Abel and Sidney's.

"You son of a bitch!"

"For God's sake, Sidney, keep it down."

"You said you'd leave her out of it! She's too precious to risk anything happening to her."

Abel lowered his voice. "I had no choice."

"Over my dead body."

Julia knew about the personality conflict between Sidney and Abel but couldn't comprehend what caused it. Yes, Sid was hotheaded, but the discord between these two all-important men in her life made her uncomfortable. She thought about the fact that Abel was a few years older, and thus a bit wiser, than Sid, as she struggled to make out what they were saying.

"You and I go back long enough to understand that this changes everything, Sid."

"Yeah, well, I told you long ago this mess would come back to bite you."

"Perhaps. But if something happens to either or both of us, someone has to know the truth. And that someone must be Julia."

They're fighting about me?

"How are you going to tell her without scaring her to death? She's had more than her share of troubles."

"I've found a way. All you have to do is deal with it."

"Deal with it? Up yours, Abel." Sid's voice escalated. "If anything happens to Julia, I swear, Abel, I'll write a whole new finale to your opening night!"

A whole new finale—what does that mean?

"The trouble with you, Sidney, is you think you're too damned important." Abel's voice was so low and menacing Julia could hardly hear it. "No one is indispensable around here. Now get the hell out of my dressing room. We've got a show to do."

"Curtain for *Don Carlo* in thirty minutes."

The sudden booming sound of the P.A. system made Julia jump. Then the door opened. Sidney stormed out of the dressing room, slamming the door behind him, and ran right into her.

"How long have you been there, kid?" he demanded.

His dark tone alarmed her. She struggled to keep calm. "What's going on, Sid? Why were you and Abel going at it again?"

"Since when do you answer a question with a question?"

"Since I'm Jewish." Julia tried to charm him with a smile, but his expression remained grim. "Can't you two just call a truce already? Please? You're acting like a jerk."

Julia could tell she'd won him over from his sheepish grin. "Look, kid, it's what parents do."

Tony disrupted their caring moment, tapping his baton against his palm in quick, tense gestures. "Time's getting short 'til curtain. You two better hustle."

Sidney glared. "Don't you ever get tired of ordering people around, Rossi?

12

Get off my case."

"I'm the orchestra manager. It's my job to be *on* it."

Sidney turned, spied Matt lurking by the pit entrance, and shot him a lethal glance. "Mind your own business, Reynolds."

Matt blanched and rushed away. Julia could see Charles approach Sidney balancing a full cup of coffee in one hand. Sidney turned abruptly, practically knocking over both Charles and the cup.

Charles clutched the cardboard container tightly. "Whoa, take it easy, *Maestro.*"

Julia knew Sid had never picked up a baton, so she couldn't quite understand Charles's reference, but when he returned Julia's shy glance with a smile, she blushed. She had to try hard not to stare at him. His movie idol looks reminded her of vintage photos she had seen of legendary tenor Franco Corelli: statuesque, slim, with a broad-shouldered frame, jet black curly hair, inquisitive eyebrows, and eyes so soulful they could make a woman melt into a puddle on the floor.

Julia was aware that Charles hung out with musicians and stagehands, supposedly to fend off his own bitterness at constantly being passed over for big roles. She sympathized with Charles's plight but couldn't understand why he blamed Abel for it.

"Hey, give me that," Sidney said, indicating the cup. "I need it more than you do."

"Can you handle it? With your diverticulitis?" Charles asked.

"It's an understudy's duty to provide overworked musicians with their 'fix.'"

"Since when?"

"Since I have to be in the pit and you don't have to be anywhere anytime soon, thanks to..." Sidney jerked his head in the direction of Abel's dressing room.

"That was unnecessarily harsh, Sid, wouldn't you say?" Charles discreetly indicated Julia and lowered his voice. "Better not bring up Abel in front of his protégée."

Sidney grabbed the cup and took a gulp.

"And don't worry about paying me back for the brew, Sid," Charles added. "You can make it up to me later. I'll think of something."

Charles's grin made Julia's heart quiver, but she kept her composure—outwardly.

Sidney scowled at Charles. "And don't call me 'Maestro.' I'm no conductor."

"It's a term of endearment."

Julia suppressed a smile at Charles's Rat Pack smirk. She, too, felt the term "maestro" should be reserved for conductors, the great ones at that. But she couldn't help thinking Charles's misuse of the phrase was apt. Sidney's strong opinions on everything gave him an air of authority.

The door to the real maestro's dressing room opened. "Julia, come in, please."

Abel did not look at the others. They all stood still, caught off guard by his unexpected appearance. Julia overcame her astonishment, walked into Abel's dressing room, and closed the door behind her. The rest of them continued their conversation as if nothing had happened.

Chapter Four

Zdes chto-nibud ne tak!
Yevo ochei bluzhdane sulit ne dobroe
There's something wrong here!
The wild look in his eye bodes nothing good.
—Tchaikovsky, *Pique Dame*, Act II

I n the intimacy of Abel's world, arguments and overbearing orchestra personnel managers were easy to forget. On her way in, Julia had caught glimpses of Abel's self-assured image, looking down from photos on the wall showing him with the world's greatest opera stars. With his slightly frizzed grey hair and rimless glasses, Julia thought Abel looked like an older version of Sidney, though she knew they were not related.

Julia was unaware that Abel had just crumpled up a piece of paper and angrily flung it into the trash. Instead, she gazed at the beautiful marble chess set he always kept on a low glass table near the door. As usual, a game was in progress. She studied the board briefly. Then she spoke.

"Rook C-5, C-7."

Abel picked up the black King's rook, positioned it two rows away, and removed a white pawn. "Your powers of observation are as keen as ever, Julia."

Julia's father, Sol, had taught her to play chess when she was five. Like Sol, Abel, a true renaissance man, was gifted in both music and chess and also found time to pursue his hobby of amateur photography. Julia's admiration for Abel's abilities was limitless.

Abel checked to make sure the door was shut. Then he turned to Julia. "I'm sure you're wondering why I called you in, Julia. First, I wanted to tell you that your work in pre-season has been outstanding. I have every confidence you will be the Met's number one violinist someday, our concertmaster." He paused and lowered his voice. "Sol would be so proud."

Hearing her father's name, she bit her lip to stem her tears. "Thank you."

Abel plucked a small box from his desk. "A modest gift, for your debut, created especially for you. May it give you blessings, for this memorable night and many more."

Julia was overwhelmed. Feeling as thrilled as Sophie, receiving the silver rose from Octavian in Act II of *Der Rosenkavalier*, Julia accepted the box and, hands shaking, lifted off the cover. Tucked inside, nestled in delicate tissue paper, was a beautifully wrought violin-shaped pin, enameled in bold colors.

She gasped. "Oh! It's magnificent."

Then Abel opened the piano bench, lifted out a manila folder, and handed it to her. On the title line was written, *"Song to Julia, by Abel Trudeau."* Added at the bottom, boldly lettered in black sharpie: "Open *after* tonight's performance."

"Maestro, I…" Julia struggled to find words. "I don't deserve this."

"But you do. I've believed in your musical gifts ever since your father brought you to play for me when you were a child. I promised him I'd look after you, to nurture your talents and gifts. Mentoring you has been one of the great pleasures of my life. This song expresses what that honor has meant to me."

Julia smiled her gratitude. She took a closer look at the bottom of the page, where Abel had scratched out some notes and scribbled in some others.

"Even Mozart made last-minute changes," Abel said with a wink.

Julia started to open the folder, but Abel stopped her. "No peeking just yet. All I ask is that you bring more of who *you* are to your playing."

"I'm not sure I know how to do that."

"Just think about it. We'll talk more next time."

"And will you also tell me 'next time' what it means to 'look beyond the notes?'"

Abel smiled. "Yes, Julia. I promise."

At that moment, Patricia waltzed in, her icy beauty emphasized by the dazzling diamonds at her ears and throat.

"I stopped by to wish you luck, Maestro." Patricia eyed Julia. "Corrupting minors, Abel?"

Julia felt herself blush. "Thank you for the gifts, Maestro. And for being my mentor."

Gathering up the box, the music, and her violin case, she hurried away, her eyes sparkling as brightly as Patricia's gems. Despite her embarrassment, Julia still felt elated.

Whatever Patricia thinks about me, or my relationship with the maestro, this is my special moment, and neither she nor anyone else can spoil it.

Abel glared at Patricia. "Is knocking not in your job description, Patricia?"

She dismissed his query with a wave of her bejeweled hand. "I certainly don't think bickering at full volume with orchestra musicians is in yours."

Patricia poised herself atop his desk, crossed her legs, and smoothed her hair. She narrowed her eyes at Abel. He recognized this as a signal that she expected him to concur.

"If you're referring to Sidney, he's my problem."

"I wouldn't want anything to spoil opening night."

"With things in your capable hands, nothing will." He sat down at the grand piano. "Now, if you'll excuse me, I have to warm up."

Abel ran his fingers over the keys with a maestro's assurance. Patricia didn't budge but remained silent. Ignoring her, he played on, rocketing through his arpeggios with an ease that would make most pianists weep. After a moment, he stopped and looked up. "Is there something else, Patricia?"

She replied evenly. "You've told me before that you had him under control."

"I do have him under control."

"Then why were you heard all the way down the hall, arguing before a performance, with the orchestra and stagehands milling about? That's not what I would call 'controlled.'"

"Stop worrying."

"Oh, but I do worry." She pulled a monogrammed silver cigarette case and matching lighter from her purse. "I worry very much. Especially about you."

"If you're referring to the latest missive from my mystery non-admirer...'" he hesitated, frowning. "I tossed it in the trash. *That's* not your problem, Ms. General Manager."

He shot a venomous glance at the cigarette case and lighter. She returned the items to her bag with an elegant flick of the wrist. "Oh? I beg to differ, *Maestro*."

"Excuse me, Maestro. Ms. Wells."

Patricia looked up to see Abel's handsome, dark-haired young valet enter from the bathroom toward the back of the suite carrying a neatly pressed tuxedo jacket and a Kevlar "Execuvest." When he started to help Abel into the vest, Patricia raised her eyebrows.

"But I see you're in good hands with Damon. And in case we don't see each other later—*merde*, darling. Or should I say, '*In bocca al lupo?*'"

"*Crepi il lupo.*" Abel didn't know whether Patricia would laugh or grimace at his retort to "In the mouth of the wolf," the phrase often used by opera aficionados for wishing luck. But no doubt she was aware that "*Crepi il lupo*" meant "Kill the wolf."

Patricia merely raised her eyebrows. "How appropriate, my dear Abel." She slid off the desk, glanced at the valet, and flashed a provocative smile. "He's cute. We should share him."

Patricia didn't see Abel's grimace follow her as she swept out of the room, closing the door behind her. Once outside, she pulled the silver case and lighter from her bag and lit a cigarette. With a toss of her head, she made her way down the empty hallway, followed by a wisp of smoke, her heels clicking on the slickly polished concrete floor.

* * *

When Julia appeared outside Abel's dressing room, she was surprised to find Charles waiting.

"I see you had a confab with the maestro, Julia. Is everything okay?

Sometimes he can be a bit brusque."

"Oh, he's been mentoring me since I was a fledgling violinist. He's never been anything but kind to me."

"You're lucky to have him in your corner. He and I have been a bit at odds lately."

"I can't imagine why, Charles. Your singing is superb."

"It's not my singing, it's—"

"Yo, Charlie."

Frank Bernini sidled over and placed his arm around Charles's shoulder. "Got a few? We need to talk about..." Frank peered at Julia. "Who's this?"

"Frank, meet Julia," Charles said. "She's a newbie. I hear she plays a mean violin."

Julia had heard about Matt's assistant Frank. He was older than Matt and nowhere near as affable. His unmistakable Bensonhurst accent, gruff manner, and coarse looks put off most people, and he especially tended to belittle the musicians. Julia couldn't understand what the handsome, talented patrician tenor had in common with a plebeian like Frank, but she imagined the stagehand lent a sympathetic ear to Charles's gripes about Abel, and probably about Patricia, too.

"Well, *Julia*, mind if I borrow Charlie?"

"Of course not."

Julia watched the two men walk off, Frank whispering to Charles as they went.

"Now you're hanging with stuck-up orchestra players, Charlie? I guess it's not her violin playing you're interested in. Am I right?"

Julia was sure Frank wanted her to hear every word. She made a mental note to stay as far away as possible from him.

Chapter Five

Un nobile esempio è il vostro...
Al cielo attingete dell'arte il magistero che la fede ravviva!
It is a noble example you give...
You draw from heaven the mastery of art to revive the faith of men.
—Puccini, *Tosca*, Act I

The women's locker room was Julia's oasis. A spacious, well-lit carpeted area with rows of lockers, mirrors, and overstuffed sofas, it was her haven from the bare concrete floors, sterile fluorescent lighting, and overall cacophony of the rest of Pit Level. Despite the female musicians changing clothes, adjusting makeup, and chatting, the space was relatively tranquil.

Julia laid her violin case on the bench in front of her locker, then perched on a sofa in a quiet corner away from prying eyes. She opened the box Abel had given her, carefully lifted out the violin pin, and fastened it to her blouse.

Then she gazed at the folder. Unable to resist temptation, she opened it. Breathless with wonder, her eager eyes drank in the notes. The thought of playing through the piece and savoring its content thrilled her.

She peered at the "Continued on Page Two" written toward the bottom of the page. But there was no page two. On further inspection, she found a hastily scrawled note underneath the "Continued" that alarmed her: "If anything happens to me, you'll find answers in the music."

What?!

"Orchestra to the pit, please," came the call from the P.A. system.

Confused and conflicted, Julia hurriedly placed the folder in the zipper compartment of her violin case. She had no choice but to rush off. Her debut performance was about to begin. She would have to wait till afterwards to return to the puzzling song. It was what Abel had wanted her to do anyway.

* * *

Julia negotiated the tangle of chairs, music stands, and noisily tuning musicians crammed into the pit. She stopped at Abel's conducting podium when she noticed his baton positioned at the top of his musical score was a bit askew.

She straightened the baton so that it would be perfectly centered. Then she continued to her chair toward the back of the first violin section, taking a deep breath to quell her butterflies, extracted her violin and bow from her case, and started to warm up. Julia was determined to perform each note with the perfection Abel demanded.

Soon every chair in the pit was filled, except the one next to Julia that was supposed to be occupied by Sidney. When he still did not appear, Julia placed her violin and bow in the case and started to get up to look for him. If he wasn't there, she needed to find out why.

At that moment, Sid rushed in and parked himself next to her. She let out a sigh of relief.

"Thank God! Where've you been?"

Sid ignored her query. Julia pulled out her violin and started to tune again, struggling with her ill-fitting, stubborn tuning pegs.

"When are you gonna get new pegs?" Sid asked.

"When you stop nagging me about the old ones."

"I've seen you lift weights. You can do this yourself." Sid grabbed the violin, easily turned the pegs, and handed it back to her. "I might not always be here to do it for you."

"Wait. What? Should I be worrying?"

Again, Sid did not reply. Julia decided to let it go for the moment when the concertmaster, Daniel, ascended the podium to tune the orchestra. In every orchestra she had played in, Julia always paid close attention to the concertmaster, whose role was of prime importance. As the *primo* violinist, he or she was responsible for leading not only the two violin sections but also for taking over when the conductor was occupied with happenings onstage, or if a "train wreck" was about to occur in the orchestra. Julia was especially aware now that Abel had planted seeds in her head of her possible future as a concertmaster.

As the house lights dimmed, Julia watched the famed crystal chandeliers ascend to the ceiling of the cavernous opera house. The glorious moment of her Met orchestra debut had arrived. It was impossible to contain her excitement.

"Here goes, Sid."

But the butterflies in her stomach escalated when she saw Tony coming toward her.

Oh, no. What have I done now?

"Last minute change," Tony told her. "Third chair just went home sick. Move up."

Julia peered at the front of the first violin section, panicked.

"What? Me, one row away from Abel? But I can't possibly—"

"Evidently, he thinks you can. Get going, it's almost curtain."

As a neophyte, it was normal for Julia to be placed toward the back of the section. She aspired to move up in the ranks gradually, but she never expected to be chosen to replace a key player on her very first night. She had no choice but to obey.

Overcome with trepidation, she rose, grabbed her violin case, and followed Tony to the front of the first violin section, trying to avoid the resentful stares from the other violinists she passed on the way. Julia glanced back at Sid, who flashed her a "you can do it, kid" thumbs up. Then she took her new position and focused on the work at hand.

This is turning out to be an opening night to remember.

Chapter Six

Die Hoffnung schon erfüllt die Brust, mit unaussprechlich süsser Lust...
Hope already fills my breast with inexpressibly sweet delight...
—Beethoven, *Fidelio*, Act I

"Conductor's cue, everyone."

The stage manager announced his orders from his microphone at stage right just as Patricia stationed herself nearby to watch, as was her usual backstage habit.

Moments later, Tony ushered Abel into the pit. The audience burst into applause as he mounted the podium. Motioning the orchestra to rise, Abel turned to the audience, acknowledged them with a gracious bow, and turned back to the orchestra. When he noticed his baton perfectly in place, he flashed a knowing smile to Julia. She returned the look, gesturing happily at her violin pin.

The musicians took their seats. The theater became silent. Abel raised his baton, and as the orchestra began to play the Prelude to Act One of *Don Carlo*, the curtain rose. Terrified of being anything less than perfect in such an exposed position in the section so close to Abel, Julia had to concentrate extra hard. But once her performance became infused with her heart and soul, her nervousness dissipated.

Giuseppe sang the title role of Don Carlo, the tragic prince whose father, King Philip of Spain, steals away Elisabetta, Carlo's intended, to be his queen. Carlo never gets over losing her, even when his closest friend, Rodrigo, urges him on to the nobler endeavor of liberating the Flemish people from Philip's tyrannical rule. Eventually, Philip conspires with the Grand Inquisitor, who suspects Rodrigo and Carlo of plotting to incite a Flemish riot, to kill both men. But the strange and mystical intervention of the ghost of Carlo's ancestor, Carlo Quinto, saves Carlo from certain death.

As Giuseppe made his entrance, Julia spied Charles watching from the backstage wings. She could see the resentment in his eyes but couldn't blame him for it. And she had to stay alert.

"*Al chiostro di San Giusto, ovè fini la vita l'avo mio Carlo Quinto,*" Giuseppe sang.

"At the monastery of San Giusto, where my ancestor Charles V finished out his life." Julia repeated silently to herself, ever conscious of the libretto she had studied.

When the time came for the Act Three prison scene several hours later, Julia's energies had flagged, but her admiration for both Verdi and Abel had not.

How does Abel do this night after night? Is he superhuman?

Julia heard a shuffling sound toward the back of the section and took her eyes off the music for a brief instant to glance behind her. When she saw Sidney clutch his stomach and hastily leave the pit, her anxiety rose. Five hours of performance were grueling under any circumstances.

But for someone with Sid's condition, it must be unbearable.

* * *

Suspended in the highest reaches of the theater, the viewing room was the exclusive domain of directors, set designers, and other company members to watch rehearsals and performances, either for critical purposes or for their own entertainment. These non-performers could observe onstage spectacles in complete privacy. The sliding glass windows overlooking the theatre allowed a bird's-eye view but were built so that outsiders could not easily see inside.

This opening night, the viewing room was closed for repairs and off-limits for everybody. That made it easy for the shadowy figure to use lock clippers to break open the padlock during the third act without being seen or heard, unfold a VAL Russian Sniper rifle, poke it through the sliding window, and aim it toward the pit.

* * *

Julia always had to prepare herself for the dramatic moment when Don Carlo's best friend Rodrigo, sung by baritone Roberto, comes to warn him of a dangerous plot against Carlo's life.

"Per me giunto il dì supremo," sang Roberto. *"Il tempo stringe. Rivolta ho già su me la folgore tremenda! Le prove son tremende! I fogli tuoi trovati in mio poter son chiari."*

"For me, the supreme hour has come. Time is short. I have drawn the dreaded thunderbolt upon myself! The evidence is damning! Your papers found in my keeping are clear proof."

An assassin wielding a medieval rifle, or *"arquebus"* moves stealthily onstage to fire at Rodrigo. Just as he sings, *"ed io morire per te—*and I to die for you," he falls to the floor, mortally wounded.

As much as she felt for Sidney, Julia snapped to attention when Abel's impassioned conducting gestures increased in urgency. It was almost time for the gunshot heralding the assassination of the baritone's character onstage. Julia girded herself. The first time she had heard the onstage shot during rehearsal, it was so loud it had rattled her. Worse, she'd missed several notes.

"Why do they make it so loud?" she'd asked Matt one day during rehearsal break.

"The decibel level of stage rifles is impossible to control. You never know how loud it's going to be," he'd explained. "At least they're shooting with blanks."

Armed with this knowledge, Julia readied herself in advance for the shock, though she was comforted that stage rifles used blanks. But as she steeled for the coming blast, something caught her eye: a metallic glint coming from the upper reaches of the theater.

For a moment, her eyes darted upward. But worried about losing her place, she forced her gaze back to her music. When the crack of the rifle burst out a moment later, it sounded twice as loud as usual, and she reeled from it.

But her discomfort turned to terror when she looked up to see Abel slumped over the podium, blood trickling down his neck.

One by one, the musicians stopped playing. A stunned silence pervaded the theater. Patrons not close enough to see that Abel was bleeding looked about in bewilderment. Then all hell broke loose. The concertmaster leapt up from his chair and stared at Abel.

Julia didn't know what was going on, only that Abel was in trouble. Without thinking of her own safety, she catapulted from her chair, thrust her violin aside, and rushed to him.

Then she saw the blood gushing from the wound in his neck. Horrified, she touched him—for the first time. Then she gasped and cried out. "Oh no! Abel—*Abel?*"

Abel toppled to the floor. A woman in the first row of the audience screamed.

Julia looked around helplessly. She knelt beside Abel and placed her hands on his neck to stanch the river of gushing blood.

"Someone, call an ambulance! Get help! Please!"

Instantly, the pit was thrown into pandemonium.

"Terrorist!" a cellist cried.

"Abel's been shot!" screeched a flutist.

Within seconds, the other musicians had jumped up from their chairs and, clutching their instruments, fled the pit.

* * *

No one yet realized that the rifle shot, perfectly timed to coincide with the gunshot onstage, had come from the viewing room. No one knew that the shadowy figure, who had ejected the cartridge manually just in case a second shot was needed, decided there was no time to retrieve it from where it had gotten stuck in a crack in the floor. Nor did anyone see the interloper duck out of the room toward the fire stairs and escape the opera house amidst the chaos.

* * *

Patrons in the audience stood up in bewilderment. One man screamed, "Terrorists!" Another man shouted him down. "Calm down, people. Don't panic!"

But it wasn't long before they all ran, screaming, for the exits. Ushers frantically tried to calm them and stop the mad rush.

Unlike her colleagues, most of whom by this time had bolted, Julia just knelt beside Abel, cradling his head in her lap, her clothes and violin pin smeared with his blood. She stared at him in disbelief until a security guard rushed to her side and tugged at her arm.

"Please, Miss. It's not safe."

She clung to her mentor, his blood spouting through her fingers, and shouted at the guard. "No! No! I'm not leaving him!"

But the guard, far stronger than Julia, pulled her away. "It's too dangerous, Miss, you have to come with me. Here..."

He offered her his handkerchief to wipe the bloodstains from her hands. Dazed, she waved him away, beyond reason, looking back at Abel. She knew he was dead.

How could this happen? How?

The house doctor and EMS personnel rushed into the pit just as Julia managed one last fleeting glance at her adored maestro. She later wished she had been able to keep something, anything belonging to him, like his baton, or his musical score.

But his baton had been shattered beyond recognition. His score, which Julia had glimpsed for a moment while the guard was tugging her away from the scene, was still open on the podium, Verdi's masterful notes now stained with blood.

Her mind was forever imprinted with the image of her beloved *Don Carlo*, tinged with the crimson blood that had flowed from her cherished fallen maestro and mentor, Abel Trudeau.

Chapter Seven

Mal qual mai s'offre, oh Dei, spettacolo funesto agli occhi miei!...
Ah! l'assassino mel trucidò.
Quel sangue...quella piaga...quel volto...tinto e coperto dei color di morte...
Ei non respira più...fredde ha le membra...
But, oh God, what dreadful sight confronts my eyes!...
Ah! The assassin has struck him down!
This blood...this wound...his face discolored with the pallor of death...
He's not breathing anymore...his limbs are so cold...
—Mozart, *Don Giovanni*, Act I

T he mass of Radio Motor Patrol cars screeched to a halt on the service drive in front of Lincoln Plaza. NYPD Officers poured out onto the plaza and raced into the opera house to find a theatre erupting in mayhem.

Cops swarmed the lobby, some attempting to prevent patrons from escaping, others forming a barrier against a mob of journalists clamoring to gain entry to the scene.

Meanwhile, a shocked and benumbed group of orchestra members silently congregated in the orchestra lounge. Some musicians lay prostrate on the sofas and cushioned benches positioned around the large, carpeted room. Some paced, while others poured themselves cup after cup of spring water from the cooler near the entrance, slaking their anxiety-driven thirst. They whispered about Abel, and about whomever the next maestro might be.

Julia, paralyzed with grief, huddled in a far-off corner, barely aware of

Sidney at her side. She ran through the events of the evening in her mind again and again. Then, as she fidgeted with the zipper pull on her violin case, she realized she had been wrong about not having anything of Abel's. She still possessed the violin pin and the song, the gifts he had given her before the performance.

I'll never have his nurturing and caring again. I'll never know what he meant by "look beyond the notes." And what if I can never find the missing page...?

She held back a sob, refusing to give in to the emotions threatening to make her break down in tears.

"Next time," he said. But now there won't be a next time, nothing but memories.

It was all gone, lost to her, disintegrated into nothingness as surely as the breath had departed from Abel's body.

Meanwhile, Sidney was trying to comfort her. Considering Julia was completely desolate, and he couldn't squeeze her shoulder or give her a supportive hug, he could only gaze at her with sympathy, and use his most soothing voice.

"I know you loved him, kid."

Julia nodded. She tried to speak, but her sobs caught in her throat.

"Shh, don't talk. Just let it all out if that's what you feel like."

She shook her head, choosing instead to grit her teeth and dig her thumbnail into her palm.

* * *

Patricia appeared at the doorway of the lounge, followed by Tony.

"How are the musicians reacting to the events of the evening?"

"How do you think, Patricia? They're in shock." Tony noticed Patricia's look of annoyance. "Unlike you, who seem to be taking all of this in stride."

"Oh?" Patricia flashed him an irritated look. "Well, I'm not. Not at all. Reporters are demanding to be let inside the house. And those two obnoxious detectives from the Twentieth Precinct are already making my life miserable. They want a list of all the personnel in the opera house, more than a thousand employees. Musicians, choristers, stagehands, wardrobe people, dancers and more. It's unconscionable."

"It's their job. How hard could it be to get a computerized list?"

"Even so, it's still a royal pain in the ass. Computers notwithstanding, who has time for such things? Impossible." She sniffed. "As if I didn't already have my hands full, trying to calm down my stars and placate the board members. Did you know they're on the verge of canceling the entire week's performances?"

Tony shrugged. "That's no surprise."

"Well, it's not acceptable, and I am determined to block them. The Met has only cancelled twice. The blizzard of '96 doesn't count."

"Whatever you say, Patricia."

The only times in the history of the Met that shows had been canceled were when legendary baritone Leonard Warren had collapsed and died onstage back in the sixties, and in 1996, when a little-known tenor had keeled over from a heart attack during the first act of *The Makropoulos Affair*. During the blizzard of that year, the mayor had closed off the entire city of New York, but it wasn't the Met that canceled.

Even when a patron had committed suicide by throwing himself off the top of the Family Circle in the middle of a performance of *Macbeth* (though he had been thoughtful enough to wait until the intermission), the show had gone on to its finish, albeit after an extended interval.

Patricia shook her head. "And as for the reporters, I suppose I'll have to allow them in."

She cleared her throat to get the musicians' attention. "The detectives will be here to interview each of you personally in a few minutes." Then she glanced around, taking note of who was showing interest and who was not. "They may want to come back later during rehearsals and re-question some of you as well."

She stationed herself at the exit, sighing in exasperation. Her fingers clutched the small cylindrical pill container in her pocket. But she knew she would have to wait until she was alone to avail herself of its contents.

* * *

Julia turned her face up to Sid and winced. He returned the look.

"Rotten luck. I really could use a drink right about now. You look like you could, too."

She found her voice and replied haltingly. "Yes, but…if we have to stay here…"

"Not to worry. Once we're done, we can hightail it to The Smith. I'll buy."

Nodding gratefully, Julia contemplated getting up but thought better of it. She still felt shaky, torn between grief and her determination not to let this disastrous turn of events undermine her usual rock-solid exterior.

Now is not the time to let any chinks show in my armor, even to Sid.

She spoke hesitantly. "Sid, I meant to ask you, where were you when… when you got up and left the pit?"

"My diverticulitis. You know how bad it gets when it kicks up."

"Yes, but—"

He grimaced, his face darkening. "What? Suddenly you're suspicious of me? You know me better than that, Julia."

"Of course I do, don't be ridiculous. I'm just worried that, well…the police don't know you like I do. If they find out you and Abel were arguing before the performance—"

"That's not your problem. It's between them and me."

Feeling the sudden need to throw some water over her face, Julia turned to Sid.

"Watch my fiddle case?"

Sidney nodded. Julia rose with some effort, moved toward the doorway, and faced Patricia with a weary expression. The general manager feigned concern.

"Anything I can do, Julia?"

"Actually, I need to go to the ladies' room."

Patricia nodded her agreement and watched the young violinist move slowly past her and through the door, her eyes never leaving Julia's shapely, velvet-clad behind.

Chapter Eight

Il duolo estremo la meschinella uccide...
Her great sorrow has killed the poor girl!
—Mozart, *Don Giovanni*, Act I

NYPD detectives Al Cummings and Buddy Cruse snaked their way through the swarm of officers who held back the mob of patrons squeezed into the Met lobby. They followed the medical examiner, along with a plainclothes officer with his camera and two uniformed officers, into the orchestra pit. Abel's body lay on the floor by the podium, where the police photographer began his task. The medical examiner studied the gunshot wound.

"Shot from behind, high angle. Can't be sure yet, but I'd check the balconies."

Al whistled. "Whew. Perp must 'a been one helluva shot."

"If the perp was actually aiming at Trudeau," Buddy said.

"Who else could he have been aiming at?" asked the M.E.

Al shrugged. "You never know."

* * *

Backstage, traumatized company members wandered about, speaking in anxious whispers, or chattering nervously. Charles Tremaine, Giuseppe's understudy, was the only one with a calm demeanor.

When the gaggle of reporters found him, Charles was huddled with Frank.

This wasn't unusual, since the two often were seen together, sometimes gabbing in full view of others but usually whispering off in a corner of an out-of-the-way hallway or corridor.

Having just consoled a shell-shocked soprano, Charles took it upon himself to be the self-possessed representative, fielding the questions of the press, who had been allowed inside the opera house and were demanding information.

"Were you backstage when it happened, Mr. Tremaine?" asked one.

"Would you care to make a statement?" queried another.

"Yes, I would." Charles drew upon his theatrical training to give the impression of being poised and self-assured. "The Met has suffered an incalculable loss in Abel Trudeau. This event has saddened all of us deeply. Its shockwaves will reverberate in New York's cultural community for years to come."

Charles presumed the reporters must have been impressed with his unruffled exterior, since they continued to compete for his attention. He smiled sadly and carried on, like the trooper he was. He'd been waiting month after frustrating month as an understudy for his chance, his moment in the limelight. Now it had finally come, and he was going to revel in it, no matter what horrific event had provided the catalyst.

* * *

After leaving the M.E. to his work, detectives Al and Buddy pushed their way through the masses of NYPD cops who clogged the hallways and into the lobby. Officers were having a difficult time managing impatient crowds of frightened and irate patrons and ushers who were milling about in mass confusion. The officers formed a barricade against the glass exit doors leading outside to Lincoln Center Plaza, preventing the patrons—their prime witnesses—from jumping ship.

Al found out who the head usher was, approached him, and identified himself. "What time did people start to arrive this evening?" the detective shouted above the din.

William, the usher, shouted back. "These doors open a half-hour before curtain. But people enter from the stage door at all hours."

Al grimaced. "That's a load of help."

A red-faced matronly woman rushed up to Al and Buddy. "This is an outrage. When are we going to be allowed to leave? My chauffeur is waiting."

"Then you might have to give him a raise, Ma'am. This may be the longest opening night in Met history," Al informed her.

"Not as long as the last act of *Die Meistersinger*, if you know what I mean," added William.

"Huh?" Al glared at him, waiting for an explanation.

William sighed. "I was referring to the lengthy Wagner opera with a third act as long as the first two acts combined. Almost six hours total."

"Six hours? Man, I feel sorry for the musicians," said Buddy. "People love opera that much?"

"If you have to ask, then you know nothing about opera," the woman huffed.

"That's putting it mildly, Ma'am," Al said.

The woman strode away. Al turned back to William and noticed Buddy pop a piece of chewing gum in his mouth. Even in the gravity of the situation, Al couldn't suppress a wisp of a smile. Buddy, the most orally fixated kid Al had ever seen, was always chomping on something. Sometimes this habit irritated Al, but in general, he found it amusing and somewhat endearing.

Buddy proceeded to grill William. "Which usher was stationed in the balcony?"

"It's called the 'Family Circle.'" Al couldn't miss the disdain in William's expression. "That would be Sergei."

William pointed out a nervous-looking young man hovering by himself in a corner. Al thought for a moment.

"Sergei. Isn't that a...*Russian* name?"

"Yes, he's our token Russian Mafia member." Al and Buddy's collective glare told William his quip was not appreciated. "Just a joke. He's new, so he gets to deal with the 'peanut gallery'—the Family Circle."

Eyes narrowed, Al peered at Sergei. Buddy leaned over and whispered in

Al's ear. "Some sniper rifles are Russian, right?"

"Yeah."

Al and Buddy walked over to the novice usher and took him by the arm. "How would you like to show us the Family Circle?" Al asked as politely as he could. The police department was getting flak these days for being disrespectful to suspects.

Sergei led them through the lobby to the interior, where they took the elevator up several levels. When the three men had reached the mile-high Family Circle, Al and Buddy noticed that the section was cramped, the seats close together.

"I tell you, this is for me first night," Since Sergei's accent was heavy, the detectives had to pay close attention to his words. "I do not notice anyone enter after curtain is up."

"Get real, how could that be?" Buddy unwrapped another stick of gum.

"Giuseppe Masini, great tenor, when he sing, nothing else important."

Al smirked. "Any true opera aficionado would agree with that, right?" He looked up toward the ceiling and pointed at a large cubicle, framed by a panel of glass windows, so high up it looked suspended in air. "What's up there, Sergei?"

"Viewing room, for company officials to watch operas. But is closed for renovation since for several weeks."

Taking Sergei by the arm again, Al nodded his head in the direction of the viewing room. The usher let out a deep breath and led on.

Once they had reached the viewing room, the first thing Al noticed was that the padlock on the door had been broken. He turned to Sergei.

"So much for renovations. Who has access to this place while it's closed?"

"Only construction workers and stagehands," Sergei replied.

"Must have been an inside job," Al said.

"If it's an inside job, why wouldn't they just use a key, boss?" Buddy asked.

"So it wouldn't *look* like an inside job, Buddy boy."

The two detectives donned latex gloves. Buddy inspected the broken lock, while Al motioned to Sergei to wait just outside the door.

Al and Buddy entered the viewing room and examined the floor. Spying a shell casing wedged in a crack, Al knelt down and tried to pry it out. It wouldn't budge.

Buddy extracted a Swiss Army knife from his pocket. "Here, try this."

After a good deal of struggling, Al finally dug out the casing and inspected it.

"VAL Silent Sniper."

Al had been first in his Police Academy class in ammunition identification. Not only was he adept at determining a type of ammunition from the casing or cartridge, he also was well versed in recognizing the more uncommon varieties. "Pretty sophisticated weaponry, very distinctive ammo. Russian, just as I thought." He eyed Sergei. The usher blanched.

Buddy peered at the casing. "Perp must 'a been in a real hurry, to leave that behind."

"I'd be willing to bet this matches the murder bullet." Al placed his find in a small plastic evidence bag and pocketed it. He assessed the extreme distance between the viewing room and the pit. "This perp knew what they were doing. Military, special ops, maybe. A real pro."

"Yeah, didn't leave anything else here, boss, not even foot scuffs," Buddy said.

Al nodded. "Rubber soles. And they knew their way around this opera house for sure."

"But even with a silencer, couldn't someone've heard the rifle discharge?" asked Buddy.

"Not necessa...sarily." Sergei tripped over the word. "There is shot on stage, very loud, then *fortissimo* passage in orchestra right after."

"Let me get this straight. The perp knew exactly when to shoot, so the noise, I mean, the loud music, would cover it up?"

"It's beginning to look that way." Al thought for a moment. "Moving on, Buddy boy. I want you to get names of everyone who isn't a musician—bartenders, program hawkers, whatever—and start interviewing them."

"On it. I already asked that, uh, general manager lady for a list of personnel."

"Good work, kid. Have the crime techs sweep the door for fibers, and for fingerprints. There's a chance the perp wasn't wearing gloves."

Buddy whipped out his notebook. "But with all the other people coming into this room, there's got to be all kinds of prints."

"From the looks of it, there hasn't been anyone else here for a while. Maybe we'll get lucky."

Buddy's notebook slipped from his hands. As he stooped to pick it up, a violent sneezing fit overcame him. "Man, it's dusty here. Hard to get prints when it's so covered with grit. Are opera houses always so dusty?"

"Who are you, the EPA?" Al shook his head. "Find out who has criminal records, too. I'll start questioning the orchestra. Got that?"

"Right." Buddy resumed his chewing. "This is gonna be one long night."

As they made their way out of the room, Al took one last look toward the extreme angle between the viewing room and the distant orchestra pit. "One way or another, it's hard to believe this could be a random hit."

"What makes you say that, boss?"

"Someone went to an awful lot of trouble. Those VAL rifles are not easy to get, and that ammo has to be special ordered. This took some planning."

"Oh yeah?"

"Mark my words, Buddy boy. This wasn't the work of some nut loaf out to get his fifteen minutes. It was done by a pro, someone who wanted the maestro dead." Al accepted Buddy's offer of a stick of gum, unwrapped it, and popped it into his mouth. "No, this wasn't random. This was personal."

Chapter Nine

Fia lunga tal notte!
It's going to be a long night!
—Verdi, *Rigoletto*, Act III

After Al sent Buddy to interview stagehands, choristers, and soloists and called for backup to cover the multitude of other Met employees, he set his sights on the orchestra members. Tony installed the detective at a table in the orchestra lounge with a list of personnel. Whipping out his notebook, Al began to question the musicians one by one.

What he discovered was fascinating. In asking the orchestra members to describe their duties, he might have concluded that they had the least interesting jobs in the opera house. They came across like factory workers, grinding out the notes, day after day and night after night.

"I just play the trombone."

"I just saw away at the cello."

"Think of me as a plumber. I bring in my tools and do my work, then I go home."

Al knew better, but not one of them had anything of interest to say. Until Harold.

As soon as Harold sat down, Al sensed the musician, a violist of indeterminate advanced age, was extremely nervous and uncooperative. Al began his inquiry by commenting on the musician's habit of gnawing on the metal clip of his pencil.

"Aren't you afraid of breaking a tooth like that?"

"Beats getting TMJ, like our tight-ass concertmaster."

It had never occurred to Al that string players, who spent countless hours with their instruments squeezed under their chins, would encounter teeth-clenching problems. But it made perfect sense that musicians, especially ones working in the Met's high-pressure atmosphere, would be prone to gritting and grinding their teeth until it became painful.

"Do you know anyone who might have had it in for the maestro?"

Harold grimaced. "Well, if you're looking for clues, go talk to that drug pusher, Sidney."

"You mean..." Al peered down his list and spotted the name. "Sidney Richter?"

"Yeah. He was always fighting with Abel, too. Hated Trudeau's guts, in fact. Everyone knew about it."

"Was the feeling mutual?"

"Yeah. I guess so." Harold lowered his voice. "They almost threw it down once in the men's locker room."

"And how do you know Sidney's a drug pusher?"

"I've seen him with sleazy guys. You know, shifty types that hang out in bars."

"But did you ever actually see him selling or buying or using drugs?"

"Well, uh, no. But it was kinda common knowledge. In certain circles."

Al frowned and penciled a note in his book, then looked again at the list. "And Richter's, um..." He fumbled over the odd pairing of words. "Stand partner, Julia Kogan?"

"Yeah, he's real thick with her." Al was not surprised when Harold got so uneasy that he broke the end of his pencil. "But she's a straight shooter. Just does her job, all business-like, ya' know? If there was one person who wasn't aware of Sid's 'activities,' it would 'a been her."

Al raised his eyebrows. "Oh?" He jotted down the info and waited for Harold to continue.

"She was Trudeau's protégée. Whenever anyone criticized him, she took it personally. She knew all about the problems between him and Sidney."

He paused. "But mostly, she just keeps to herself, doesn't trust, or rely on anybody. Don't know why. I guess I wouldn't trust anyone either if I had been raised in foster homes."

"I see." Al decided it was more important to keep the dialogue focused on Sidney than do a character study of Julia Kogan. "Anybody else who might have had it in for Trudeau?"

"Well, there's a lot of back biting around this place, but...I'd talk to Sidney."

"Okay." Al looked up from his writing. "Thanks for your time."

"Don't mention it."

Harold got up and sauntered away. The next to sit opposite Al was Tony, who fidgeted with his baton.

Al asked, "Can you show me the closest pit stop?"

Al saw Tony's face flood with relief. "Follow me."

* * *

In the men's room, Tony stood by as Al leaned over a sink, splashed water on his face, and toweled himself dry.

"It's gonna be a long night. Mind if I ask you some questions while we're here, Tony?"

"Shoot. Oh, sorry. Bad choice of words."

Al overlooked the gaffe. "Did you see all the musicians before the show tonight?"

"It's my job to make sure they're all here."

"And where did you first see Sidney Richter?"

"He was coming out of Abel's dressing room before the show. Hopping mad."

Al reached for his notebook. "Oh? About what?"

"Looked like they were having an argument. No surprise. Sid and Abel had a major personality conflict. Always arguing, those two."

"Do you know why?"

Tony shrugged. "They just rubbed each other the wrong way."

"Did you hear their conversation?"

41

"Not really, behind the dressing room door, it just sounded like shouting. But I definitely made out the word 'son-of-a-bitch.'"

Al paused to write. "Anyone else in the orchestra have problems with Abel?"

"Nah, are you kidding? They were all in awe of Trudeau, me included. The man was a genius. Had the whole music world in the palm of his hand." Tony watched as Al wrote with a vengeance. "Am I done?"

"Oh...Yes, thanks for cooperating." Al paused. "By the way, where were you when Abel was shot?"

Tony swallowed hard. "If you must know, I was in Abel's dressing room."

Al's sharp look demanded an explanation.

"He had some custom-made batons. I liked to practice conducting with them. It made me feel like..." His face reddened. "A real conductor."

Al scrutinized Tony's humiliated expression and felt badly for him. It couldn't have been easy for the personnel manager to admit such an intimate detail. But then, criminals sometimes confessed to petty crimes to cover up larger ones.

"I'll take that under advisement for now."

Chapter Ten

Se udir brami il resto,
discaccia i sospetti, che torto mi fan.
If you want to hear the rest,
drop those suspicions that do me such wrong.
—Mozart, *le nozze di Figaro*, Act I

Al headed for the door. Then, realizing he would never find his own way back through the maze of hallways, he looked to Tony for help. Nodding his understanding, Tony led Al out of the locker room and back down the hallway. Just as they had reached the orchestra lounge, Buddy appeared at the entrance and leaned toward Al. They entered the room, speaking softly.

"Too many people in this opera house, boss. I've called for backup. You got anything yet?"

"Not much. How 'bout sitting in on this next one?"

He pointed to Sidney's name on the list. Buddy pulled up a chair next to Al.

"Send Sidney Richter over, please, Tony."

Tony motioned to Sidney. Al noticed Sidney was in no hurry to come in and sit in front of the two detectives.

Out of the corner of his eye, Al also saw a young woman, a violin case sitting on the floor next to her, lingering by the water cooler, acting nervous and on edge. Noticing her hand was shaking when she filled a paper cup with water, he was willing to bet she was Julia Kogan, even though he hadn't been introduced to her yet. By her attentive expression, he guessed she was trying to listen to the exchange between him and Sidney.

"You were heard arguing with Abel before the show, Sidney. What was that about?"

"We had our differences."

Al eyed Sidney with suspicion. "What kind of differences?"

"Artistic ones." Sidney peered at Al, eyes narrowed. "Like, I personally don't think we should be playing Wagner on the Jewish high holidays, especially Yom Kippur. I wasn't shy about letting him know."

Buddy rolled his eyes. "What's so bad about that?" he asked.

"Wagner was an anti-Semite. It was his music they played when the Jews marched into the concentration camps." Sid scowled. "Want more detail, Mr. Detective?"

"Was that the only thing you and Trudeau were fighting about?" asked Al.

"Nope. You want a laundry list?"

Buddy eyed Sid's defiant expression. "Were you the only one in the orchestra who had that kind of disagreement with him?"

"I was the one who told him to his face. You got a problem with that?"

Al ignored Sidney's confrontational tone. "You and Trudeau had personality conflicts?"

"Yeah, so what? It happens. A lot of musicians do battle with the conductor. It doesn't mean they're going to kill him."

"I didn't say anything about that."

"You didn't have to. Your attitude is obvious. Can I go now?"

Al knew his questioning was going nowhere. "Yeah. But stick around, just in case. And maybe you could point out your stand partner, Julia."

Sidney did what he was asked to do. "Okay. But she doesn't know anything."

"Oh? How do you know?"

"She's just a kid. Why don't you ask Tony-the-*wunderkind* wannabe Toscanini where *he* was during the murder?"

Before Al could reply, Sidney pushed back his chair, got up, and walked over to Julia. Sid gently plucked the paper cup from her trembling hand.

44

"You're next, kid," Al heard Sidney say. "Don't let them get you down. I'll wait for you in the hallway, and we can blow this joint, okay?"

Julia nodded. Al motioned her toward the chair opposite him and cleared his throat.

"Was there anything special about your relationship with Abel Trudeau?"

"He was my mentor. I wouldn't be at the Met if not for him."

"Did he ever talk about any enemies, any threats to his life?"

She shook her head. Al regarded her shrewdly. He could see her frayed nerves already starting to show.

"What about Sidney? How close are you with him?"

"Close enough to know he would never harm Abel."

"Who said anything about that, Julia?"

"I could tell from his expression you were giving him a hard time."

Are you close with Sidney in any other way?"

Julia bristled. "If you mean physically, it's none of your business."

"I wasn't implying that."

"Oh, weren't you?" Julia's face reddened. "If you must know, Sid's like a big brother to me. He took me under his wing when I first got here. That's all I have to say."

There was an uncomfortable silence as they locked stares. Buddy got up and leaned over Al. "I gotta go back upstairs. Whaddya' think so far?"

Al murmured in Buddy's ear. "Not much to go on here, except maybe Richter. Didn't believe a word he said."

They exchanged glances of understanding. Then Buddy walked off.

From Julia's anxious look, and the way she was clutching her violin case, Al could tell she was worried, even if she hadn't been able to hear what he and Buddy had said. Whether that worry was about Sidney remained to be seen.

Al cleared his throat again. "Did you hear Abel and Sidney arguing before the performance?"

Julia nodded.

"Were you aware of their personality conflicts?"

"Yes. But if you think Sidney—"

45

"Forget Sidney for the moment. Is there any reason why you might want Abel Trudeau dead?"

"Are you accusing *me*? For God's sake, Abel got me this job. He's been like a father to me since my own father died when I was a kid. Why would I want to harm him?" She became more agitated. "Look, I know where this is going. First my mentor is murdered, and then you want to accuse my best friend of being involved, and now me."

Julia stood up abruptly, spilling the contents of her water cup all over her sweater. She burst into tears. Al studied Julia's distraught face. He felt sudden sympathy for her. "We can finish this later, Julia. You can go."

Julia rose and fled the lounge. At that moment, Patricia strode in, scowling, and gave Al the evil eye.

"Are you quite finished, detective?"

Al looked up at Patricia. "And you are…?"

"Patricia Wells, general manager of the Met."

Al scanned his list. "I don't see your name here."

"Of course not. I'm not a musician."

"Got something against musicians?"

"Look, detective," Patricia said, "I'd appreciate your letting my players go. Can't you see they're exhausted and upset?"

"Sorry, Ms. Wells, but these few will need further questioning."

"Couldn't you continue tomorrow?"

"I can't risk them skipping town overnight."

"If they want to keep their jobs, they're not going anywhere."

"Okay, Ms. Wells, you win. For now."

"Thank you, detective." Patricia addressed the remaining musicians. "You may go."

Al watched the musicians' exodus, then scooped up his papers and left without uttering another word.

* * *

Julia was devastated. The detective's questioning had shaken her to the core.

46

She had escaped the lounge, shoving the violin case under her arm, fighting off tears as Abel's last words again echoed in her ears.

"Just think about it. We'll talk more about it next time."

Rather than console her, the after-effects of Abel's promise had only made her feel more hopeless.

But there won't be a next time. And this is turning out to be the worst night of my life.

Chapter Eleven

Vissi d'arte, vissi d'amore, non feci mai male ad anima viva!...
Nell'ora del dolore, Perchè Signore, me ne rimuneri così?
I lived for art, I lived for love, I've never harmed a living soul!...
In this hour of suffering, why, oh Lord, do you repay me this way?
—Puccini, *Tosca*, Act II

At two a.m., Julia and Sidney were still sitting at the bar in The Smith, a restaurant on Broadway directly across Lincoln Plaza from the Met. The bistro/ bar was a favorite haunt of Lincoln Center musicians; though Julia, who was compulsive about her work and made a point of staying away from booze and late-night carousing, was not a regular patron there.

Sidney, however, certainly was, and his frequent hits from his glass of Scotch reminded Julia of a needy baby with its comforting bottle. She nursed her own glass, not saying much, then turned to her colleague and spoke with slow deliberation to keep herself from breaking down.

"It's my fault he was killed."

"How do you figure that?"

Julia gazed at Sid, her lip quivering. She began fidgeting with the zipper on the violin case, which was positioned upright next to her bar stool. "He was supposed to go on sabbatical to Vienna. I asked him to stay for my first season. He changed his plans for me. I'm responsible for his...his..."

"Don't be so hard on yourself, Jul."

But Julia wasn't listening. "Here I am worrying about myself, when Abel—"

A loud booming coming from the TV screen on the wall above the bar interrupted Julia's self-recriminations. She sat bolt upright and looked up at the screen to see a newscaster positioned in front of the Met.

"Tragic opening night at the Metropolitan Opera," the journalist declared. "Musical Director Abel Trudeau was gunned down..."

Distraught, Julia sank back on her barstool. Then suddenly she sat straight up, crying out.

"Oh no! Sid! It just came back to me. I saw—"

"Saw what?"

"A weird flash of something shiny, like...like metal, coming from the direction of the viewing room, just before Abel was shot. It could have been from the rifle that killed him!" She broke down, sobbing. "I could have done something! I could have stopped it!"

"Julia, stop berating yourself. There was nothing you could do. Shh..." Sid reached for her but abruptly pulled his hand away as she recoiled oh-so-slightly. "Abel's gone now, kid. But wherever he is, he'll be watching out for you. All you can do for him is to be the violinist he wanted you to be."

Accepting Sidney's proffered handkerchief, Julia blew her nose until she became calmer.

"He had high hopes for you, kid. And so do I." Without thinking, Sidney tried to pat her hand in a comforting gesture. She hastily withdrew it. "You shouldn't blame yourself, Julia. You idolized him, and he appreciated it more than you know."

But Julia, lost in thought, wasn't paying attention. "That must have been the reason Abel told me to wait till after the performance to look at his song!"

"Wait a minute. What song?"

"The one he wrote. For me."

"Julia, you're not making any sense."

"But I looked at it anyway. And do you know what he wrote at the bottom of the first page? 'If anything happens to me, you'll find answers in the music.' But then we were called to the pit. I didn't have time to figure out what Abel meant. Now I know! He was worried something terrible might happen to him. Why didn't he just tell me, instead of—"

But the sudden appearance of a sleazy-looking guy approaching from the opposite end of the bar interrupted her, and she couldn't keep herself from staring. His five o'clock shadow gave a Cro-Magnon cast to his grizzled features, and he looked as if he had been sleeping in his clothes since the Dark Ages. Julia became uncomfortable when he ogled her.

Sidney shot the man a lethal glance. "Not now, Geraldo," he hissed.

Geraldo grimaced. "But we need to talk about—"

Sidney cut him off, his tone menacing. "We need to talk about *nada*. Now beat it. And leave the girl alone."

He waved Geraldo away. But as the interloper turned on his heel, muttering under his breath, Sid leaned over to him and murmured. "My place. Later."

The brief exchange went sailing over Julia's muddled head. She watched Geraldo slink away, turned to Sidney, and grabbed his arm.

"What was that about? Who was that guy?"

Sidney dismissed her concern with a wave of his hand. "Sometimes, I give him a handout. Now every time he sees me, he thinks I owe him." He looked at her, his brow furrowed. "You look beat, kid. I think I'd better get you home now."

"But I'm not tired!"

"Listen to your big brother. I'm the closest thing to a family member you have left."

Julia realized he was right. It was three a.m., and suddenly she felt exhausted. All she wanted to do was sleep.

"Come on," Sidney said. "I'll take you home."

In a daze, Julia followed Sidney outside without saying a word, clutching her violin case under her arm, as he hailed a taxi. Julia knew she was capable of getting her own cab, but she also knew better than to protest. She decided it was easier to accept Sidney's offer and allowed him to help her into the cab.

"Do you want me to come with you?" Sidney asked.

"Thanks, Sid, but I think I just need to be alone."

"I totally understand. Get some rest, okay?"

Nodding his sympathy, Sidney gave the cabbie an address and watched as the cab took off. Julia was in such a fog she hadn't noticed the shady-looking guy with the grizzled beard who was watching from the shadows.

* * *

Julia let herself into the entrance of her building at that unreasonably early hour of the morning and mounted the stairs to her abode, the weight of sorrow pressing down on her thin shoulders.

She passed through her living room, not allowing time to take in the atmosphere she always found comforting after a long workday: its cushiony furnishings, softly draped window treatments, muted rosy color scheme, and stuffed animals decorating the mantelpiece over the non-working fireplace, broadcasted femininity. Light weight dumbbells sat on the bookshelf.

When she trudged into her bedroom, she gazed around at a tidy space filled with her favorite mementos and most treasured objects. Met opera posters adorned the walls. Bookshelves with violin sheet music and novels from her favorite authors, from Agatha Christie to Isabel Allende and Gabriel García Márquez, shared space with light exercise equipment.

Julia firmly believed in keeping both her mind and body fit. She loved to read, but she also was convinced that the strength she had developed from exercising helped her keep her violin upright during hours-long rehearsals and would make her feel safer walking the streets of Manhattan, when performances ran late.

Too wired to sleep, she set her sights on deciphering Abel's song. She laid her violin case on the bed, extracted her instrument, along with the music from the outside zippered compartment, and placed the music on her music stand. Regarding the page with profound sadness, she lifted her violin and bow and slowly started to play. But when she spied Abel's hasty scrawls at the bottom of the page, she abruptly stopped.

"If anything happens to me, you'll find answers in this music."

Bitter tears obscured her vision. She placed the violin back in the case. Too paralyzed by grief to remember to close it, she set the case and music on the floor and sank down onto her bed.

Answers? Where? On page two? Will I ever find it?

Julia looked over at her nightstand and gazed at her most cherished photos: her kind-faced father Sol; herself, age eight, violin under her arm, with Sol looking on proudly; as a ten-year-old, playing the violin, Sol and Abel watching and smiling.

She picked up the photo of Sol, slowly traced her finger around his image, and gently put it down. Then she unclasped the chain at her throat, opened the gold locket dangling from it, and regarded tiny images of herself and Sol. Overcome with sadness, she laid the locket on her nightstand, reached for the music box next to it, and opened the cover.

Julia fought back tears as she read the engraving on the inside cover: "Love always, Dad." The familiar, graceful "Anniversary Waltz"—the tune her parents had danced to on their wedding night—wafted from the box.

With a mournful shake of her head, Julia thought of her mom and dad. Her mother, Sylvia, had preceded Sol to the grave when Julia was five. Most of the young girl's memories of her mom were those told to her by her dad. At least the music box, which her father had given her for her tenth birthday, kept those memories alive. But in her dreams, she still was reliving those horrific moments when she'd lost him on the streets of Manhattan.

* * *

The mutual adoration between Julia and her father was well known to her classmates at Juilliard Prep. Julia's teacher, famed violinist Itzhak Perlman, had often remarked to Sol how exceptional it was to see so much affection flow between father and daughter. Nor could he remember having seen a father so willing to participate in a daughter's weekly violin lessons.

Julia was ecstatic to be studying with Perlman, but her most fervent wish was to make Sol feel even prouder than he already was. He had told her many times about his imagined vision of her onstage in a top professional orchestra or performing in the pit at the Metropolitan Opera. Thus, on that radiant autumn day when he and his ten-year-old daughter emerged from the school at midday after her lesson, she had returned his proud gaze with wide-eyed innocence.

"Did I play the 'Meditation' good, Daddy?"

"You played it well, Precious. Very well."

"Could Mommy hear it in heaven?"

"Yes, dearest, I'm sure she could."

Massenet's "Meditation" from the opera *Thaïs* was one of the most celebrated solo pieces in violin literature. Despite its technical and interpretative challenges, Sol was convinced Julia could play it, even at her tender age. He was right. Everyone who heard Julia play the piece was astounded at her ability to interpret it with such maturity.

"Julia, I'm so amazed and so proud of the way you play it," he told her. "And do you know why?"

"Why, Daddy?"

"Because of how you've continued to devote yourself to your music and to master the violin, despite losing your mother five years ago. In fact, I told Maestro Trudeau how impressed everyone is with the way you play the 'Meditation.'"

"You did?" Julia knew her father and Abel Trudeau were close friends.

"But if, when you grow up, you decide to audition for the Met, I'm not going to ask him to help you. You'll have to do it all on your own."

"I know, Daddy." She paused, thinking. "Do you think I can?"

"I think you can do anything you set your sights on, Precious."

Julia kept her hand grasped tightly in Sol's as he led her across the traffic-choked intersection to the opposite side of Broadway. She and Sol both hated this intersection, with its badly timed traffic lights and multitude of streets crisscrossing at angles. They always breathed a sigh of relief after dashing precipitously across to avoid being hit by cars or taxis. Julia dreaded the thought of ever negotiating the dangerous junction by herself.

Once they had crossed safely, Julia looked at Sol again and smiled.

They hadn't noticed the swarm of NYPD cops jumping out of patrol cars and the confusing throng of onlookers staring in fright. And when the hirsute man came tearing out of the revolving door of the Chemical Bank on the corner of 65th Street and came close to knocking Sol down, Sol reacted immediately, despite the man's drawn revolver. He did as any father would do to stop someone from doing harm to his little girl. Thrusting Julia out of the way, Sol grabbed the gunman by the arm.

Julia watched, horrified, as the bullet slammed into her father's chest at close range, and he collapsed on the sidewalk. Before anyone could stop her, she rushed to her father and sank down next to him, her violin case tumbling to the ground beside her. Within seconds, an NYPD officer felled the offender with a shot to the shoulder. But it was too late.

Cradling Sol's head in her arms, Julia sobbed, tears streaming down her face, as her father's life was extinguished before her eyes.

"Daddy! Daddy!"

In a minute, it was all over. The incapacitated bank robber was not going to hurt anyone else. Several other policemen gathered around Julia, asking if she was hurt. An officer tried to gently wrest her away from her father's prostrate form, but her strength, surprisingly powerful for such a young child, defeated his efforts.

"No, no! Leave me alone!"

How dare they try to pull me away from Daddy? I'll never let anyone touch me again!

Julia remained on the ground, unwilling to move. She rocked herself back and forth, eyes glazing over in shock. In her view, the police were all useless. They couldn't bring back her dad...

* * *

Now Abel was gone, too. Julia listened to the music box for a moment. She unclasped the violin pin from her blouse and made a silent vow.

I'll wear it every day, Abel, I promise.

She thought of washing the pin but reconsidered. The blood was the symbol of her pain and her loss. It was more appropriate to let it remain, at least until tomorrow. She placed the pin on the night table on top of a tissue, taking care not to touch those scarlet-colored drops, the last vestiges of Abel's ebbing life.

Suddenly she felt completely worn out. Collapsing on the bed, she gave in to grief-induced exhaustion. Then, blinded by tears, she shut the music box and curled up in fetal position on the bed.

* * *

Just inside the stage door, a man was sitting in the ancient phone booth, speaking into the phone.

"West 67th Street and Central Park West," he said under his breath. "That's all I can tell you."

He hung up, looked around to see if anyone was watching, and slipped away unnoticed.

Chapter Twelve

Menzogna! Nego. Le prove? Al fatto. Chi mi accusa? I vostri birri invan frugar la villa

Lies! I deny that. What proofs have you? In vain your spies ransacked my villa

—Puccini, *Tosca*, Act II

Al and Buddy, accompanied by a SWAT team of armed NYPD cops in protective gear, burst through the door of Sidney's apartment, guns drawn, at three-thirty a.m. Sidney and his "guest" for the evening, Geraldo, were entertaining themselves: Sidney, by practicing a Mozart violin concerto; Geraldo, by availing himself of a generous line of coke on the coffee table.

They both stood by in helpless shock as Al strode to Geraldo, swiped his finger in the white powder, and sampled it. He then confronted Sidney.

"What would your friend Julia think about *this*?"

"You keep Julia out of it," Sid growled.

But when an officer threw open a closet door, revealing cartons filled with a cache of assault weapons and multiple boxes of ammunition, Sidney's astonishment rendered him speechless.

"And this, Richter?" Al demanded.

Sid started to protest. "I've never seen that before. Someone must've planted it there."

"Oh, really?" Al said. "And who would that be?"

Buddy patted down Geraldo, reached into his pocket, and extracted a handgun. "9 mm Luger. I'd say you've seen this ammo before."

"Hey, Boss," an officer yelled. "Look what I just found."

The officer handed Al a packet of handwritten letters tied with red ribbon that had been squirreled away at the bottom of one carton. Al pulled out one missive, scanned its contents, and addressed Sidney.

"Well, what do you know. Love letters. Between you…and *Abel Trudeau.*"

Fear transformed Sidney's face into wide-eyed terror. "I'm innocent! This was a set-up!" he shouted. "I'm calling my lawyer."

"Given the amount of coke we found," said Buddy, "It better be a high-priced one."

* * *

It wasn't long before the officers dragged Sidney and Geraldo through the entrance of the Twentieth Precinct and upstairs, where they shoved them into separate interview rooms.

Bedraggled and in a daze, Sidney slumped into a chair and leaned, head in hands, over a table. Within seconds, Al and Buddy appeared. Despite the late hour, Al was on a roll.

"Strike one, you're busted for coke. Strike two, the ammo found in your apartment matches the casing of the bullet that killed Trudeau."

"I don't know anything about ammo."

"I somehow doubt that," Buddy said.

"It'd be easier on you if you cough up a statement now, Richter," said Al.

"Yeah. Your pal in the next room might beat you to it, and where would you be then?"

"Statement? About what?"

Al wasn't buying Sidney's bewilderment. "Those letters, all nicely wrapped in red ribbon. How romantic. You and Trudeau were lovers. He was about to throw you over. A jealous lover raging over being dumped. That's motive…" Al raised his eyebrows. "For murder."

"Are you freaking kidding me?"

Buddy smirked. "Strike three, you're out, Richter."

"What is this, a baseball game?"

"Yeah. And your cohort in the next room is about to hit a homer."

"Not another word, Sidney." Sidney's attorney, Herb, swept into the room and faced Al and Buddy. "Herbert Cafferty, defense attorney for Sidney Richter. I want my client released immediately."

"Not so fast," Al said. "He's in major trouble here."

Herb tapped his foot. "What kind of trumped-up charges are you trying to pin on him?"

"Possession of unregistered weapons and controlled substances. And murder."

"What!" Herb shrieked.

Buddy smirked. "Ammo found in his apartment matched the type and lot number of the casing from the weapon that killed Abel Trudeau."

"It wasn't mine!" Sid's face reddened. "I'm being framed!"

"Shut up, Sidney, I'm the lawyer here."

Al continued. "And he was hiding love letters from Trudeau, who was about to dump Richter for another guy. A jealous lover, killing for revenge."

Herb faced Al. "Ammo notwithstanding, you still don't have the murder weapon itself. The letters are circumstantial. And on what grounds did you raid my client's apartment? He has no previous record."

The lawyer's indignant expression didn't faze the detective. "FYI, Mister Attorney, we got an anonymous tip, and a search warrant from a judge. Richter had a heated argument with Abel Trudeau just before the opera. *And* he has a relationship with a known drug dealer, who happens to be in the next room."

"I'll ask for a bail hearing. Sidney is a respected musician, in a world-class musical organization. He has no priors."

Al's voice remained calm. "Your client is suspected of a major, high-profile crime. He's a flight risk, a Russian émigré with no local family ties. We'll get the judge to deny bail."

Herb raised his voice. "My client is a Manhattan resident with ties to the community and a prestigious job. We'll see what His Honor has to say."

"I'd say Richter's pretty much nailed. Open and shut case. The love letters, the drugs, Sidney's known conflicts with Abel. Those alone are enough to detain him." Al paused. "But the fact that Sidney was absent from the pit during the assassination pretty much clinches it, I'd say."

"*You'd* say? I think I'll wait for the judge."

Al modulated his voice, attempting to be civilized. "If he cooperates now, the D.A.'ll talk to the judge about cutting him some slack."

"You're involved in this, Richter, whatever you try to say," Buddy told Sidney. "And we can't help you if you won't help yourself."

Sidney just hung his head.

Chapter Thirteen

Perdon...l'affanno mio, le pene...
Forgive me...my grief, my distress...
—Mozart, *Don Giovanni*, Act I

Getting out of bed the morning after Abel's murder was the greatest trial Julia had suffered, since her father's death. After a fitful sleep, she awakened, her head throbbing and her lips tasting of salt from the tears she had shed during the night. Exhausted, she arose and pulled on the cuddly terrycloth robe, and furry "wolf" slippers Sidney had given her for her birthday.

As soon as her eyes opened all the way, Julia spied the open violin case and Abel's song lying on the floor and was seized with a sudden determination to get past her grief and play through, at least to the end of the one page in her possession.

She grabbed hold of the instrument and the music and began to play the song. But a strange, jarring note stopped her cold.

That's weird. It's so dissonant. Could this be right? It's not like Abel to make mistakes.

Puzzled, she stared at the music. There was no second page to compare with the strange sound on the first page. But once stopped, she couldn't bring herself to make another attempt.

Sighing with frustration, she put down the violin and shuffled toward the window. The morning sunlight pouring through, which she usually welcomed with gratitude, only hurt her eyes.

Thank God there's no rehearsal this morning.

The Met had allowed the theater to darken in respect to their maestro. But given Patricia's track record, like docking her own pay to attend her father's funeral, Julia suspected one day's respite was about all the company would get.

Suddenly Julia felt a craving for fresh air to combat her lethargy. She opened the window, which was more than tall enough for her to climb out of, clambered onto the fire escape, and sat as close to the window ledge and as far away from the outer railing as possible.

She heard the front door slam, followed by the familiar clatter of clunky heels on the living room floor. After a moment, a young Asian woman about Julia's age poked her head out the window.

"Have you even moved from here since I left on my tour, Jul?"

"Katie! Thank God you're back!"

Julia looked over to see her buddy and roommate, Katie, *New York Times* in hand, grinning from the window. Julia's face lit up at the sight of her.

"Yep. Didja' miss me? And am I the best, or what? I brought you your newspaper."

Julia eyed the crumpled document and shook her head.

"Okay, I admit I read some of it first," Katie said, grinning. "But oh my God, what a nightmare!" she declared. "Can you believe those scumbag reporters accosted me at the airport trying to pump me for info on Abel?"

Katie Ma was Julia's best female friend and confidante. The two young women were more like sisters, for Katie's Korean family had taken care of Julia at Abel's behest after the efforts of other foster families had failed. The two girls had shared everything, from violin fingering secrets to their most intimate adolescent fears and hopes.

Even at a young age, Katie had been aware of Julia's characteristic determination not to show her vulnerability and had done her best to make Julia feel as if she belonged with an Asian family. But Julia was so insecure, so terrified of losing someone else she loved, she kept her distance and convinced herself she was, and always would be, an outsider. She decided she would never fit in, and though she made little effort to adapt to her new environment, she eventually warmed, if only slightly, to the other family members.

Meanwhile, Katie adjusted to living with the young girl who always felt the need to prove herself and fight for her own space. She showed infinite patience with Julia's self-esteem issues, recognizing her new "sister" as a spunky, determined person who would not allow anyone to step on her or come between her and her chosen career.

If not for her closeness with Katie, Julia would have set off on her own when she reached eighteen. Instead, she chose to stay with Katie and family until she and Katie graduated together from Juilliard. At that point, they decided to share an apartment. Julia and Katie practiced together, challenging each other. Though Julia was the better player, she inspired Katie to discover and utilize her own talents to the max.

Katie, too, had auditioned for the Met when Julia won the coveted position. Julia was afraid Katie would resent her success, but she was relieved to find the opposite was true.

"You deserved it," Katie had told her. "If I had to lose to someone, I'm glad it was you."

Due to her outstanding showing, Katie was placed on the roster of extras in the Met orchestra and was hired quite often as a substitute. Attendance tended to be spotty at times, especially during flu season, and as a result, Katie's presence was ubiquitous.

Katie climbed out the window and perched next to Julia. "I came as soon as I could, Jul. They let me go early when I heard about…about Abel." Katie's voice softened. "I'd hug you, but I know you'd never allow it."

Julia's eyes welled up.

"I'm so sorry, Jul. I can't imagine what you've been through. Are you okay?"

"Do I look okay?"

"Sorry, dumb question." Katie pulled a granola bar from her pocket. "Here, have a bite. You need your strength. Though having seen you lift weights, I imagine you've got plenty of that. In any case, here's your newspaper. Not sure you should read it, though."

Katie handed Julia the newspaper and, chomping on the bar, moved to the edge of the railing and leaned over. "Man, I missed that view."

"For God's sake, Katie, get away from there. You know it freaks me out."

"Aren't you overreacting just a bit?"

"Have you forgotten I almost fell off the top deck of the Staten Island Ferry?"

"Sure, when you were two years old. Shouldn't you have gotten over it by now? Just read your *Times* and ignore me."

Julia decided to follow Katie's advice. She had no doubt what the headline would be.

"MURDER IN THE PIT—Opera Conductor Slain."

Julia stared at the photo of Abel appearing with the front-page article.

"It gets worse on page two."

Julia's eyes widened in alarm. "What?"

Katie read aloud. "'Acting on an anonymous tip, NYPD officers arrested Met Opera violinist Sidney Richter at his Upper West Side apartment last night at three a.m. Boxes of 9mm Russian sniper ammunition were found in his apartment, along with quantities of cocaine—'"

"Oh my God! Ammunition? Cocaine? How is that possible?" Julia shook her head in disbelief. "I thought I knew Sid."

Julia saw by Katie's expression that there was more to the story. She continued to read.

"'...And a packet of love letters, said to be between Richter...and Maestro Trudeau. Richter is now considered a prime suspect in the murder case.'" Katie searched Julia's ashen face. "Those letters don't prove anything, Jul."

"Are you just saying that to make me feel better?"

Katie didn't answer.

"Whatever his drug activities, or his...personal problems, Sid could *never* have harmed Abel. Those accusations are groundless. And inexcusable." Julia held Katie's gaze. "I've got to help him, K., to prove he's innocent."

Katie recognized a familiar determination in Julia's expression. "Oh, no. You're not about to take up another one of your causes."

Julia bristled. "This is not just another cause. This is Sid."

"Look, Jul, I've always admired your highly developed sense of justice. But it was one thing when we were growing up, and you adopted stray kittens or defended kids whose parents were yelling at them in the park. Sid's innocence, well, that's something else altogether."

"Why?"

"Because you have no control over whether he's innocent—and even less possibility of proving it."

"Katie Ma, I'm surprised at you! Sid's been like a brother to both of us. He fought for me to get this job and convinced Abel that *you* should have first crack at substitute gigs. He showed us the ropes. He gave us a shoulder to cry on when things got tough. We owe him."

"You're right," Katie said. "And I know you're terrified of losing Sid. But I'm willing to bet the NYPD won't appreciate your trying to do their job."

"I don't care. Sid's life is on the line. He's my friend. I believe in his innocence."

"But if Sid didn't do it, then who did?"

"That's what we have to find out."

"Wait a minute. *We?*"

"He's your friend, too."

Katie groaned. "Oh, Lord."

"We both know Sid better than any cop could. We have to do whatever it takes to clear his name. For starters, there's no way he could have collected all that illegal stuff. I think he's being framed."

Katie gasped. "Framed? By whom?"

"I don't know yet. But we're going to start by texting every musician in the orchestra and urging them to DocuSign a petition protesting Sid's arrest. Then we're going to print it out, go to the Met and hand it over to Patricia."

"Good Lord, Julia, the last thing you need is to rock the boat with Patricia."

Julia ignored Katie's admonition. "And we're going to insist she demand the NYPD assign a new detective to the case. One who knows about opera."

"Are you kidding? You seriously believe such a thing exists?"

"This is New York, remember?" Julia moved quickly toward the window. "Come on."

Julia climbed through the window into the living room, followed by Katie. She took her phone from her purse and swiped the screen. A list appeared: "Met Orchestra Members, cell phone numbers." She clicked deftly, then held up the phone to Katie.

"I just texted you the second half of the list, *M* to *Z*. I'll do *A* through *L*. That'll be good enough for starters."

"Can't it wait until I unpack?"

But Julia already was punching buttons on her cell phone. "Then I'll email a DocuSign to everyone who says yes and print it out."

Julia was thankful having something to occupy her thoughts. She'd always had her music to inspire her, and playing the violin gave her a purpose in life. Now, saving Sidney was an equally important cause. Faced with a legion of musicians represented by Julia, Patricia would have no choice but to put her considerable influence at work in pressuring the NYPD to hire a different detective. Even if it meant going all the way to the Board of Trustees.

* * *

Julia had never been in the well-appointed, wood-paneled Met boardroom. Intimidating, luxurious, it had floor-to-ceiling windows with killer views. An immense rectangular mahogany table dominated the space.

Poised at one end of the table, Julia and Katie eyed the gathering of board members on each side, who in turn regarded Patricia, standing guard at the opposite end.

Clasping the petition Julia and Katie had worked so hard to create, Patricia addressed Julia. "How many names are on the petition, Ms. Kogan?"

Patricia's officious manner didn't faze Julia. "Every member of the orchestra, except for Harold, Ms. Wells."

"Very well. Thank you, Ms. Kogan and Ms. Ma, for presenting us with this mandate. We will let you know our decision shortly. If approved, you will have the full weight of the Metropolitan Opera behind you."

Nodding their thanks, the young women rose and departed. Once the two musicians had left the room, Mrs. Tallman, a stately older woman, turned to Patricia.

"Patricia, dear, wouldn't we be overstepping our bounds, intervening for a...criminal?"

"Let me put it this way, Mrs. Tallman. A quick call to the mayor's office is a small price to pay to avoid mutiny in the ranks."

Patricia cast a meaningful glance around the room. The other members nodded their agreement—Mrs. Tallman included.

Chapter Fourteen

Wer du auch seist, ich will dich retten...du sollst kein Opfer sein!
Gewiss, ich löse deine Ketten, ich will, du Armer, dich befrei'n!
Whoever you are, I will save you...you shall not be a victim!
Surely I will loose your chains, I will free you, poor man!
—Beethoven, *Fidelio*, Act II

When Police Commissioner Ted Branson reached for the phone, he had just finished slipping into his pajamas. His private line never rang unless something important was happening. Ted was overworked, but he had assumed that it went with the territory when he'd accepted the appointment from the mayor. He had been in a constant state of raw nerves ever since, and despite his choice to stay on with the new administration, calls from the mayor's office always made him jumpy. He was not a night owl and disliked having to deal with major crises in the late evening hours. Who knew the source of this one would come from the Metropolitan Opera?

Deputy Mayor Susanna Aguilar's voice sounded regretful but resigned. "This is a tough one, Ted. High profile case, you know."

"You don't have to tell me that, Ma'am."

"But I don't want any excuses, and neither does the mayor." Susanna paused. "He wants you to find a detective who knows something about opera."

"What difference would that make?"

"Who knows? But it couldn't hurt to make the new mayor happy."

"With all due respect, how the hell am I going to find an opera-loving detective?"

"That's your problem, Commissioner."

* * *

Officer Larry Somers was a closet opera buff, though as far as his colleagues at the NYPD's Twentieth Precinct were concerned, there was nothing closeted about Larry's absolute and unquestionable love for opera. When the inspiration hit him, he was known to start conducting to some music known only to him. He never burst into song, however. He reserved that for the privacy of his shower. He was not about to allow his coworkers any such peek into the way his mind worked. Singing was too intimate, too revealing, something to be kept to oneself—unless one was an opera star.

Larry spent endless hours haunting the lower level of Westsider Records on 72nd Street near Broadway, where he searched for the latest releases of his favorite opera stars, of which tenor superstars Jonas Kaufmann and Lawrence Brownlee, soprano Sandra Radvanovsky and upcoming diva Erin Morley were at the top of his list. He also combed the aisles of the Strand Bookstore on Columbus Avenue, searching for vintage LPs.

Despite his rough-hewn good looks and eyes that twinkled, in his younger years, Larry had lost the interest of many prospective girlfriends by regaling them with the sounds of one of his rare classical LPs from the '50s, '60s, and '70s. He sensed he might be better off trotting out the tunes of U2, Fish, or the Grateful Dead, which were more likely to be successful in seducing the women's musical palates. But he had no patience for anything else but opera, preferably Italian.

His mother, *née* Angelina Morone, called Lina by those closest to her, had emigrated from Italy, the birthplace of opera. She had exposed her son to the art form day and night while he was growing up in the North End of Boston. Even her Boston P.D. husband, Richard, didn't seem to mind the constant resonating of Verdi and Puccini through the Somers's modest second-floor apartment. Despite the fact he didn't quite understand opera, Richard once told Larry that he associated the music with his adored wife.

Larry had a particular affection for Saturday afternoons, when Lina would open the windows and blast the Met Opera radio broadcasts for the whole neighborhood's benefit. His street buddies made fun of Larry's professed love for all these operas, but he didn't care.

The only opera for which he felt ambivalence was Verdi's *Don Carlo*. It was during a Met broadcast of this brilliant work that his mother, her face bathed with tears, called him in from his street hockey game to tell him his dad had been killed in the line of duty. After that, Larry associated his father's death with that beautiful and noble music and could not bear to listen to it.

After Richard Somers's funeral, Larry and his mother moved to New York City to live with Lina's sister, his Aunt Maria. Larry was thrilled to be living in the city the Met called home. Every weekend, he and his mother waited in line for hours to score standing room tickets for Met matinees. His heart raced when they were able to get tickets and perch at the rail in the Family Circle with other standees to absorb the atmosphere along with the glorious music.

By then, his favorite opera was Beethoven's *Fidelio*, much to the chagrin of his mother, who was devoted to the Italian repertoire. He immersed in Hildegarde Behrens's rendition of *Der Treuen Gattenliebe*, convinced she was singing it to him alone. The sound of her high "B" at the end of the aria thrilled him in ways no one else's could do. Only when Larry reached adulthood, and after his mother had passed away, was he able to listen to *Don Carlo* again. He saved it for evenings when he was in a bleak mood. Seated on the floor in his darkened apartment, he listened to the poignant aria, *Ella giammai m'amò*, weeping softly to himself.

But other than those rare black days, Larry generally was cheerful. He listened to opera each day, and evenings when he was on late duty, in the property room of the NYPD. For as many times as he had tried, Larry just could not ace the detectives' exam, or at least score high enough to make the cut. Some of the personnel in the precinct told him one night over beers that he was too distracted by opera to concentrate on the exam. For whatever reason, year after year, Larry remained at his post in the property room.

Larry had been there the evening Detective Al Cummings got the call about the assassination at the Metropolitan Opera. Buddy had stopped by the prop room on his way out. Larry, listening to Pavarotti let loose on *La Donna È Mobile*, from Verdi's *Rigoletto*, had been conducting along with the music, enthusiastically waving his arms, until he noticed Buddy gesticulating at him.

Larry ignored him in favor of Pavarotti. Buddy waved his hands in front of Larry's face. The opera buff was so absorbed in his music, Buddy had to yank out his earbuds.

"Hey!" Larry was indignant. "That was Pavarotti's high 'B' you interrupted."

"Sorry to intrude, Toscanini. I thought you might want to know Al and me are assigned to a murder case."

"That's nothing new."

"But this one's at the Met Opera. Conductor's been assassinated."

"What! You mean, Abel Trudeau?"

"Yeah, I think that's the guy's name."

"JesusMaryJoseph." Larry was stunned. "Abel Trudeau assassinated. This city has truly gone ape."

Now Buddy had Larry's attention. Larry had followed every detail of the prodigious Maestro Trudeau's career. And now he was dead. How was it possible?

"So, when am I gonna hear you sing, Caruso?" Buddy asked.

"How many times do I have to tell you? I only sing in the shower."

But before Larry could ask about the case, Buddy was out the door.

* * *

Larry followed every detail of Abel Trudeau's murder and the subsequent arrest of violinist Sidney Richter, who was being charged with the crime, and constantly pumped Al and Buddy for information. There was, understandably, a run on Trudeau's recordings in the Westsider Record Store near

Lincoln Center, and Larry was there to snap up any Trudeau CDs he didn't already own. He assumed his involvement with the Met case would end there.

He was careful to stash his earbuds out of sight, to give the impression he was hard at work studying for his detective's exam, when he saw his chief, Donald Darnell, approach the prop room several nights later. Larry knew Darnell was no dummy and probably sensed what he had been doing. He gave the chief credit for not upbraiding him about it.

"So, here's the deal, Somers." Darnell said. "You're on the Met Opera case, with Cruse."

Larry peered at his boss in disbelief. "Is this supposed to be a joke? If so, it's not funny."

"It's not a joke. Cummings is off, and you're on. "

"Can you do that?" Larry was still unconvinced. "Go over the head of a first grade?"

"It's been done, when the situation calls for it, Somers. In this case, the higher-ups at the Met lobbied for the change. Truth be told, I'm not happy about it, either."

"Cummings will have my ass. He'll never let me live it down."

"Cummings doesn't know squat about opera. You do. That's what the Met management wants, and that's what we're delivering. And FYI, you're lead, too. Cruse admitted he's still too green to handle that. But he is willing to bring you up to speed."

Larry swallowed hard. "Lead? But I've never investigated a case. I haven't even passed my exam."

"We're making an exception this time. The detective supervisor reviewed the case for solvability factors. Detectives are assigned to investigate crimes based on their expertise. You were chosen as lead because of your solvability potential, given your expertise in opera."

Larry took a long moment to wrap his head around what Darnell had said.

"Just so you know, Cummings threw a fit at being passed over for you. Someone who hasn't even made lowest echelon detective and likely never will. But there was nothing I could do. When it comes to the power of the

Met's influence, there's nothing *anyone* can do."

"Ya' got that right," Larry murmured under his breath.

"Report to the Met stage door tomorrow morning. That'll be all, Somers."

Larry watched as the chief departed. He wasn't sure when the reality of the situation was going to hit him.

When it does, I won't know whether to be thrilled or terrified.

He also sensed, with the evidence against Richter so compelling, he was being brought in merely as a decoy to pacify the Met Management. Thanks to the inside information Al and Buddy passed along to him, even Larry could recognize the case was pretty much sewed up.

It didn't matter. Despite his sadness and anger about Trudeau's demise, Larry had every reason to rejoice.

One way or other, my dream of entering the Met by the stage door is about to come true.

Chapter Fifteen

Und ist die Arbeit abgetan, dann schleicht die holde Nacht heran
And when the work is finished, then blessed night will creep on.
—Beethoven, *Fidelio*, Act I

W hen he and Buddy arrived at the Met stage door security station the next morning, Larry was showing the effects of his lack of sleep. Buddy had brought him up to date since Al was still sulking about being taken off the investigation. Despite his red eyes, Larry took in his surroundings with a child's fascination.

Finding themselves face to face with a surly security guard, whom Larry thought must have been chosen expressly for his suspicious nature, the two detectives flashed their NYPD badges. But Larry could see that this guard took his job of keeping the Met backstage terrorist-free seriously and was determined to make sure the two men truly were from the NYPD.

"Haft 'a see ID."

"But I already showed you," Larry protested.

"Lemme see it again."

"We're on the list. From the NYPD. Larry Somers and Buddy Cruse. For Patricia Wells, the general manager."

The guard checked his clipboard. "Yeah. Okay. End of the hall, turn left, go past the artists' area, elevator to your right, if it's working and you're not claustrophobic," he mumbled. "Otherwise, take one of the three stairways to the sixth floor. She'll be waiting."

Larry frowned at the guard, bleary-eyed, wondering how he and Buddy would manage to locate this sequestered ivory tower. The guard picked up a phone.

"Detectives Somers and Cruse on their way up, Ms. Wells…Yes, Ma'am, I'll find someone to show 'em the way."

"How hard could it be?" Buddy flashed his affable grin. "Maybe we should Map-Quest it."

"Wait here," the guard said. "I'll find you someone soon enough."

Before long an attractive young woman carrying a violin appeared. The guard turned to her. "How 'bout you show these detectives how to get to Ms. Wells' office, Julia?"

Julia remembered the younger detective from their brief encounter in the musicians' lounge the night of Abel's murder. She didn't recognize the older one, however.

He must be the opera one. Good to know my request was taken seriously.

She turned to the guard. "You mean I can come in without showing my ID?" Her own sarcasm startled her. She lost no time in chastising herself.

Here I am, facing the opera-savvy replacement detective I asked for, and I'm being flip. What was I thinking?

Julia could see the guard disapproved of her harsh tone. "What do you think?" he asked.

"Right." As Julia extracted her card from her bag, she caught sight of Larry's badge and noticed at once that it read "Inspection" and not "Detective" as Buddy's did. Her heart sank.

He's not even a detective?

Buddy turned to Julia. "I'm Buddy Cruse. We met the night of—"

"Yes. I remember."

"This is my colleague, Larry Somers."

Larry turned to Buddy. "This kid plays the violin?"

Julia peered more closely at Larry. She guessed he was around forty, which she considered ancient. Still, the small flecks of salt in his curly peppercorn-colored hair gave him a surprising attractiveness.

Nonetheless, Julia always had a retort ready for "older" skeptics who thought she wasn't mature enough to belong at the Met.

"Excuse me, but Mozart was a 'kid,' too, and no one questioned his violin playing," Julia replied haughtily. "I know my way around. But if you prefer, I could just drop breadcrumbs, like Hänsel and Gretel. Do you want the fast track to the elevator or the travelogue?"

Julia was annoyed at Buddy's barely suppressed grin as he observed the not-so-subtle repartee going on between her and Larry. But she chose to suppress her displeasure.

This stranger represents my only hope for Sidney. I'd better toe the line.

"Oh, definitely the travelogue." Larry turned to Buddy. "You search Trudeau's dressing room. I'll meet you later."

The guard buzzed all three of them inside the gate. None of them heard him when he picked up a phone and dialed upstairs, announced Detective Somers on his way up, hung up the phone, and sniffed, "Your Highness."

* * *

Julia saw that Larry had difficulty keeping up with her as they hastened down a long, winding hallway on Stage Level. She was unfamiliar with the high floors of the opera house, but she had visited the Artists' area on countless occasions.

Each time she and Larry sped past a room, she explained its function with expertise, aware of his wide-eyed fascination. "Wardrobe, coaching, and rehearsal rooms on the right. Green room on the left."

"How'd you learn about all this? Don't you spend most of your time in the pit?"

"I've been coming here since I was a kid to coach with Abel Trudeau. After my dad died."

"Oh. I'm sorry."

Julia sensed from Larry's sincere apology that he had experienced a parent's death. But she kept her thoughts to herself.

They soon arrived at a carpeted space where large numbers of people were rushing about in different directions. Seeing Larry's bewildered expression, Julia continued her tour speech.

"This is the Artists' area. Stage is in that direction, soloists' dressing rooms over there."

Larry watched the activity, wide-eyed. "So many people. Who are they?"

"Singers, wardrobe people, stagehands. The usual."

"Where are they all going?"

"With six evening performances and one matinee a week of different operas, and rehearsals for upcoming repertoire during the day, there's plenty to do, believe me."

Julia pointed to a door on one side of the corridor and explained it led to Orchestra Level, where the pit and cafeteria were. Then she led Larry to an elevator at one end of the artists' area.

"That's it. Sixth floor. She'll be waiting, no doubt."

"She?"

"Patricia, the general manager." Julia's impatience was escalating.

This is the guy who's going to help me save Sidney?

"Oh, right. Sure you don't want to see me to her door?"

For a brief instant, Julia was tempted to accept his offer. After all, being sequestered with him in a slow-moving elevator for a few extra minutes would give her an opportunity to plead her case for Sidney's innocence. But she thought better of it.

There'll be time for that later.

"I only go there when I have to."

"By the way…thanks."

"No problem."

Julia smiled, determined to be nice to him for Sidney's sake. But she suddenly felt shy. She wasn't sure why, but she went to the trouble to fix a stray hair as she took off, leaving Larry to fend for himself.

Larry exited the elevator and bumped right into Patricia. He immediately felt intimidated.

"Ms. Wells?"

Patricia extended her hand with a calm, unruffled smile. "Generally speaking, yes."

"I didn't quite expect you to be right here to greet me."

"We wouldn't want you to lose your way, would we?"

Her brusque manner and air of superiority gave him pause, but he managed a rejoinder. "I'm touched you would go out of your way to help out one of New York's Finest."

"Finest what?" Patricia asked.

Before he could respond, she turned around and led Larry down another long hallway.

"Do you have that list of personnel that Buddy...er, Detective Cruse requested?"

Without missing a beat, Patricia turned and faced him. Larry almost felt ice dripping from her tone. "I'm going to need more time, Detective. There are over a thousand people working here at any given moment. Between performers and stagehands and wardrobe people...Well, I'm sure you understand I'm overwhelmed."

The atmosphere between them remained awkward. The first thing Larry noticed in the office was the floor-to-ceiling window with its spectacular view. Spread out below them were Lincoln Plaza, its celebrated fountain, and the microcosm of New York City populace that passed through the famous square day in and day out.

Larry realized he needed to change the subject. "That's quite a vista. You must rate."

"Isn't it? And yes, I do."

When will she stop talking down to me?

"Good thing you're not scared of heights."

Uneasy at her lack of response, Larry cleared his throat and tried a different tack. "You've got your hands full, running the opera at this difficult time, dealing with a murder on top of your usual problems—"

"Problems, you say? Try notifying an insurance company they're going to be paying for psychotherapy for hundreds of employees." She paused. "Detective Somers, I'm a very busy woman. Did you have some *specific* questions?"

"Ah, of course." Larry could see Patricia was irritated and was surprised at his own delight over it. "Did you notice anything or anyone unusual backstage before the murder?"

"No, I didn't. Frankly, I was too busy trying to calm our lead tenor—"

"Giuseppe Masini?" Larry whipped out his notebook and began to write. "I saw him perform *Ernani*."

Larry noticed that Patricia seemed both surprised and taken aback by his apparent knowledge of opera.

Wasn't she the one who requested a detective who knows opera?

He continued before she had an opportunity to react. "I'm an opera buff from 'way back. My mom used to listen to the Met on the radio every Saturday. She and I did standing room whenever we could get tickets."

"Oh really?"

Ignoring Patricia's apparent lack of interest, Larry allowed himself a moment of nostalgia and continued.

"Where were you when the murder occurred, Ms. Wells?"

"Oh? Am I a suspect?"

"We're required to ask. Procedure."

"I was backstage. That's *my* procedure."

"Anybody see you?"

"Don't be ridiculous. Of course. Everybody sees me."

"What was your relationship to the deceased?"

"We were professional colleagues. Nothing more."

"Any rivalry? Bad blood between you?"

"Rivalry is rampant in an opera house. That shouldn't surprise you."

"But you and Trudeau must have been the most high-powered of all of them."

"Your point being?"

"Just high stakes." Larry paused. "He ever mention any threats? Did he have any enemies you knew of?"

Patricia waved her hand in an offhand manner. *"Entre nous,* who doesn't?"

Larry persisted. "Was he involved in anything shady?"

"How would I know about such things? I have an opera house to run."

If Patricia knew I wasn't technically a detective, she would eat me for breakfast and ask for a hand towel.

Patricia picked up a ringing phone and spoke into it. "Yes? She is? I'll be right down." She turned to Larry. "Please forgive me detective, I must go handle a diva problem. Are you familiar with Dorothy Muir?"

"Are you kidding? I have all her CDs."

"Well, as you can imagine, she's a very difficult personality. I'm the only one who can handle her. So, if you'll excuse me—"

"You don't mind if I tag along, do you?"

Larry saw that Patricia's lack of surprise at his rhetorical question didn't change the fact she had been hoping to be rid of him sooner rather than later. He also knew she wasn't about to rock the boat any further. It was already tilting.

Chapter Sixteen

Se non muove par la sua dolor, ha non il cuor
If he's not moved by her grief, he has a heart of stone, or no heart at all
—Mozart, *Don Giovanni*, Act II

Abel's valet, Damon, watched Buddy and the accompanying crime techs search through the late maestro's effects. As Buddy pulled photos of Abel with famous conductors and singers from the wall, he eyed the scowling valet with suspicion. Having seen too many Coppola movies when he was growing up, Buddy always had a visceral, if unfounded, reaction to inordinately handsome, unhappy-looking young guys with black curly hair who stood by silently.

"Be careful how you handle his things, will you, detective? Try not to paw them to death. They're collector items now. Especially the baton. It's priceless."

Buddy ignored Damon's supercilious tone. "I recognize the Three Tenors, but who are these other photos of?"

"Giuseppe Masini and Dorothy Muir, of course," the valet sniffed. "Naturally, we change them according to who the guest artist is for any particular week."

"Naturally." Buddy didn't have a clue what the valet was talking about and gestured at a third picture. "Who's this good-looking dude with Trudeau?"

"Charles Tremaine. Tenor."

"Another biggie?"

"Actually, no. You might say second-string."

"Then why'd Trudeau have his photo taken with the guy?"

"*Maestro* Trudeau was kind, magnanimous," Damon said. "He was happy to be photographed with even the most insignificant of artists. Charles was just an in-house *comprimario* who got lucky."

"'Comp'...*what?*"

The Valet rolled his eyes. "*Comprimario*. That's what we call the singers who do secondary roles. Charles eventually became an understudy for larger roles."

"Right." Buddy was completely in the dark but didn't share that with Damon. "So, where's the one of Trudeau with you?"

Damon glowered. "The nerve of this philistine," he muttered under his breath.

He collapsed on the piano bench, weeping. Buddy allowed himself a *frisson* of sympathy for the valet. Then he continued his search.

* * *

Buddy later met up with Larry and huddled with him in a backstage corner, comparing notes. "I did Trudeau's dressing room and Richter's locker, too. Couldn't come up with much. Though that valet was acting pretty weird."

"We can keep an eye on him. But unless Richter can explain his way out of those jealous love letters," said Larry, "It's open and shut."

Buddy's eyes opened wide. "You mean...you already know...?"

Larry flashed a crooked smile. "I can recognize irrefutable evidence when I see it. Or, in this case, hear about it. From you, as it happens."

"Right." Buddy lowered his voice confidentially. "Then how do you feel about...?"

"Being a walking, talking detective decoy?" Larry again finished Buddy's thought. "It got me into the Met, didn't it?"

* * *

The memorial gathering that evening took place at Charles Tremaine's

81

apartment. Located a short walk from the Met, in a landmark building off Central Park West and up the street from the ABC Network studios, the spacious, upscale co-op was a perfect venue for the ceremonies. Whatever his feelings about his talents not being appropriately recognized at the Met, the singer considered the volunteering of his abode his own generous gesture to the company in their collective time of need.

Inside the elegantly furnished living room, a large glossy photo of Abel was positioned on a dais surrounded by flower arrangements. In the background, a recording of "Siegfried's Funeral Music" from Wagner's *Götterdämmerung* alternated with the "Entry into Valhalla" from *Das Rheingold*. Charles thought the pieces appropriately somber for the fallen hero. Musicians, choristers, stagehands, and other company members hung about, downcast, conversing in subdued whispers.

Ever the gracious host, Charles circulated through the crowd, alternating between offering drinks or solace, whichever seemed suitable for the situation and people he addressed. Seeing Julia linger in a corner by herself, he approached her, gazing with concern at her eyes, swollen from crying. He knew Julia's devotion to Abel was legendary.

"Anything I can get for you?" he asked in a gentle voice. Charles saw that his kindliness had touched off a threat of tears from the overwrought violinist, even though he could tell she was putting on a brave front.

"Oh. Thanks, Charles. I...just need to find the powder room."

"Of course. Why don't you use the one in my bedroom? It's more private."

Julia acknowledged him with a grateful smile. He pointed toward the rear of the apartment, and she moved off. He was impressed at her having kept her composure, at least in public.

Ushered in by a maid, Larry and Buddy remained at the entrance, scrutinizing the action, and taking discreet notes. They had agreed even if the case was open and shut, it wouldn't hurt to get a sense of the feelings, positive and negative, of the attendees toward their departed maestro. They both watched closely as Patricia moved to the dais and waved her hands to get attention.

She spoke in a subdued tone. "I'd like to make a few announcements."

82

All faces turned toward the general manager. Even Charles stopped what he was doing. He knew Patricia's calm, self-assured confidence was the result of years of experience as an important figure accustomed to addressing boards of directors as well as rich patrons.

"I'd like to start by thanking you all for coming," she said, as she surveyed the room. "If anyone has a problem with performing at tomorrow's rehearsal, please inform me, and I will see an alternate is found for you."

Several people raised their hands. Patricia acknowledged them with a nod.

"On that note, I'm sorry to report our tenor, Mr. Masini, is grieving profoundly and will be unable to sing tomorrow."

Hearing this, Charles started to step forward toward Patricia, a stalwart expression on his face.

Patricia waited a moment for the appropriate disappointed murmur from her listeners. "However, as a special favor to the Met, Mr. Jonas Kaufmann has agreed to take Mr. Masini's place tomorrow."

The crowd gasped collectively and started whispering to each other. Charles stopped still, his expression darkening. Patricia cast an eye in his direction.

"I also wish to thank Charles Tremaine for so graciously offering us his home as a venue for this gathering."

Patricia gestured toward Charles, applauding, and the others joined in. Beneath a gallant smile, his face was etched in frustration.

Buddy muttered to Larry. "Who's that Kaufmann guy?"

"Only the most famous tenor in the world today."

"Guess he's gonna be the next one to have his face plastered on the dressing room wall."

The detectives gazed around the room once more and left without making a sound.

* * *

Julia emerged from the bathroom adjoining Charles's bedroom and sank down in a chair by his desk, dabbing at her eyes.

I should have known how hard this would be. I should have taken a tranquilizer. If only Katie was here.

Julia knew Katie's AA meetings took precedence over everything else, even death. But she missed her just the same. At that moment, Charles hurried in and closed the door behind him. He poured a tall glass of Scotch and chugged half the contents in one gulp.

Noticing his distress, Julia cleared her throat. When Charles saw her sitting at his desk, his face flushed a bright red. He set his glass on the wet bar by the door and turned to her.

"Are you all right, Julia?"

She could tell by his expression he was anxious to cover up his embarrassment and replied with as much conviction as she could muster. "Fine, thank you, Charles. But you look upset."

Charles took another gulp of his drink. "Oh, it's nothing..." He hesitated for a moment. "Giuseppe canceled tomorrow's rehearsal, and Kaufmann is replacing him. Which leaves me odd man out. Again."

"That's a shame. But don't worry, you'll be in the limelight soon, I'm convinced."

She smiled her encouragement through misted eyes. He approached her, perching on the ottoman by her chair.

"How sweet you are to worry about me in your time of grief. No wonder Abel was so fond of you."

Julia blushed. Then sighing, she said, "I miss him so much, Charles. He was the best mentor I ever could have asked for."

"He was my mentor, too," he said. "My very first coach. Though we did have our differences at times."

"I'm sure that happens to everyone sooner or later. Right?"

Charles nodded. "I suppose."

Julia was seized with a sudden urge to confide in him and gestured at the violin pin fastened to her sweater. "He gave me this for my first opening night, the night he...he died."

He leaned in close to her, eyeing the pin. "He must have had immense faith in you. He certainly had exquisite taste. And not just in jewelry," he added, holding her gaze.

Julia disregarded his compliment, which made her uncomfortable. "Not only that. He wrote a song for me and gave it to me that night, just before the performance."

"Oh? What kind of song?"

"That's a good question. I tried to play it, and it just sounded weird. And the second page was missing."

"Maybe Abel was distracted. Opening night jitters and all. Would you like me to look at it? It might help to have a second pair of eyes."

"That's very generous, Charles, but...it's kind of personal."

"I understand. I didn't mean to pry."

"You weren't."

Uncomfortable at his closeness, Julia shifted in the chair. Charles responded by moving back several inches.

"I could use some help, though, with something else...if you wouldn't mind."

"Anything for you, Julia."

"It's Sidney, I'm so worried about him. He's been in that horrid Tombs place for a whole day now. I thought..." She groped for the words. "I thought I could help him by getting a new detective assigned to the investigation. But now I don't know if it will do any good at all." She lowered her voice. "I just know Sid couldn't have harmed Abel. I'm convinced he's being framed for Abel's murder. But I don't know how to prove it."

"What can I do to help?"

"If you hear of anything, any gossip around the opera house that has to do with Sid, could you please let me know?"

Charles smiled warmly. "I'd be happy to."

With a great effort, Julia rose and turned to go. Charles took her arm, but she shrank away from him. "I'm sorry, Julia. I should have been more sensitive."

"It's okay. Really."

"No, it's not. I know what Abel meant to you and how close you are with Sidney. I can only imagine how you're suffering right now. I'll do whatever

I can to help, even if it's only to offer you a shoulder to cry on."

She nodded her thanks. But as she moved toward the door, she noticed him watching her, admiring the way she walked. It made her nervous.

How could he look at me that way, when he knows how vulnerable I am right now?

Suddenly aware of the clinginess of her black jersey skirt, she chastised herself.

It's probably my fault.

She quickly slipped through the door, resolving to be more careful about her attire from now on.

Chapter Seventeen

Dolce signora, che mai v'accora?...
Darei la vita per asciugar qual pianto
Gracious lady, whatever is it that grieves you?...
I would give my life to wipe away those tears.
—Puccini, *Tosca*, Act I

The next morning, Julia sat in the visitor center of "The Tombs" staring out the window at the slate gray sky.

How appropriate for a visit to jail.

Julia was not a morning person, but to see Sidney before getting to rehearsal by eleven a.m. meant arriving at the prison by eight o'clock, which she considered an ungodly hour.

She looked around, trying not to be disturbed at the brutal, low-life atmosphere surrounding her. But it was difficult. The place reeked of human misery and unhappiness. She could not deny it, even in her befogged state.

The first thing Julia noticed when Sidney came in was his haggard, sweating face. There was something wrong with him, something beyond the customary wretchedness of an imprisoned man. She could tell by the way he avoided her gaze when he sat down opposite her.

Suddenly she felt anxious and afraid. "Are you okay, Sid? You don't look too great."

"I...I think someone is trying to poison me."

"What? Oh, Sid!" Julia cried out. "Who would do that? How do you know?"

"Haven't a clue. I just suddenly got sick, and it's not my diverticulitis." He shook his head. "I should 'a been out 'a here by now."

The difficulty with which he spoke made Julia feel even more concerned. Though being touched was anathema to her, she felt an urge to take his hand, or stroke his forehead to see if he had a fever. But the Plexiglas barrier between them prevented it.

Sidney waved away Julia's concern. "Rossi overheard me calling Abel a son-of-a-bitch. Suddenly I'm a murderer. I was set up, Julia. Someone planted that ammo and those love letters in my apartment."

"I totally believe that, Sid, but...what's going to happen to you?"

He lowered his voice. "The D.A. is talking life without parole. *Life without parole*. It's the 'new death penalty.'"

Julia felt the color drain from her face. "'New death penalty?' What does that mean?"

"More people have died in New York State prisons in the last decade than in the three hundred years capital punishment was allowed. More than twelve hundred the last ten years."

"Oh, my God. How is that possible?"

"More punitive sentencing, constant parole denials, keeping older people like me locked up longer. It all adds up to a new kind of death penalty. The D.A.'s office uses their power to push for the longest possible sentences. If I can't prove my innocence, I'm screwed. I'm going to die here!"

Julia had never seen Sid in such a vulnerable state. His wild-eyed expression terrified her.

"The grand jury meets tomorrow. If they indict, the D.A.'ll pressure me to make a deal, otherwise, I go to trial with a life sentence—a *death* sentence—hanging over my head." Sid began to sob. "Julia, I can't make any deals. I'm innocent. I didn't do it!"

Suddenly Sidney's breath started coming in halting spurts. He doubled over, groaning. "God, I feel so nauseated."

Julia leapt up and made a frantic gesture at the guard. "Help! Come here! He's sick!"

Sidney collapsed on the floor. The guard rushed over, followed by another guard. Julia stood motionless, watching in helpless disbelief as the two men dragged Sidney off. She felt the beats of his life ticking away like the pendulum on a metronome.

* * *

On the subway going home, Julia wracked her brains for some means of helping Sid, but she came up with nothing. When she returned to her apartment, she was still upset. Once back in her bedroom, she decided to clear her head by again trying to play Abel's song. There was still time before she had to be at rehearsal.

Facing her music stand, she stared at the notes, as if willing them to make sense. But the strange, incongruous dissonance stopped her just as before. She was still poised in front of the music when Katie peeked in.

"Still practicing that thing. Are you obsessed or what?"

Julia ignored the question. "Did you hear those notes? Do they sound skewed to you?"

"Actually, yeah. Obviously, there's some mistake. Maybe Abel was in a rush when he was copying it. It was opening night, after all."

"Abel didn't make mistakes. He was the most meticulous person I ever knew. He must have known what he was doing." Julia pointed to the bottom of the page. "Though he did tell me there were some last-minute changes."

"Yet he neglected to include the second page. Why?" Katie asked.

"That's the question of the century."

"It's an awful lot to deal with right now, Jul. Why not just bag it until later?"

"With Sid in prison, wasting away, there's no 'later.' There's only now."

"But what does the song have to do with Sid?"

"Abel gave me this song for a reason, K. My gut tells me those wrong notes might be pointing to a clue in here somewhere, tied to Abel's murder. Maybe I can use it to prove Sid is innocent. I'm going to keep playing until I figure out what it is." Julia eyed Katie's dubious look. "You'll help, won't you?"

Julia gave Katie her best puppy dog gaze. Katie groaned in surrender.

Chapter Eighteen

E perche piangi...onde contanta senti pieta della mia vita?
But why do you weep...why do you feel such pity for my life?
—Verdi, *Un Ballo in Maschera*, Act III

E ven with Katie's help, Julia's efforts to decipher Abel's composition proved fruitless, and before long, she gave up in frustration. She hid the music away in the zipper compartment of her violin case, in the event she found an extra moment to practice at the Met.

Julia had left Katie behind so that she could take her time walking to work. Soon she was marching down Broadway, her fiddle case strapped to her shoulder. When she found herself at the corner of West 72nd Street, she could not resist turning toward West End Avenue and ended up in front of Westsider Records. There was more than enough time before rehearsal to stop in and browse a bit.

After witnessing the disturbing spectacle with Sidney that morning in The Tombs, Julia felt a need to indulge herself. In times of stress, she often escaped to the comforting womb of the Westsider and lost herself amidst the myriad of consolatory favorites in the classical CD section. It soothed her to be sequestered among the plastic discs representing her dear friends Mozart, Beethoven, Brahms, and Verdi. As a child, one of her favorite treats was to wander the aisles with her father after her violin lessons at Juilliard Prep.

Sol Kogan had been Julia's first violin teacher. Though he never became a professional musician, he had enough mastery of the violin to start her off in the right direction. But within the first two months of his pedagogy, he realized she would quickly surpass him, and he lost no time in sending her to Juilliard Prep, the Lincoln Center institution famous for preparing talented young children for professional musical careers. He always accompanied Julia to her lessons, and the two of them spent hours afterwards searching through the bins at the record store for "little bargains," as Sol called them.

The display in the familiar window commanded her attention. All of Abel's recordings, labeled "Homage to a Fallen Maestro," were there, beckoning to her. The word "fallen" again brought into sharp focus the realization that he was dead. At first, Julia did not know whether she could handle the emotional pangs of being surrounded by these reminders of Abel, a mentor who, like her father, had passed from her life with such violence. But her indecision disappeared when she overheard the conversation of the two guys next to her.

"Do you think we should snatch up some copies?" one asked.

"Of course. Trudeau's recordings may be worth a lot of money someday."

Without waiting to hear another word, Julia hurried into the store, headed for the opera section, and began to scoop up CDs of Abel's performances. But as her distress about Abel came bubbling up to the surface, she put the CDs back with a sigh of defeat and berated herself.

Julia, you're being ridiculous. You're acting like a child. When are you going to get your inner strength back?

In the midst of her silent diatribe, she spied Larry Somers approaching her from a few rows away. Her self-punishment shifted to a sudden desire to flee.

The last thing I need is to chitchat with this guy in the middle of a public place.

She decided it was better to pretend not to see Larry. But it was too late. He was already at her side, flashing her a look of mock bravado.

"You're not going to buy them all, are you? I was gonna buy some."

Julia couldn't resist a retort. "I'm not going to let a bunch of Philistine thrill-seekers snatch them all up because they want a piece of scandal they can sell on eBay."

"Hey, not all of us want to profit from the maestro's death."

She felt regret for her hasty response. "Oh. Sorry."

"Apology accepted."

The awkward silence between them was palpable as Julia picked up a CD with Abel's picture on the cover. From the corner of her eye, she spied Larry's intense gaze. It made her uncomfortable.

"*Fidelio* is sublime, don't you think?" he asked. "One of my all-time favorites, in fact."

Despite her hostile feelings toward Larry, Julia found his smile engaging. Disarming, in fact. And she was impressed with his taste. In general, even self-professed opera aficionados stuck to the so-called bread and butter of the opera repertoire: Verdi, Puccini, Donizetti, and Bellini. Most devotees proclaimed Beethoven's only effort at writing opera to be inferior to the Italian school. But Julia loved *Fidelio* as dearly as any other, though she resisted feeling a connection with Larry because of it.

"It was one of my dad's favorites," Julia said.

"I knew that."

She was taken aback. "You did?"

"He was also partial to '*Thaïs*,' wasn't he?"

Despite the sudden memory and wistful thoughts about the last piece her father had ever heard her play, Larry's detailed knowledge of her and her father startled her.

How can he know about this?

"You're a graduate of Juilliard, worked at the Willowstream Music Camp in the summer of '18, were mugged on upper Central Park West last year. You volunteered to teach some kids in Harlem about opera."

Julia let the information sink in. She was aghast at Larry's knowledge of the intimate aspects of her life, but she had to admit he did his research.

Larry broke the silence. "I lost my mom when I was a child, too."

"I'm so sorry." Now Julia's barriers were beginning to break down. She was feeling genuine sympathy for him.

"My mom was the one who turned me on to opera. Now I just sing with Pavarotti. In the shower, of course."

Julia managed a smile. For the first time, she took a good look at Larry.

Like her father, he was not too tall, maybe five feet-nine inches, and slender, and had a twinkle in his eye. There was something about him, something she couldn't quite identify, that made her rethink her initial negative impression of him. It was as if a link had been uncovered, allowing them to reveal their private lives to each other. Suddenly she felt more comfortable and relaxed.

Maybe there's hope after all. He might be open to discussing Sidney's innocence.

Julia decided it was time to ask. "Is it true that Sidney's case is closed?"

Larry sighed, shaking his head, and Julia immediately regretted her question. His look told her he knew some sad truth that he felt badly about having to reveal. She girded herself.

"Look, I feel for you and your friend. But the evidence against him is compelling."

Julia's face fell.

"Sidney was a rejected lover. He and Abel were at each other's throats. They found letters..." He paused. "And weapons. And ammo."

Julia swallowed hard. "I don't care, Sid's not capable of murder."

"How do you know?"

"He's my best friend. He's looked out for me ever since I joined the Met."

"Hey, you think you know somebody, then it turns out you don't. You've got to be careful who you trust, Julia. Look what happened to Abel."

Julia looked at him in distress as he spoke in a firm but gentle tone. "My hands are tied. I hate to tell you, but they sent me here because they wanted to comply with the Met management's request for an opera-savvy detective, and they knew I wouldn't rock the boat."

Each word nauseated Julia. All her efforts, to collect the musicians' signatures on the petition, to sway Patricia and the board, to plead Sidney's case to this new detective, were for nothing. Sid would be found guilty, and there wasn't a thing she could do to help. To make things worse, Larry was trying to be nice to her.

"There's going to be a Grand Jury hearing soon, maybe even today. It's a high-profile case, and it'll be on a fast track. I...I'm so sorry, Julia."

He really does seem sorry. But I still wish I'd run when I had the chance.

"I have to get to rehearsal now."

"How 'bout I tag along with you? I have to go there, too."

Julia had second thoughts about Larry's sincerity. "Oh? I thought the case was closed."

"I still have to show up."

"Suit yourself."

Julia reached over, plucked the *Fidelio* CD from a bin, and proceeded to the cashier.

Larry followed. "Once you make up your mind, kid, you're off and running. It's impressive."

Julia was too mired in thoughts of Abel and Sidney to hear him and, within seconds, had paid for her purchase. She declined the offer of a bag and instead placed the CD in the zipper compartment of her violin case. As she unzipped it, Abel's song fluttered to the floor.

Larry bent down and retrieved it, eyeing it with curiosity. "Ooh, how interesting." He examined the title. "Dedicated to you?"

"Abel gave it to me the night he was murdered."

"Have you played it?"

"Of course. But—" She snatched the song from him, pointing out the scribbling at the bottom of the page. "These notes don't make sense. I think he put them there for a reason. Like he was trying to tell me something."

"That's a bit of a stretch, don't you think? Messages in music?"

Julia ignored his skeptical look. "That shows how much you don't know about music history." Julia considered another tack. "If I can prove it's not a 'stretch', will you consider the chances of Sid's innocence? Even let me team up with you to find the real killer?"

Larry whistled. "Easy does it, Nancy Drew. You may be a brilliant violinist—or so I've heard—but you need sleuthing skills, developed over time. And investigating is riskier than you think."

"I have great instincts. I know more about the opera house than you ever could. I can talk to the people there in ways that you can't. And you just called me brilliant."

"Did I?" Larry smiled. "I'll take it under advisement. Meanwhile, how about we call a truce, in any case, kid?" Larry asked.

Julia mused on the mixture of admiration and resentment she felt for this cop, whose intelligence was engaging. She was reluctant to ally herself with the enemy, but she also felt it unwise to give up her efforts to convince Larry of Sidney's innocence.

"I'll think about it. And don't call me 'kid.'"

Chapter Nineteen

La vita mi costasse, vi salverò!
I'll save you, even if it costs me my life!
—Puccini, *Tosca*, Act I

When Julia and Larry appeared at the stage door, company members were gathered around a sign tacked to the bulletin board near the security post.

"*Tosca revised rehearsal time, 12:00 p.m.*"

"Later, Julia." Larry flashed his badge to the guard and headed through the gate.

Charles, who was retrieving an envelope from the mail cubbies on the wall, approached Julia. "Who was that?" he asked.

"The new detective on Abel's case."

"He doesn't look much like a detective." Charles gazed at Julia's exhausted, stressed face. "How's my favorite violinist today? Looks like you haven't slept?"

Julia shook her head. "I was up half the night trying to figure out Abel's song."

"I have a practice studio reserved this morning. We have time to go there and try singing it together before your rehearsal."

Julia didn't know what to think. On one hand, the song was deeply personal and intimate. On the other hand, Charles was an accomplished musician who knew Abel and might have some insight into the strange, bewildering notes eluding her own efforts. And the thought of singing even a few notes with one of the Met's outstanding tenors was too tempting to resist.

"Okay. But I can't stay long."

"Follow me."

The Artists' Practice Studio was more impressive than Julia had imagined. Its high ceilings and elite atmosphere broadcasted *luxe*. A scrupulously polished Steinway Grand, cushy upholstered settee, and autographed eight-by-ten glossies of renowned opera singers on the wall completed the effect.

Julia gazed around in awe. "I've never seen such a magnificent space."

"Then it's about time you did."

Charles sat on the piano bench and patted the space to his right. Julia obeyed the gesture as Charles placed the song on the music rack. He played the first few notes, and then hummed them. Julia joined him but stopped suddenly.

"Am I crazy, or is that note weird?"

"It does sound odd. And you're not crazy. Lovely, sweet. But not crazy."

His admiring glance made Julia feel self-conscious. "So, what now, Charles?"

"Why not lend it to me for the day? I can try to make sense of it, and we can discuss it later, maybe over dinner. If you're off tonight, that is."

Is he asking me out?

Julia had been told the Met stayed out of their employees' dating affairs. Management weren't thrilled when people dated "in-house" but didn't interfere either. Several marriages had taken place, usually between employees of the same genre: musicians with musicians, singers with singers, ballet dancers with other ballet dancers. Daniel, the orchestra's concertmaster, had married a well-known solo singer, but no doubt his prominent position helped him cross the genre line. Plus, their love story was both touching and legendary.

The one unwritten rule was not to accept already-married couples into the orchestra. Nepotism was frowned upon, at least on the surface. Better to support two families than one, was the policy. The stagehands were an exception, but they were part of the Teamsters, and their union had more clout than any other in the opera house.

Julia's guard went up. "Dinner?" She looked at the people around her, but no one seemed to be listening. "Well, I am off, actually, but—"

"Just a get-together, no strings." He waited while she considered. "How about we meet at *Café des Artistes* at eight?"

Julia glanced at the wall clock. She was still hoping to talk to Matt before rehearsal. Ultimately, despite her misgivings, Charles won her over. She nodded.

"Wonderful. See you tonight, Julia."

She listened, transported, as he warmed up his voice and the lush tones soared up into the high-ceilinged space. Then, with a backward glance at the precious music perched on the piano rack, she slipped out of the room.

* * *

Matt was supervising the placement of sets for the day's rehearsal along with Frank and other assistants when Julia arrived at the busy backstage area. Other stagehands adjusted scenery and props as solo singers and choristers loosened up their voices.

"More to the left!" Matt shouted. "Lower it slowly!"

Groaning at the effort, the stagehands let down a backdrop with great care and stopped for a much-needed breather. They all managed to smile, however, when they spied Julia coming toward them.

Julia returned the greeting. She knew they were nice to her because she was new, and she didn't perceive their appreciation of her as a threat or sexual innuendo in any way. She got along well with all the stagehands except for Frank, who seemed to have been born with a nasty disposition. After a few attempts at being friendly with him, she gave up and decided to stick to the more genial members of the International Alliance of Technical and Stage Employees.

Striding toward Matt, Julia didn't notice the cloth-covered table placed in her path. Finding herself face-to-face with the bloodied severed head of Saint John the Baptist on a silver platter, she gave a little gasp, bumped right into it, painfully stubbing her toe, and uttered a soft cry. She looked around and saw Frank smirking at her. Suppressing a shudder, she limped toward Matt with as much dignity as she could manage.

He gave her his usual affable grin. "Hey, Julia. What's up?"

Julia got right to the point. "Matt, can we talk…about Sid?"

Matt lowered his voice. "Let's go somewhere else." He motioned to Frank. "Can you take over for a few?"

Frank frowned. "We're awful busy right now. It's not a good time." He fired an unfriendly look at Julia. "But yeah, sure thing, boss."

"Thanks, pal. Don't know what I'd do without you."

As Frank took Matt's position, Julia noticed him watching her and Matt out of the corner of his eye as they walked off. Julia thought Frank probably knew about the little love notes Matt penciled by her name on the sign-in sheet and resented Matt's crush on her. She sensed there was something about her that grated on Frank's nerves, but she couldn't fathom what it could be. He was either jealous of Matt, or he thought she was distracting Matt from his job. But Matt had never mentioned that Frank had made any complaints about her.

I'll never understand the world of stagehands.

As usual, the backstage wings were a zoo. Stagehands, the stage manager, his assistants and lackeys, and other assorted company members were all jockeying for space and attention. Matt led Julia to a dark, quiet corner at the rear of the stage.

Julia nodded in Frank's direction. "I don't think he likes me."

"Don't take it personally. He's surly with everybody. It's just his army training."

That explains a lot. The military is even more incomprehensible than stagehands. Some sort of feral tribe.

"I, on the other hand, like you a lot."

She was not surprised at his declaration but didn't know how to respond. There was a tense silence as she tried to summon up the courage to broach a subject which, she sensed, Matt would not be comfortable discussing.

"So, what's up?" Matt asked, smiling.

"Sidney."

"Gee, Julia, I'm disappointed. I was hoping for maybe dinner and a movie."

"This is serious, Matt. He needs your help."

Matt's smile lost its luster. "Me? What could I do?"

"We both know he's not capable of harming Abel. I think he's being framed. I thought you could help me find out who's framing him. And who the real killer is."

His face darkened. "I don't know, Julia. Isn't it up to the police to investigate?"

"They've already decided he's guilty. If we don't come up with evidence to clear him, he could spend the rest of his life in jail."

From his gloomy expression, Julia could see that her pleas had an effect. "Understood. But it's not the time or place to discuss this, Julia."

"Then when? Or where?" Julia became frantic. "Sid's chances of beating the charges are fading away as we speak. He's sick, too, thinks someone in the jail is trying to poison him."

Matt groaned. "Oh, man..."

Julia held his gaze. "Will you help, *please*? I don't know where else to turn. You're his friend, you've known him, like, forever, right?"

"Yeah. But we had a falling out recently." Matt hesitated. "Okay, we can talk, but later. And anywhere but here." He lowered his voice to a faint whisper. "The walls have ears."

"It's got to be soon. There's going to be a Grand Jury hearing any moment."

"I promise to find us a time and place, ASAP. And I'll ask around, try to pick my coworkers' brains."

"Thanks." Julia struggled to maintain her composure. "I've never been so scared, Matt."

"Don't worry, we'll get to the bottom of this." He thought for a moment. "Okay, meet me in the stagehands' locker room after rehearsal. We can find a quiet corner there."

She let out a sigh of relief. "I will. Thanks."

"Meanwhile, you need to let go of things you have no control over, okay?" Matt returned to his upbeat smile. "Now get into that pit and be the violinist you're meant to be."

He reached over to give her shoulder a reassuring squeeze. She instinctively stepped back and noticed Frank hurrying toward them.

"Sorry to interrupt, boss, but the stage manager's on my case."

"I'm on top of it, pal. One minute, okay?"

"I'd better go. Catch you later." Julia made her best effort to return Matt's smile. "And thanks, Matt. You won't be sorry."

"Something tells me I will," he said. "I wouldn't do this for anyone but you, Julia."

"I know."

With an uneasy glance toward Frank, Julia walked off. After taking a few steps, she tripped over a floor rail. Though she managed to maintain her balance, Matt was instantly at her side. "I'm okay," she said, righting herself.

"I knew that. You can take care of yourself, right?"

She flashed him a small but sincere grin and continued on her way. When Matt returned to Frank, he noticed the stagehand was regarding Julia with a disdainful sneer.

"Can't figure out why you hang around with those snooty musicians," Frank said. "Under-worked and overpaid if you ask me."

"Oh? I don't think they're so bad."

Frank smirked in Julia's direction. "Yeah, I have to admit that one is quite a piece of ass."

After Frank had sauntered away, Matt hurried off, anxious to complete a final check of the stage before the first act curtain. He wasn't watching where he was going and accidentally brushed against Patricia, who was making her way toward the wings.

He sensed from her glare of annoyance that she was ready to pounce, but instead, she just muttered, "Watch where you're going, Matthew."

"Sorry, Patricia." He rushed away, aware that she probably was following the sway of his boyish shape as she took her position in her favorite observation spot.

Just before he reached the wings, Matt spied a book of matches lying on the floor. Without hesitation he leaned over and picked them up as Frank was approaching him. He straightened up and grimaced at the assistant. "So much for a 'smoke-free' environment, right, buddy?"

Frank nodded. "Those guys will never learn until they burn down the place."

The passage of the law banning indoor smoking in New York City was ancient history, but some stagehands still demonstrated their reckless attitude by sneaking cigarettes wherever and whenever they could. It was something even Matt was powerless to control. In response, he kept a collection of all the matchbooks he had accumulated over the years and displayed it in its full glory on a bulletin board in the stagehands' locker room. His "guilt board," he called it.

"But did they have to leave this where the general manager can see it? Just one more reason for Patricia to be on my case," Matt complained.

"Nah, she's got a few other things to tick off her list first. No worries."

"I suppose so."

With a hopeless shake of his head, Matt pocketed the offending matchbook, intending to add it to his ever-growing collection, and sped away to survey a newly repainted backdrop.

Chapter Twenty

Akh! Istomilas, istradalas ya!...Istomilas ya gorem...nochyu-li dnyom, tolko o nyom dumoi sebya i terzala ya

Oh! I am weary and worn out with suffering!...I am weary with sorrow...night and day only of him I think and worry.

—Tchaikovsky, *Pique Dame*, Act II

When Julia hurried into the orchestra pit Katie was already sitting there, tuning her violin. Most of their colleagues were seated in their chairs, looking up with apprehension toward the balcony. News had spread quickly that the shot that killed Abel had come from that direction. The substitute conductor stood on the podium, tapping his baton on his music stand, waiting for stragglers to take their seats for rehearsal.

At the sight of Katie, Julia's face lit up. "If anybody was going to replace Sid, I'm glad it could be you."

Katie smiled. "Aw, you say that to all the subs."

"Rumor has it everyone's going into therapy, you know, after seeing Abel..." Julia's voice choked. "I'm not sure I can do this, K."

Katie stopped tuning, made a quick, discreet sign of the cross, and fingered the small gold crucifix around her neck. "Of course, you can, Jul. You've got me to lean on. And who else could put up with you?"

"You have a point."

As Julia started to tune, Katie noticed Julia's hands trembling but didn't comment. Instead, she looked upward toward the pit rail to see Larry leaning over. "Who's that guy up there staring at you, Jul?"

Julia glanced in Larry's direction and frowned. "The new detective."

"Oh? You mean the opera one? He's cute."

"Oh, please." She wasn't about to admit that she agreed with Katie.

The appearance onstage of the stage manager interrupted their dialogue. Glancing toward the wings, he waved his hands. "Quiet, please, ladies and gentlemen. Quiet."

Right on cue, Patricia strode toward him and positioned herself at the apron of the stage. She scanned the stage, pit, and theater and cleared her throat.

"I understand the difficulty of working in these stressful circumstances and applaud you for your courage in this time of grief," she said. "I want you to know I have faith in your ability to overcome your distress and to make sure the show will go on. Thank you for your service."

Patricia exited to murmurs and whispers among the company.

Julia turned to Katie. "She seem nervous to you? I mean, like, she's being even more 'business-as-usual' than usual."

"Jul, you're imagining things. *As usual.*"

With a brisk clapping of his hands, the stage manager shushed the Company. "Quiet, please. *Tosca*, Act One. Places."

The conductor tapped his baton on the podium. A collective sigh emanated from the musicians as they poised themselves to play. Julia could tell that, like her, they were reluctant, not quite ready to plunge back into work after recent trying events.

Julia and Katie sat at attention, responding to the conductor's downbeat with as much enthusiasm as they could muster. The tragic irony of the situation struck Julia. Whatever the circumstances, she and her cohorts were expected to play their instruments as if nothing had happened. It reminded her of the tenor agonizing in *Pagliacci*:

Recitar! Mentre preso dal delirio

Non so più quel che dico e quel che faccio!

Eppur...è d'uopo...sforzati!

Perform! While I am so plagued with grief

I don't know anymore what I say and what I do!

And yet...I must...force myself!

And the show goes on.

* * *

The stage manager appeared in front of the curtain as soon as it drew to a close after the first part of the rehearsal. "Twenty-five-minute break, ladies and gentlemen."

He disappeared behind the curtain, and the conductor climbed from the podium through the small door in the pit wall and into the theater. The musicians placed instruments in cases and raced out of the pit, like horses at a starting gate, to beat the lineup at the cafeteria.

Julia stepped up on the podium, gazed at the first row of seats, and peered at Larry. She couldn't help but notice that the color of his tie brought out the blue of his eyes. She chastised herself for going there. "I see you're doing your job."

"How kind of you to notice. By the way, has that guy conducted at the Met before?"

She shrugged. "Who, the substitute conductor? Yeah, I guess."

"How often?"

"I don't remember exactly. Why?"

"Do you think he was after Abel's job?"

"You mean, you're thinking of someone else to pin the murder on?"

"You never know. So, the conductor...?"

Well, this is encouraging. At least he's thinking of suspects other than Sid.

"Very self-involved, like most conductors. Capable of planning a murder? I sincerely doubt it," Julia said. "But while you're at it, how about looking into a few other things."

"Such as?"

"Such as, the general manager is acting funny, in my opinion. So is that assistant stagehand guy, Frank. Have you checked them out?"

"Whoa, slow down. Let's take this one step at a time."

"Aren't we working together?" Julia went on without waiting for a response. "I mean, for instance, everyone knows Patricia resented Abel."

"They do?" Larry pulled out his notebook and started writing. "How come?"

"Simple. She wanted all the power."

"Oh. I see. And the stagehand guy, what's his name...?"

"Frank. He's always lurking around, shooting nasty expressions at people."

"That's no reason to suspect him of murder, Julia, is it?"

"But what about that creep who was arrested with Sid? I bet you didn't even read his file."

"I don't have to. He's a small-time pusher, already copped a plea. Your friend Sidney, on the other hand, refuses. Meanwhile, I found out Sid learned to be a crack shot with a rifle from hanging around with his uncle after he left Russia as a teenager. That's all I need to know."

"What?" Julia reeled. Another setback. "I don't believe you."

What else hasn't Sid told me?

As she struggled to overcome her dismay, Julia noticed a tinge of sympathy had crept into Larry's voice. Nonetheless, she returned his look with a defensive glare.

"What if someone else in the company is a 'crack shot?'"

"We haven't found any evidence of that. Yet."

Avoiding her glare, Larry picked up the conductor's musical score from the podium and started to flip through the pages.

Julia was outraged. "What do you think you're doing? A conductor's score is private. You don't just invade it."

"Whoa, take it easy. My bad." Larry replaced the score to its rightful place and turned his gaze on the lavish sets onstage. "You may not believe it, but being so close to Puccini is a real treat for me." He turned back to Julia. "Do you think *Tosca* is a perfect opera?"

Julia's stomach started to rumble. "Pardon me, but I have to eat something before I keel over from hunger."

She turned to go. Larry glanced down into the pit and eyed her violin in its open case. "Before you go, how about playing something for me?"

"What?"

Sidney's in prison, and this guy wants me to play for him.

"Sorry, but I'm on break."

"Please, just a little excerpt? It would mean a lot to me. I love the violin."

She searched her mind for an excuse. "But I don't like playing for strangers. When I was a little kid, my dad always roped me into playing for company."

"He probably just wanted to show you off."

"Yeah. And I hated it." Julia climbed back into the pit, put her violin in the case, snapped it shut, and grabbed her small libretto of *Tosca* from the zippered compartment. "If you ever sing for me, detective, I might consider playing for you. Now, if you'll excuse me—"

"Okay. Some other time. And you can call me Larry. We're working together, after all."

She started to retort but stopped and reconsidered. With Sidney's life on the line, she couldn't afford to be nasty to him. "That's nice of you."

Julia began to walk away but stopped to check out the bottom of her shoe. "Damn!" She noticed Larry staring at her. "Why are you looking at me like that?"

"You don't seem like the type to use a four-letter word."

"You're right, but whenever I get a nail in my shoe, I get frustrated. This place is like a hazardous waste site. Nails, splinters, frayed carpets everywhere."

"Really? The venerable Met?"

She extracted the nail from the bottom of her shoe, taking great pains not to injure herself. "It's not as glamorous back here as it is on the patrons' side. There's—"

Julia suddenly felt guilty and stopped herself from describing the litany of hazards to be found in the opera house. She loved her job at the Met so much, yet here she was, about to let loose with her frustrations. In all fairness, every theater had its own physical dangers, not just the Met. It went with the territory.

I must be feeling the stress of the murder, of Sid's being arrested.

"Fascinating, Julia. How come you know so much about this place?"

"I already told you, I've been coming here since I was a kid. I know it better than you ever could. You have an awfully short memory for a detective."

Julia didn't want to offend Larry. She suspected he wanted to know more, but the precious few minutes of her break were ticking away. Her stomach was protesting, and she needed to do something about it. She held the nail at arm's length and eyed it in disgust.

"Yeah, we musicians do suffer for our art. To quote the late, great Beverly Sills, 'What a way to make a living!'"

He pointed to the offending piece of metal. "Can I keep that, as a souvenir of the Met?"

"I'm sure you can find a much better reminder of the Met than this ancient artifact. See ya," she said, tossing her head, as she hopped down from the podium and made her exit.

* * *

Larry watched Julia's hasty departure with concern. He was beginning to worry about the safety of this young, surprisingly rebellious artist who was too smart for her own good.

I better look out for her. Doesn't look like anyone else will.

But he couldn't help but notice the sheen of her long chestnut hair as she tossed her head. And he had to suppress a smile at the thought of a new name for her: *Drama Queen.*

Chapter Twenty-One

Egli e innocente, voi sapete.
He is innocent, and you know it.
—Mozart, *Le Nozze di Figaro*, Act II

J ulia dropped the wayward nail in a trash barrel outside the company cafeteria and slipped onto the lunch line. She was beginning to regret her agreement to meet with Charles that evening. She had heard through the opera house grapevine he had a thing for the ladies, particularly the petite dark-haired ones.

Such knowledge made it easier for Julia to resist the advances of this reputed Lothario, though only a bit, for he was as handsome as any male she had ever met. She had promised herself, when she won the Met audition, to stay away from men in general, since her priority was to prove herself in the big leagues of the musical world. But more importantly, she couldn't deal with the thought of physical intimacy. She contented herself with being in awe of Charles's musical talent, which he had demonstrated with distinction in any number of rehearsals.

The only man Julia trusted, now that Abel was dead, was Sidney, her surrogate "big brother." He had championed her since day one, and she had long ago gotten over the fact that he had hit on her constantly when she first arrived on the scene.

Sidney was on the auditioning committee and had heard her play, albeit from behind a screen. Using an opaque screen or curtain in orchestra auditions had been the practice since the early 1970's to counteract the sexual discrimination pervasive in the male-dominated world of orchestras. It was no coincidence that after this change in procedure, the number of women in orchestras rose exponentially.

Julia later learned that Sidney was so impressed with the musical gifts of the violinist whose identity was hidden he was convinced the player should and would win the position. Sidney proved correct, and once Julia had been chosen and was presented to the committee as the new first violin section member-elect, Sidney offered to coach her over the next six months to help prepare her for grueling pre-season rehearsals.

Thrilled to have an experienced Met violinist for a mentor, Julia accepted Sidney's offer. He spent time with her, going over the music she would need to learn for the coming season and giving her a heads-up about the difficulties, both musical and personal, she was apt to encounter as a brand-new violinist in the Met orchestra pit.

But it didn't take long for his hormones to take over, and he couldn't resist hitting on her. Julia was taken aback at first, but once they had become close enough for him to admit his rationale, she had no problem understanding it.

"My ma told me all my life to find a nice Jewish girl."

"And that would be me?"

"Well, you did admit to me that your father was from a *shtetl* in the Ukraine. You don't fool me with those WASP manners and that turned-up non-Jewish nose and your non-New York Jewish accent. You're a JAP waiting to happen. No offense."

Julia had taken Sid's flirtations in stride at first, bemused that an "older man" thought he had a chance with a twenty-two-year-old girl. But when he started asking her out on a daily basis, she had no doubts how to put him in his place. A lifetime of avoiding physical contact and developing the toughness of a Manhattanite fending for herself had prepared her for that.

"You. Me. Not going to happen." She softened the blow, adding, "But you know I adore you, right?"

After some time, she managed to set Sidney straight, and once she made him understand he had to refrain from hugging or other demonstrations of physical affection, they became close friends. Happy enough with a platonic relationship, Sidney began in earnest to cultivate Julia's potential as a violinist.

He also looked after her with avuncular concern, and she returned his caring with true devotion. Aside from Abel, who Julia considered more God than human and therefore unapproachable when it came to her personal life, Sidney was the only male she had been able to trust since her father's loss. After years of feeling abandoned, she, at last, had found someone whom she could count on in times of personal need.

Once the issue of sex was ruled out, Sid demanded nothing of her except a friend's loyalty, and she depended on him for moral support. Other than Sidney, Julia was afraid to let anyone else into the deep recesses of her heart. She had allowed her father and Abel there, and they had both left. She kept her feelings hidden away and enclosed in a protective shell to avoid being hurt again. Then Sid was arrested, and her carefully constructed personal life had collapsed.

Charles sidled up to Julia in the cafeteria line. She returned his smile, though not in too friendly a manner.

"So, what are you up to today, Charles?"

"Oh, you know, the usual. Covering Giuseppe. My best-known role is 'frustrated understudy.'"

"You'll get your chance to shine soon, I'm sure of it, Charles. You're so talented."

"Oh, yes, do keep the flattery coming." He paused. "Sometimes I wish I were a baritone, so I could take out my frustrations by singing the role of 'Scarpia' in *Tosca*. It's one of the greatest villain roles in all of opera."

"Oh, yes, I agree." Trying to impress him, Julia quoted a classic passage. "*E avanti a lui tremava tutta Roma*...And before him, all Rome trembled.'"

Charles sang his response. "'*Tosca...finalmente mia.*'"

* * *

As Julia and Charles conversed, Larry came in and watched, unnoticed by them. There was a slight tinge of envy in Larry's glance as he eavesdropped on their conversation. Though nearly twice her age, he was physically attracted to Julia, but something about her also made him want to protect her. Larry recognized a Don Juan when he encountered one, however, and he saw right through Charles's pretense at affability.

I hope Julia won't fall for it. But of course, there's nothing I can say.

At Charles's "*'Tosca...finalmente mia'*" declaration, Larry grumbled to himself. He knew what it meant.

Oh, right. Finally yours? In your dreams, Casanova.

* * *

Julia noticed that Charles was eyeing the *Tosca* libretto she held close to her breast.

"A libretto? I'm impressed," he said. "Most violinists don't bother with words."

"In opera, words and music are equally important. Abel always taught me that."

Having studied the libretto in detail, Julia knew that the phrase "*finalmente mia*" translated as "finally mine." She also knew it was the villain Scarpia's declaration just before he's about to rip Tosca's clothes off, though in the action onstage, Tosca murders him before he can accomplish the deed. Julia smiled to hide her discomfort and embarrassment at the sexual innuendo behind Charles's quote. She hoped to steer the subject into more secure territory.

"Can I join you?" he asked. "For lunch, I mean."

Julia was relieved that Charles had changed the subject. She found his self-effacing grin appealing.

"Thanks, but I'm just going to grab a sandwich and eat with Katie."

"Oh. But there's still tonight, yes?"

"Of course. Have you had a chance to look over the—?"

Julia spied Tony on his way over and left the question unfinished.

Uh-oh. Trouble ahead.

Generally, personnel managers never bothered with pleasantries. In her experience, Julia suspected they lived for the opportunity to stick it to the poor slobs who labored in the pit.

Tony lost no time in handing Julia the bad news. "Patricia wants to see you in her office."

Julia groaned. "Now? What reason?"

"She didn't say." He fidgeted with his baton. "Just go, you've got time."

"Oh, right," Charles said. "What's ten more minutes out of a twenty-five-minute lunch?"

Tony glared at Charles, but Julia hoped to avoid further conflict. She smiled her gratitude to Charles for defending her, decided to forgo the sandwich, and moved toward the exit.

Just as well, putting some distance between Charles and me. He's much too attractive.

* * *

Charles hungrily eyed Julia as she left. He had noticed Matt slipping into the line and eavesdropping on his conversation with her. But Charles did not feel threatened. He knew that if Matt was angling for attention from Julia, he was reaching for something unattainable. For Matt was steeped in the nitty-gritty world of wrenches, nails, and splinters. How could a stagehand, even the head stagehand, compete with a real stage performer—one who, hopefully, was about to become famous?

My major role may be pinch hitter, but at least I'm backing up the big guns.

* * *

The door was half open when Julia arrived at Patricia's office. Julia looked inside and saw the general manager seated at her desk, *tête-à-tête* with famous soprano Dorothy Muir, who was leaning closely over her. Together the two women were perusing a print copy of *Opera News*.

Julia knew that, much as for the Hollywood set, the head of a major opera house absolutely had to keep up with the trades. No other opera company in the world held a candle to the Met in terms of prestige, and everyone who worked there reveled in seeing the Met name glorified in print. But she sensed intimacy between the two operatic superstars and hesitated to interrupt, though she could hear every word they were saying.

"*Brava,* what a performance at the memorial service," Dorothy said. "They hung on your every word."

"They had no other choice, did they?"

The two women ceased talking as soon as they caught sight of Julia.

"Did no one ever teach you to knock, Julia?"

From Patricia's acid smile, Julia knew the encounter was not going to be pleasant. She felt physically and emotionally depleted from the week's events and didn't have much mental stamina in reserve.

"The door was open. I wasn't sure what I was supposed to do."

She was the one who called me here, but I don't dare remind her.

"Never mind." Patricia turned to Dorothy. "I'll join you at rehearsal."

Dorothy swept out of the room, brushing past Julia. Patricia gestured to Julia, who, gathering every possible shred of her remaining calm, stepped inside and closed the door.

"You wanted to see me, Patricia?"

Her smile fading, Patricia laid down the magazine. "It's been brought to my attention that you've been hanging around backstage, interfering with the stagehands. That is unacceptable."

Julia was taken aback. "But people go backstage every day. Since when is that a problem?"

"Since Abel's unfortunate murder."

There was a brief, uncomfortable silence. Julia steeled herself. She knew that as a novice, she had to be as diplomatic as possible, a mere cog in the colossal wheel propelling the Met ever forward. Still, Patricia was being unnecessarily harsh, even for Patricia.

"But I don't understand. The stagehands all know me. I wasn't bothering them."

"Frank told me you waylaid Matt, taking up his valuable time, getting in the way of the scene changes." Patricia raised an eyebrow. "Your job is to play the violin, in the pit. Not to loiter backstage. Any deviation is just cause for dismissal."

"Are you threatening me?"

"Let's just say I'm advising you, shall we?"

Frowning, Julia eyed Patricia. "Why are you so concerned about musicians going backstage all of a sudden?"

"There are dangers backstage. Things you are not aware of, Julia. I wouldn't want anything to happen to you."

Dangers? Something happening to me?

"I'm touched by your concern, Patricia."

Patricia moved to the window and leaned out, admiring the view. Julia started to hyperventilate.

Patricia turned back to face Julia. "Are you unwell, Julia?"

"I suffer from vertigo. And that's a long way down."

"Or an enviable view, depending on how you look at it."

Julia bit her trembling lip to quell her nausea. "Will that be all?"

Patricia nodded, and Julia departed without a word.

* * *

Once Julia was gone, Patricia pulled a silver vial and a minuscule plastic straw from her desk drawer. She shook some white powder from the vial onto a small mirror on her desk, inhaled the powder, and sighed with relief.

"As Sills once famously said, 'What a way to make a living.'"

In a few minutes, the fine white crystals took their effect, and Patricia forgot why she had allowed herself to become so upset about an insignificant little neophyte such as Julia Kogan.

* * *

Meanwhile, in a secluded corner of the backstage area, Matt was having a hushed conversation with several stagehands. "Any of you guys remember who the last stagehand in the viewing room was the night of the twenty-ninth?"

They all shook their heads.

"Well, if you remember, or think of anything, just get back to me, okay? It's important."

Nodding, the stagehands dispersed and went back to work, as did Matt, who didn't notice Frank watching closely from the opposite corner.

Chapter Twenty-Two

La ci darem la mano...
Vorrei, e non vorrei, mi trema un poco il cor
Let's give each other our hands...
I want to, and yet I don't, my heart just won't be still
—Mozart, Don Giovanni, Act I

A fter rehearsal was over, Julia put away her violin with uncharacteristic haphazardness. She was preoccupied with thoughts of Abel and worries about Sidney.

"Whoa, you're in a rush," Katie said. "Is prison closing early?"

"Oh. Sorry, K. I guess I just want to get there ASAP. Don't look so worried."

"Me, worry? Nah. Just say hi to Sid for me."

"I will."

Julia ran off. She knew Katie would understand her abrupt departure. Julia had received word that Sidney's condition had deteriorated, and she wanted to get to him as soon as possible. Since she was the first one out of the pit, the hallway was still empty, and she was able to sprint toward the locker room unimpeded. As she passed by Abel's former dressing room, however, a familiar voice she couldn't ignore popped into her head.

"You're talented, but you have a lot to learn. I can help you..."

Julia's eyes misted over. It was as if Abel were with her again, out of nowhere.

Or maybe he never left me.

On impulse, she stepped inside the dressing room door and wandered slowly around the room. Other conductors had been using the space since Abel had been killed. Yet it resembled a sort of shrine, with everything just as he had left it. Julia gazed at Abel's photos, still on the wall, his chessboard, with the pieces somehow suspended in time, and envisioned him running his fingers along the keys of his piano.

"Remember, look beyond *the notes."*

She was reminded that she had not yet made sense of the song he had written for her and resolved to go back to it after she saw Sidney. Meanwhile, she glanced around the room, studying the walls, the cabinets, and the hidden corners.

Is there a clue here somewhere, Abel, something that will point me to your murderer? If so, please tell me.

But silence was her answer. She turned to leave but suddenly turned back. The chessboard. There was something weird, something different, about it.

Julia scrutinized the board's configuration and noticed the king was in "check-mate" position. She knew Abel hadn't left it that way. Out of instinct, she began to remove the king. Then she realized she had better leave things as they were and instead alert Larry to her discovery. Then a sudden urge to look inside the piano bench overcame her.

She looked around, anxious, and listened for a moment. Satisfied there was no one in the vicinity, she leafed through the pages of sheet music inside the bench cushion. Buried among the papers, she discovered a hand-written sheet of music paper. Astonished, she removed the sheet and gazed at it. Her heart quickened.

"Song to Julia, Page 2." The missing page! But did he hide it on purpose?

She quickly squirreled the page away in the zippered compartment of her violin case and left the room. Now, at least, she had another part of the puzzle, which might help her make sense of the song.

First, see Sid. Next, try to play the new page.

* * *

In her haste to reach the locker room, Julia didn't notice the man watching her from around the hallway corner, shadows obscuring his face. In her agitated state, after picking up her sweater from her locker and heading toward the exit, she didn't see that same man in the phone booth by the stage door.

"I don't think she took anything," the man spoke *sotto voce* into the telephone. "She was just snooping around. Let me know if you want me to do something about it."

He hung up the phone, just as Julia rushed by on her way out of the theatre.

* * *

After he had inspected her violin case for contraband, the prison guard walked Julia through a locked cage into the sick ward and stood watch at the foot of Sidney's bed as Julia approached her ailing colleague. Aghast at the sight of his pale and worn face, and his much thinner-looking body tossing in a fitful sleep, Julia bent over Sidney's ear and whispered.

"Sid...Sid."

"Sorry...I'm...not too..." He struggled to open his eyes. "Medicine...makes me woozy."

Julia tried not to show her alarm at his bloodshot eyes and sickly state. "I...I brought my violin in case you wanted to play." She extracted her violin and bow and extended them toward Sidney.

He reached for the bow but was too weak to hold it. "Sorry, kid. I just can't."

Hiding her worry, Julia tucked the instrument under her chin and played a lush melody, the violin solo from Act Four of Verdi's *La Traviata*. When she had finished, she looked at Sidney. "Abel coached me on this one for my Met audition."

Sidney smiled weakly. "I know, kid, I was there."

"Oh, right. I knew that."

He managed a feeble nod and focused his heavy-lidded eyes on her. "Beautiful playing, kid. Abel'd be proud."

"Sid..." Her voice trailed off. She wanted to ask the nagging questions in her head, about his relationship with Abel, about his drug dealing, about where he was during Abel's murder. Unable to bring herself to trouble her beleaguered friend, she could only gaze at him, especially when he made the enormous effort to raise himself up.

Sid's eyes began to droop. He fell back on the pillow. "Can't talk anymore. Talk...later."

In an instant, he closed his eyes and was out. Julia bit her lip, distressed and confused.

I wish I could ask him why someone would frame him. I wish he would get better. I wish all of this had never happened.

* * *

Julia thought she owed her admirer, Matt, a peace offering.

His fast reaction when she almost fell flat on her face in front of the sign-out sheet the night of Abel's murder wasn't the first time he had saved her butt. He always looked out for her in ways even Sidney had never done. Plus, he had pledged to help her find a way to clear Sidney.

She wanted to show Matt her gratitude, without giving him the idea she had a romantic interest in him. She also needed to ensure that the other stagehands were still on her side. She hoped some of them would help her gather more information for Sidney's defense.

Food is always a safe bet.

After her visit with Sidney, Julia stopped by the stagehands' locker room with a large pizza box in hand, hoping to find Matt. When no one answered her knock, Julia opened the door a crack, peeked in and, after a moment, tiptoed in.

"Hello?"

There was no sign of life. She had been inside the orchestra men's locker room, but she had never seen the stagehands' private, closed-off hangout and could not resist looking around.

The room was Spartan and exuded testosterone, just the opposite of the sophisticated comfort of the women's locker room. The one wall devoid of gray metal lockers held Matt's infamous bulletin board of matchbooks. She approached the board and read the label:

"Matt's matchbooks, collected exclusively at the Metropolitan Opera House. You are guilty as charged."

Chuckling, Julia plucked a matchbook from the board and roamed around the room. A locker displaying a "Gulf War Vets, '92" sticker caught her attention. She stopped to inspect it more closely when a tap on her shoulder made her jump. The pizza box careened to the floor as she pivoted around to find Frank glowering at her.

"This locker room is off limits. For...musicians."

Frank's menacing tone caught Julia off guard, but she quickly recovered. "Matt asked me to meet him here."

"Oh yeah? He thinks 'cuz he's head stagehand he can bend the rules? Well, he's not here. So you can just beat it."

Julia held up the matchbook. "I've been hearing about his bulletin board for so long, I had to check it out."

"That piece of crap?" he sneered. "He's always messing with it, like he probably was the night of the murder, when he should 'a been backstage with his crew."

Blanching at the mention of that night, Julia quickly stuffed the matchbook into her pocket and stooped over to retrieve the disheveled food. "I thought you guys might like some pizza."

Julia watched as Frank opened the locker with the Gulf War sticker and proceeded to take off his muscle shirt. Bare-chested, he turned and came toward her, backing her into a corner, an intimidating gleam in his eye. She flushed with embarrassment.

"What's your real business here, anyway, chickie?"

She held his gaze without flinching. "I already told you, I just brought some pizza for you guys."

"And didn't *I* already tell *you* it's off limits for anyone but stagehands?"

Julia opened her mouth to reply but seeing him start to stretch his hand toward her, she realized she needed to avoid at all costs a confrontation about the "touch" issue.

"I'll just leave this here."

Laying the box down on the bench, she retreated, too soon to see Frank dump the box into the trash, strip off the rest of his clothes, and head for the showers.

* * *

Sidney slumped in a chair at a table in an interview room of the infamous Tombs, sweat pouring down his gaunt, haggard face. A grim Buddy leaned over him.

"Ballistics report came back. The murder bullet came from your box of ammo, Richter."

"I already told you, I was set up."

Sidney's voice trailed off as Herb, his attorney, entered, a smug look on his face.

"The Judge has set bail and agreed there's no further reason to detain my client."

Buddy ignored Herb's pronouncement and kept pressuring Sidney. "Set up? By who?"

"I don't know."

Recognizing Sidney's desperation, Buddy upped his menacing tone. "I think you do."

Herb grabbed Sidney's elbow. "Let's go, Sidney. You don't have to say another word."

Sidney got up with great effort and glowered at Buddy. "I shouldn 'a had to spend one night in this place, much less pay bail."

Sidney staggered out, followed by Herb. As he watched them leave, Buddy cursed under his breath and left the room.

In the adjoining viewing room, Assistant District Attorney Richard Magnus turned away from the two-way mirror and intercepted Buddy. "We kept him locked up for as long as the law allowed, Buddy. There was nothing else we could do. I'm sorry."

Buddy gritted his teeth. "But I thought he was a flight risk."

"He's also been a member of one of Manhattan's most prestigious arts organizations, for a number of years." The A.D.A. smiled. "Don't worry, we'll still convict. The evidence is undeniable."

Buddy flashed a look of disgust at A.D.A. Magnus and walked away.

* * *

Unnerved by her run-in with Frank, Julia was hastening toward the double doors leading to the switchboard and security post when she felt a tap on her shoulder. Assuming it was the abrasive stagehand, she wheeled around.

"I'm out of your territory, what more do you—" When she saw Larry grinning at her she heaved a nervous sigh. "Don't you know you can terminally scare someone doing that?"

"A bit on edge, are we?"

Larry's look of mild amusement grated on Julia's nerves. "Ever hear of post-traumatic stress syndrome? You'd be on edge, too, if your best friend was in a heap of trouble," she said, and started to walk away.

"No time to chat? Just yesterday, you couldn't wait to bend my ear."

"That was yesterday. Today I..." She hesitated, realizing she was being needlessly snappish to him. "I'm just feeling hopeless, that's all."

"Yeah, I hear ya."

Larry's sympathetic glance consoled her somewhat, but Julia thought better of confiding in him, twinkle in his eye notwithstanding. "I'm sorry I can't stop and chat. I have to go home and get ready to...uh, go out tonight."

"Oh? I'd have thought you too upset to be socializing just yet."

"It's not socializing, it's business. Don't ask. Just doing my part to investigate, as promised." She paused. "On that note, I had some further thoughts."

"Well? Don't keep me waiting."

"What if it was Patricia who framed Sid?"

"And you say that because...?"

"Abel was the only one standing in the way of Patricia being top dog at the Met. Now he's gone, she's running the show. But she also wants his allies out of the picture. She just called me into her office and upbraided me, his favorite mentee, threatening me with dismissal. I wouldn't put it past her to do the same to Sid."

"She's not exactly the sharpshooter type."

"Right. But she could have been scheming with someone else who is. She could have ordered the hit on Abel."

"You've been watching too much *Blue Bloods*."

Julia was too frustrated to reply.

"By the way," Larry continued, "I interviewed that guy, what's his name, Geraldo. You know, the one who was arrested with your friend-in-a-heap-of-trouble. He and Sidney have been in cahoots for years, supplying drugs throughout the Met. It didn't just start yesterday."

Speechless, Julia stared at Larry in disbelief.

"Like I said before, you think you know someone…" He peered at her agitated face. "You okay?"

But all she felt was anger and bitterness. This was not the kind of news she had hoped to hear. Nonetheless, she tried to take it in stride. It was neither the right time to bring up her chessboard discovery, nor to mention having found the missing page of Abel's song.

"I'm fine." She started to walk away and once again turned back. "By the way, thanks."

"For what?"

"For taking the trouble to follow up on a suggestion—from a 'kid.'"

She didn't stop to see his reaction but was happy to leave him standing in the middle of the hallway.

Chapter Twenty-Three

Perdon, perdono...quello non sono, sbaglia costei...
Il delitto mio non è. L'innocenza mi rubò.
Oh, spare me, spare me...I'm not your man, you're mistaken...
The fault isn't mine. I was led astray.
—Mozart, *Don Giovanni*, Act II

J ust as she was rushing out the stage door, Julia bumped into Matt.

"Gee, you don't look so happy to see me."

"But I am, Matt. In fact, I was looking for you."

"You were? So, there's hope after all."

Julia smiled. "No, I didn't mean...There's just something I wanted to give you."

Matt's eyes grew wide. "Ooh, I love surprises. Lay it on me."

"Actually, I left it for you in your locker room."

"Uh-oh. Never do that, Julia. Nothing stays around there for long."

Julia checked her watch. "Oh. Sorry, Matt, I have to go home and practice."

"But what about my surprise?"

"Just look for a big white cardboard box from Anthony's."

Matt licked his lips. "Ah, Julia, you're a woman after my own heart."

"Yeah, I know. I've seen your rendition of it on the sign-in sheet."

Julia ran off, violin case in hand. Matt headed for the locker room to retrieve his surprise.

* * *

Larry hovered over his desk, earbuds in his ears, lost in thought. Even his favorite Verdi aria from *Luisa Miller—Quando le sere al placido*, in his preferred version sung by José Carreras—failed to distract him from his anxiety about the Trudeau case.

Buddy, too, was not his usual upbeat self. Always ravenous, he tossed his sandwich into the trash uneaten. Seeing this, Larry took the buds out of his ears and looked at Buddy, surprised.

"So, what do we do now, boss?" Buddy asked. "Now Sidney Richter's out of jail, I mean."

"We'll still get him, I'm not worried. I'm thinking about Patricia, though."

"The general manager? You got a thing for her? She is kind 'a hot."

Larry was pleased to see Buddy's expression turn mischievous. "No, you dope. I meant, from what I hear, she's been acting more hostile than usual to her employees. Suspiciously so."

"That could mean something. The music world does have the largest number of sociopaths, after all."

"How did you know?"

"You'd be surprised at what I know." Buddy smiled. "You like her for the murder? Accomplice, maybe?"

"Just a hunch," Larry said. "I want you to surveil her, just in case."

"Happy to. For how long?"

"As long as you can stand it."

"Sure."

They grinned at each other for a moment, but Larry was sorry to see Buddy's expression return to its former distressed state.

"Something bugging you, pal?" Larry asked.

"I was fine until you brought up the subject of women."

"Oh, I get it. Feel free to get it off your chest."

Buddy hesitated. "You sure?"

"Go for it."

"Okay." Buddy took a deep breath. "I went to see my ex-girlfriend after work last night."

Larry raised his eyebrows. "Go on."

"We dated a long time ago, but I been carrying a torch for her for years. She broke up with me because I wanted to become a cop. Then she married a fireman."

Buddy wrinkled his brow. Larry was surprised to see his young colleague so troubled. And he had an uncomfortable feeling about what was coming next.

"He was one of the first guys to start up the staircase in the World Trade Center." Buddy's voice choked. "It's so ironic. She throws me over 'cuz she thinks my job is too dangerous..."

Both detectives became silent, reliving their personal and collective traumas associated with the 9/11 catastrophe. Though, by now, the horrific event was in the distant past, any New Yorker with a soul would always feel humbled in its shadow. Larry knew many of those lost from the Fire Station near Lincoln Center, and he imagined Buddy did also.

Larry tried to brighten the atmosphere. "That's really nice of you to talk with her."

"Well...I'm afraid my intentions weren't completely unselfish. Ya' know what I mean?"

"I do. And I know you too well to believe that."

"Thanks." Buddy gave him a sheepish grin. "How about you, Lar? You have a girlfriend? You don't seem to get out much. With chicks, I mean."

Larry frowned. "Not many 'chicks' like opera. I'd rather spend an evening with Mimì."

"'Mimì?'"

"She's an opera character, Buddy boy."

"You mean, like, you stay home and listen to opera?" Buddy sighed. "That's sick, man. You should be out there meeting chicks. You're not gay, are you? You been holdin' out on me?"

"Nah, I just prefer the company of Carmen, or Lucia. Or Mimì."

"Maybe we should go out on a double date sometime, me and 'Carmen,' and you and 'Mimì.'"

Larry felt the tension ease. He appreciated Buddy's effort to lighten up the mood.

"Anyway, Mimì, Carmen, whatever twists your top," Buddy said. "But do me a favor. Lose the sour face. I liked you much better when you were conducting along with Pavarotti."

* * *

Julia stood in front of her music stand, feeling the anticipation of a novice violin student tackling her first concerto. With Katie out of the house for an AA meeting, Julia had some uninterrupted time to ply the depths of Abel's song. Even if Charles still had the first page, she had not yet explored the newly discovered second page. She eyed the pile of clothes in one corner of the room and the stack of books on the floor by her bed. Since Abel's death, she had lost her usual drive to keep things tidy and in place. She shrugged.

It'll all still be there tomorrow.

She placed the music on the stand and started to play through the second verse. But the second strain was even more jarring than the first. Julia let out a shriek of frustration.

What was Abel thinking? I'll never get this right.

Then a voice came to her as if from the grave.

"You've got it right...You have the gift of an artist's soul."

She wanted to believe Abel, but doubted she possessed that gift. And if she did, it was slowly trickling away, whereas time was moving far too quickly.

* * *

Julia found the atmosphere inside the elegant *Café des Artistes*, with its French artwork on the walls, subtle lighting, and air of privacy, intimate and personal. Ensconced in a quiet corner booth, Julia and Charles lingered over cognacs. In general, Julia stayed away from liquor, but she felt it would be impolite for her companion to drink alone. Every so often, she glanced at the envelope containing page one of the song which lay on the banquette next to Charles, but she tried not to be too obvious about it.

She had avoided bringing up the subject of Sidney's drug activities, but even after a few sips of the golden liquid had relaxed her nerves, it was still foremost in her mind.

"Charles, did you know about Sid's...drug dealing?"

"There were rumors. Among the company."

Julia's heart sank. "Oh my God. How could I not know?"

"You haven't been at the Met that long. Give it time, you'll learn all the secrets."

"But I trusted Sid. He was my best—" She choked back a lump in her throat.

"It's not good for you, being so preoccupied with this, Julia. Mind if I change the subject?" Charles leaned toward Julia's bodice to inspect her violin pin. "I see you wear it all the time. Abel would have been pleased."

His closeness made her uncomfortable. If he was attracted to her, he was not being subtle about it. But for some reason, she didn't pull back. She began to fidget with the pin.

"You were about to tell me how you became so passionate about chess, Julia."

"Oh. Right. My father taught me chess. Abel and I used to play. My dad and Abel were close friends. Abel took me under his wing after my dad—"

She paused for a moment, her eyes closing as the painful memory resurfaced. Swallowing hard, she blinked her eyes open, saw her companion's encouraging smile, took a deep breath, and went on. "After that, Abel taught me everything I know. About chess, about music. He even showed me the different ways of naming musical notes in various languages."

"You and I must have a chess game someday. I'm always looking for a challenge."

Now in familiar territory, Julia began to unwind. She felt much better knowing she had something in common with Charles that didn't involve his physical attraction to her.

"So, besides Scarpia, which roles are on your wish list?"

"Just Scarpia forever." He modulated his voice from conversational to dramatic. "*'Tosca, finalmente mia'*...Julia, finally mine!"

Julia felt the color drain from her face. His operatic misquote made his intentions all too obvious.

Charles frowned. "Oh, I'm so sorry. Of course. I meant '*Tosca*'—"

Julia rose, pulling her jacket around her shoulders. "You know, I suddenly feel so tired. I should go."

"But we haven't had a chance to look at the song." Charles reached beside him on the banquette and picked up the sheet of music. "Perhaps if you come back to my place, we can try it at the piano..."

"It's getting late, Charles. Why don't you just keep it for tonight. We can discuss it tomorrow."

"Are you sure you don't mind my having it a while longer?"

"No problem. I can't make heads or tails out of it anyway." Julia's jacket slipped off her shoulders. Charles leapt up to help her with it. "Would you like me to see you home?"

"No, thank you, I'll just grab a taxi," she said, her smile tense. "Thanks for dinner."

Clutching her purse, Julia beat a hasty retreat. She was conflicted about leaving the song in Charles's possession, but she had to trust someone, and it might as well be Charles.

Nonetheless, she felt relieved she had only given him the first page and had hung on to the second. And there was something oddly satisfying about hearing Charles curse under his breath as he watched her go.

Chapter Twenty-Four

Pervoi già possente la fiamma d'amore
Inebria, conquide, distrugge il mio core
For you the flame of love, already powerfully kindled,
intoxicates, overwhelms, consumes my heart.
—Verdi, *Rigoletto*, Act I

Julia tiptoed into the living room to find Katie curled up on the sofa with a bag of chips.

"So, where have you been, Missy?"

Switching on a light, Julia dropped her bag on the table by the door and peered at Katie. "What are you doing sitting in the dark?"

"Unfair, answering a question with a question."

"Okay, you win. I had dinner. With Charles."

A mischievous smile lit up Katie's face. "A date?"

"It wasn't a date, just a meeting. To discuss Abel's song."

"Oh, right. Where'd you go?"

"Des Artistes."

"Yep." Katie chortled. "It was a date."

Julia rolled her eyes. "Katie, the last thing I need is to 'date.'"

"Maybe. But something's up with you. I can see it in your face."

"As usual, you're right. It's…it's about Sid." Julia held back tears. "That detective told me Sid's been supplying drugs to the company. For years."

"What?"

Katie started to choke on a chip. Panicked, Julia pounded her friend on the back until the coughing fit subsided.

Julia sighed with relief. "Don't ever do that to me again, K."

"Sorry, Jul, but the thought of Sid pushing drugs kind 'a shocked me."

"Shocked *you*? I'm beside myself. I'm beginning to doubt my trust in him."

"Think about it. He just made a big fat mistake. No one's perfect."

Julia thought for a moment. "You're right. I shouldn't let that keep me from clearing his name and finding the real killer."

"Which reminds me, while you were out—not on a date—the NYPD called. They're letting Sid out on bail," Katie said. "But he's still sick, and they need a family member to pick him up. He listed you as next of kin."

Julia grabbed her bag. "Why didn't you tell me sooner?"

"Hey, you were the one who stayed out late—"

But Julia was already out the door.

* * *

It didn't take more than a cursory look around for Julia to realize Sidney's apartment was still in the same disarray as when the police had raided it. Sofa cushions, books, notebooks, papers, and what looked like the contents of the front closet, were strewn on the floor. She quickly gathered the cushions and arranged them on the sofa as Sidney, too tired to complain about the mess, collapsed on it.

Julia covered him with the Afghan throw she found on the arm of the sofa and settled next to him. He appeared exhausted and ill. She hadn't liked the looks of him, so pale and thin, when she had picked him up from The Tombs. And he didn't look any better now.

"Can I get you anything, Sid?"

"A new life, maybe?"

Sidney didn't say anything more, just shook his head. Julia tried to distract him with gossip about work.

"Do you believe Patricia threatened to dismiss me, just for talking to Matt backstage?"

"I don't want to talk about it."

The sudden abruptness in his manner startled Julia. "Oh. I understand. You must be so beat. We can talk about it later." Julia waited a few seconds to speak again. She was afraid of tiring him, but she needed to stay with him long enough to make sure he was able to spend the night alone. "You okay?"

"Sure."

But when he groaned in pain, she frowned at him. "Why are you still sick, Sid? Is it your stomach?"

"It's those damned drugs they've been pumping into me. They make me woozy."

His eyelids fluttered and closed. Julia watched his face, her anxiety escalating. She leaned closer to him. "Sid, who do you think framed you?"

He sighed. "Stop with the questions already, kid. I've had enough of that in jail."

"But if we don't come up with an explanation before the grand jury decision—"

His eyes flew open. "For God's sake, Julia, you have no idea what you're getting into. Leave it alone! And leave *me* alone, too!"

Julia was stunned. Sidney, so unlike his usual self, made her gasp. She turned away from him, distraught. A heavy silence fell over them.

"Oh, kid, I'm sorry. Forgive me, please. I shouldn't have jumped on you like that. I know you're only trying to help. I'm an idiot. I'm sorry I yelled. You know I love you, kid." He closed his eyes again, sighing. "Just let me sleep off the drugs. I'll be better tomorrow, I can answer all your questions. I promise." His voice lowered. "I'd never do anything to harm Abel, you've got to believe me, Jul."

Julia could see he was struggling to keep his eyes open and gazed at him in sympathy. His words had wounded her, but she understood the magnitude of the strain he was under. She removed his shoes and planted a gentle kiss on his forehead. "Shh, sleep now."

Pulling a notepad from her purse, Julia wrote down a number, ripped off the sheet of paper, and placed it on the end table. "Here's my cell phone number, so you have it close by in case you need me. Just call, anytime. Good night, Sid."

He closed his eyes and murmured, "You touched me. I'll be damned."
Still smarting from his outburst, she left the room in silence.

* * *

As soon as Julia arrived at the Met the next morning, she headed backstage to look for Matt. She wanted to return his matchbook and fill him in on the unpleasant exchange between her and Frank in the stagehands' locker room.

But she couldn't find him. Instead, she found Charles lingering in the wings at stage right, watching stagehands place the impressive backdrops for Act Three of *Tosca*. She, too, loved to gaze at this elaborate set, with its pre-dawn sky behind the terrace of Rome's Castel Sant'Angelo Prison and Saint Peter's Basilica in the background.

Julia had no desire to see Charles now, and turned to leave, but he caught sight of her.

"Julia, do you have a minute?"

She looked at him. "Well, not really. Rehearsal's about to start—"

"You won't be late, I promise."

Julia nodded and followed Charles to a far-off back corner.

"I wanted to apologize for coming on so strong to you last night, Julia. I couldn't help myself. But I feel I owe you an explanation."

"It's okay, Charles. Don't worry about it." Her tone was ambivalent, and she made no effort to hide her uncomfortable feelings.

"But I do worry. I care what you think of me." He paused, searching her face. "You know, I think fate brought us together. You came to the Met exactly one year after me."

"How do you know how long I've been here?"

"I noticed you the very first day you walked in the door. I've been admiring you ever since." He paused. "But that's no excuse for being so forward. Please forgive me."

Julia was taken aback. She wasn't used to such overt male attention, even from Matt. It made her ill at ease. But coming from Charles, she somehow didn't mind it.

Maybe I've let the gossip about him influence me too much. Maybe I've been too quick in judging him.

There was something about him.

Something that makes me want to trust him. To let him care about me.

Flushing with embarrassment, Julia glanced around to make sure no one was eavesdropping. "Nothing to forgive. I completely understand."

Charles searched her face. "Do you? You still seem upset."

"Oh, it's not you. I'm just worried about Matt. He's usually here." Julia looked about anxiously. "Have you seen him?"

"I haven't, but I wouldn't worry. Matt can take care of himself. He's probably off on some official 'head stagehand' business. Meanwhile, it looks like Frank's got things well in hand."

Julia turned toward the stage and spied Frank, barking orders to several crewmembers. She squirmed, uncomfortable, at the thought of their last encounter.

It's Matt who should be in charge.

The P.A. system interrupted her thoughts.

"Fifteen minutes, ladies and gentlemen. Act Three *Tosca* rehearsal in fifteen."

"I'd better get to the pit, Charles."

"Are we okay?"

"Of course." She smiled. Something about him made Julia think of Abel. Perhaps it was his eyes, the same clear blue, or his look of intelligence. She wasn't sure, but she felt a sudden jolt of pain.

"What is it, Julia?"

"Oh, nothing." She hesitated. "I just thought I saw…Well, for a moment, there was just something about your face that reminded me of…of Abel."

Charles laughed. "I'm flattered, Julia. No one's ever told me that before."

"Maybe it was the light. Anyway, I've really got to go."

With a wary look at Frank-in-charge, Julia took off and ran right into Larry and Buddy, just on their way in.

Julia acknowledged Larry with a brief nod. Then she hurried away.

* * *

Buddy raised his eyebrows at Larry. "What's her problem?"

"Damned if I know." Larry shrugged and turned to the stage as cast members began to assemble for the dramatic last act of *Tosca*.

How lucky am I to be seeing this firsthand?

He pinched himself to make sure it was real.

Chapter Twenty-Five

È qui che voglio dirtelo, e tu m'ascolterai,
che t'amo e ti desidero, e che tu mia sarai!
Here and now I want to tell you, and you shall hear me say,
that I adore you and desire you and that you will be mine!
—Leoncavallo, *I Pagliacci*

s Julia and Katie tuned their instruments, Julia struggled as usual with her violin pegs. Julia responded to Katie's sardonic smile with a pout and vigorously twisted the recalcitrant tuning apparatuses, casting a nervous eye on the *conductor-du-jour*, who was ascending the podium. Finally, the pegs cooperated, and Julia sighed with relief.

The stage manager appeared in front of the curtain. "We start with the Act Three Firing Squad scene. Maestro?"

Act Three of *Tosca* contained a great deal of violence, as did much of the opera. A squad of supernumeraries (non-speaking individuals called "supers" for short) dressed as soldiers and bearing rifles filed onto the scene. Tenor Giuseppe, who had managed to get over his opening night trauma, positioned himself at stage left, where he awaited his "execution." Legendary diva Dorothy Muir, the Met's current *prima* lyric soprano, crouched at stage right. Her role was to watch the action and sing *sotto* while she waited for her lover to fake his death and steal away with her after the firing squad had exited.

Giuseppe had stood in front of this firing squad dozens of times and knew the supers carried dummy rifles. Dorothy, who had occupied her position at the side of the stage at least as many times, was also aware of that fact. Still, Julia knew that the tenor and soprano disliked the sound of the rifles. When fired, the shots distracted the audience from the music; and the noise frightened everyone, Julia included, whether onstage, in the pit, or in the house.

The conductor raised his baton. From his position in the wings at stage right, Larry had a perfect view of Dorothy and could not help but gasp upon seeing her. Having listened to her recordings and watched her performances on TV and in the Met's live HD presentations for so many years, he was in awe—not only of her artistry, but also her beauty.

I can't believe I'm just a few yards away from her.

He elbowed the stagehand standing next to him. "That's Dorothy Muir. Oh my God."

From the dirty look the stage manager flashed him, Larry could see that disturbing the respectful silence backstage was a cardinal sin. Embarrassed, Larry responded with an apologetic glance and focused on the dirge the orchestra was playing.

This scene, with its foreboding orchestra theme rising in crescendo to a passionate climax, was one of Larry's all-time favorite moments in opera. He girded himself for the anticipated crackling of rifle fire that shattered the atmosphere and watched in hushed expectation for Giuseppe to fall to the floor at the appropriate moment.

The supers took aim and blasted away, and Giuseppe collapsed convincingly.

"*Là! Muori! Ecco un artista!*" Dorothy sang in triumph. "There! Die! What an actor!"

But the tenor did not fall in silence. Instead, he uttered a blood-curdling scream.

The stage director scurried onstage from the wings, waving his arms in wide gestures. "Cut!!" he shrieked. "What's going on here, Giuseppe? You're supposed to fall down. Dead, not screaming."

Giuseppe clutched his leg, wincing with pain, as the infuriated director raced to his side.

"What's going *on* here?" Giuseppe spluttered. "I've been shot, that's what!" He lifted his hand from his leg, revealing a large gushing, bloody wound.

Gasps of shock emanated from the onstage company, as the thick red liquid spurted out in copious quantities. The director gaped, horrified. "Get a doctor!"

Buddy, who had been watching from the wings at stage left, raced onstage to join Larry, who already was assessing the damage. "I've called E.M.S., boss."

Larry shouted out the kind of orders he had anticipated having to give in panicked situations. "Everybody, stay where you are! We've got this under control."

But he had never handled the kind of all-hell-breaking-loose assemblage of the theater people that surrounded him. His commands were as useless as those of a Roman guard trying to keep Pompeiian citizens from fleeing a wall of pyro plastic smoke and ash hurtling toward them. Supers fled the stage in terror. The stage manager and stagehands came running. Giuseppe wailed. The director paced back and forth, head in hands, moaning.

"People, people!" the stage manager yelled. "Calm down, please!"

Dorothy spat fire. "Calm down? Are you insane?"

Larry saw that the stage manager's efforts to make order out of chaos were useless, as were any attempts to soothe Dorothy, who looked as if she were on the verge of a murderous diva-driven tantrum. He also sensed that the beleaguered stage manager was willing to insist, beg, prostrate himself, or all three, to quash the intractable diva's temper.

"But Miss Muir—"

Ignoring the stage manager's entreaties, Dorothy stomped offstage, her long satin skirts rustling with each receding step.

With all the pandemonium onstage, the music in the pit had come to a precipitous halt. Larry watched the orchestra members stand up abruptly. He recalled that they had been unfortunate enough to witness not only this entire episode but Abel's murder as well. He could see fear in the eyes of those who stayed rooted to their spots, looking up toward the balcony or gawking at the stage. The others fled the pit in droves.

Julia and Katie remained in their chairs, eyes glued to the stage, watching stagehands carry off the wounded Giuseppe.

Buddy and Larry followed the sizeable stream of company members making their mass exodus. "You go left, I'll take right," Larry directed, hoping between the two of them they could corral as many potential witnesses as possible.

Before long, Patricia hurried into the fray, waving her arms at the bedlam surrounding her.

"Quiet, everyone!" she called out. "Rehearsal is postponed. We will continue where we left off tomorrow. With understudies."

The conductor shook his head vehemently. "With all due respect, Patricia, after what just happened, don't you think the company needs more of a break?"

"It was only an accident. He'll be fine." Patricia lowered her voice, eyes flashing. "May I remind you that the Met has only twice canceled due to an unforeseen adverse event, and only with a death involved. Giuseppe was injured, unfortunately, but he will recover. We've already closed the opera house once this week. The board of directors will not tolerate any further interruption in our usual schedule. Do I make myself clear?"

The conductor turned to the concertmaster and whispered. *"Is she crazy?"*

Patricia flashed a look of menace toward the conductor. Then she strode offstage.

* * *

In the wings, mayhem still ruled. Supernumeraries and company members crowded the backstage area, talking among themselves in panicked whispers.

Scoping out the turmoil around him, Larry grabbed the stage manager's arm. "Who's in charge of munitions here?"

"That would be me," said a tall man in cargo pants and a field jacket. "I'm the property manager."

Larry peered at him. "Don't you check the stage rifles before they're used?"

"Of course I do, multiple times. I can't imagine what happened here, or why."

From the corner of his eye, Larry spied a young, good-looking supernumerary carrying a stage rifle steal toward the exit. "Buddy, take the prop manager to H.Q. and question him about why there was a loaded rifle used onstage. I've got a runner."

Larry strode to the super and grabbed his arm. "Going somewhere, uh… what's your name?"

The young man flushed. "P-Paolo."

"Come with me, Paolo."

Larry steered Paolo through a set of double doors into the foyer outside the wings. He whipped out a pair of latex gloves and relieved Paolo of the rifle. Then he opened the ammunition chamber, extracted a bullet, and examined it.

"This cartridge has a projectile. It's live ammunition."

The super blanched. *"What?"*

"Don't act so surprised." With his free hand, Larry quickly snapped a pair of handcuffs on the super's wrists. Then he dialed Buddy. "Better get here pronto."

Buddy appeared with the prop manager in tow. "Buzz CSU, Buddy," Larry said. "We've got big time evidence to bag."

"Okay, boss." Buddy stopped short when he saw Paolo, the rifle, and the cartridge. "Wait a minute, I know you. You're the valet from Abel Trudeau's dressing room." He turned to Larry. "They let this guy carry a rifle? What kind of place is this, anyway?"

"You take our friend Paolo down to H.Q. with the prop manager," said Larry. "I'll call for backup to handle the *'artistes'* onstage."

Buddy stared at the super. "Paolo? But I thought your name was Damon."

Paolo shrugged. Larry gestured toward them, holding the rifle carefully. "Whichever it is, someone is taking his stage duties too seriously."

Buddy turned back to Larry. "And doing double duty," he said as he led the super and prop manager away.

Chapter Twenty-Six

Badate! Questo è luogo di lacrime! Or basta! Rispondete! Ed or la verità!
Beware! This is a place for tears! Enough now! Answer me! And now the truth!
—Puccini, *Tosca*, Act II

A t the precinct, all the cops stared, wide-eyed, at the sight of Buddy dragging the hapless, uncommonly good-looking Paolo/Damon up the stairs to the interrogation area. Buddy, who imagined the young man was accustomed to such attention, was surprised at how uncomfortable he looked.

"Aren't you used to being 'admired,' Paolo? Or do you prefer Damon?"

"I'd rather be admired onstage than be gawked at in a police station. And I prefer Paolo."

Buddy cast Paolo a withering glance. "Oh, right. So many admirers, so little time." He shoved Paolo into an interview room. "Stay here until my boss gets back."

"How long?"

"Ya' never know. Just whistle a few opera tunes to pass the time," he said, and locked the door behind him.

* * *

Larry arrived several hours later having interviewed dozens of company members and come up with little significant information. He believed the prop manager when he said he didn't know how a loaded rifle had made its way onstage. He also assigned a special ops team to investigate the matter more thoroughly and thanked his lucky stars that no one had been killed. Now he was more than ready to fire off some pointed questions at the young man who had been carrying the loaded weapon.

Larry sat opposite Paolo, notebook in hand. "So, which is it, Paolo, or Damon?"

"Paolo."

"Which are you, valet or super? Tell the truth this time."

"I was a super when Maestro Trudeau offered me the valet job. With him gone, I had to go back to supering."

"Would you like to tell me what you were doing with a loaded rifle onstage?"

Rivulets of sweat ran down Paolo's neck. "I didn't know the bullets were real, I swear."

"Oh? I'm told you switched rifles with another super, that his had your number on it."

"I...I didn't check the number, it...it must have been the prop manager's mistake."

"The prop manager says otherwise." Paolo's response did not fool Larry. "Were you trying to kill the singer, or just wound him?"

Paolo jumped to his feet. "I don't have to tell you anything!"

"Yes, you do. That is, if you don't want to see your so-called 'stage career' go down the tubes."

Paolo turned his face to the wall, muttering under his breath. "I turned tricks on the street."

"What? I couldn't hear you."

The super wheeled and faced Larry. "I was a hooker, okay? I sold my body, to guys, some of them from the opera. One of them got me in."

"Which one?" Larry asked.

"I don't remember, I swear."

"Maybe twenty-four hours in a cell will jog your memory."

"Oh, no, please! I can't be locked up. I'm claustrophobic."

"Don't worry, you'll be cured fast." Larry eyed Paolo coolly. "We're booking you for first degree assault. D.A.'ll probably add criminal assault with a firearm." He watched Paolo's eyes widen with panic. "Don't complain, it's a class 'B' felony instead of a class 'A.'"

Paolo turned pale. "But I didn't do anything, I was set up."

"My advice, plead guilty to the first count, and they'll likely drop the second one. First offense, they might even let you out without bail until your hearing. Meanwhile, make yourself available for questioning. And keep your nose clean. Although if you ask me, you shouldn't be out on the street."

Despite his field inexperience, Larry knew the rights of a suspect counted for more than the rights of a victim at times. It was close to impossible to keep someone locked up for very long; these days it was all the NYPD could do to detain a suspected perp overnight. However, once Paolo was back out on the street, Larry decided to have him surveilled.

He'll slip up, sooner or later.

Chapter Twenty-Seven

Ah...soccorso...son tradito!...L'assassino...m'ha ferito...

Ah...help me...I am undone!...The assassin's blade has pierced me...

—Mozart, *Don Giovanni*, Act I

The next day, rehearsal was set to continue from where it had left off before Giuseppe's "unfortunate accident," as Patricia had called it. She was waiting at the entrance to the wings for the action to begin when Sidney rushed by with his violin case under his arm.

She glared at him. "A word, Sidney."

Sidney stopped and glanced around as nearby stagehands stared. Patricia took his arm and led him off to a secluded corner.

"What are you doing here?"

"What does it look like? I came to rehearse."

"How can you even show your face after what you've done?"

"I have as much a right to be here as anyone else."

"No, you don't. Not anymore."

"Why do you even care, Patricia? Does my being here remind you too much of Abel?"

Without waiting for a reply, Sidney stormed off. Patricia watched him, quaking with fury.

* * *

As Patricia strode onstage, she saw that the musicians were still milling about.

She flashed a look of menace toward the conductor.

"Maestro, please."

Patricia brusquely made her exit. The conductor waved his arms at the staring, shell-shocked musicians, who slowly took their seats.

The stage manager cleared his throat. "Understudies, please! Quiet, onstage!" He continued his directive in hushed silence. "Covers for Tosca and Mario, please. Charles, Sarafina!"

Charles rushed onstage, followed by Sarafina, a diva soprano of the Wagnerian "Valkyrie" body type. Charles resumed Giuseppe's exact position on the floor with machinelike precision.

Once seated, the distracted musicians began to play—without any enthusiasm whatsoever.

Julia leaned over to Katie. "How does Patricia stay so bulletproof?"

Katie shrugged. "Don't know. I'm guessing she has some help from her 'friends.'"

She mimed popping a pill into her mouth.

Julia's eyes grew wide. "You mean...antidepressants?"

"Maybe something stronger, if you get my drift."

Julia thrust the violin under her chin and obeyed the conductor's beat. She still felt terrorized by the events of the previous day. But her trepidation disappeared when she looked up to see Charles onstage.

It's about time he got his chance.

Sarafina made the most of her fifteen seconds of fame by belting out her last solo phrase with all the dramatic power worthy of her girth. "*O Scarpia! Avanti a Dio!*" She turned to the nearest stagehand. "That means, 'Oh Scarpia! Before God!'" Then she proceeded to walk nonchalantly toward the wings.

The director threw up his hands. "Cut!" he screamed. He grabbed Sarafina's beefy arm before she could complete her exit. "What was that? You're supposed to throw yourself off the parapet!"

With Sarafina's considerable dimensions, a leap off the edge of the parapet, even with stacks of mattresses waiting below, was dicey at best. Legendary but hefty diva Monserrat Caballé was notorious for making her leisurely strolling exit to stage left without risking the precipitous vault. No one would be surprised if Sarafina followed suit.

"Are you kidding?" Sarafina asked the open-mouthed stage manager. "There's no way I'm jumping off that mother."

She continued to stroll offstage, smiling broadly.

* * *

Julia appeared at the stage door that evening in concert attire and found Larry hovering near the security guard. Both guard and detective were double-checking IDs.

"After what happened at rehearsal, Julia, I figured you'd be too upset to show up tonight."

"Cops have no idea what musicians go through," Julia said. "I still have to play, even under the worst circumstances. The show must—"

"Go on? I honestly had no idea you guys were so plucky." He cracked a friendly smile.

Encouraged, she took the opening. "So, tell me about that super you collared today. Is it true his rifle had real bullets?"

"'Collared?'" Larry studied her eager expression. "My, aren't we the resourceful one?" He leaned toward her, lowering his voice. "I can't reveal details about the ammo, though. That's classified. You know what ammo means, right?"

"Of course. I watch *CSI*, just like everyone else," Julia said, annoyed.

"I have a feeling you do a lot more than just watch it. You've made a study of it."

Julia wasn't sure how to handle the backhanded compliment. "Thanks, I think. Maybe you're not such a bad guy after all."

"Careful, I blush easily."

Feeling the atmosphere between her and the detective lighten up, she decided to share some of her recent finds. "If you promise to be very nice to me, I'll share a secret with you."

"I'm all ears."

"Somebody moved the pieces on Abel's chessboard in his dressing room.

You should dust for prints."

"You've been watching too much TV, Julia. I'm not sending in my crime techs just because you think I should."

"But whoever moved the pieces could have been the real killer, returning to the scene of the crime. That's what they do, don't they?"

Larry narrowed his gaze. "Okay, I'll look into it. Happy now?"

"Delirious. By the way, Matt never showed up for work today. I haven't seen him since I asked him who he thought might have framed Sid. Now I'm really concerned. It's not like him to be MIA."

"Okay, I'll send in Buddy to check."

"Now that's what I call partnership. Nice working with you," she said, as she walked off.

Chapter Twenty-Eight

Perdon...l'affanno mio, le pene...Ah! vendicar, se il puoi, giura quel sangue ognor!
Forgive me...my grief, my distress...Ah! swear that, if you can, you will avenge his blood!
—Mozart, *Don Giovanni*, Act I

After the final curtain fell on that evening's performance of *Don Giovanni*, the musicians emitted a collective sigh of relief and made their hasty exits from the pit. But Julia just sat motionless.

This opera always had a profound effect on her, even more so since Abel's demise. The sufferings of Donna Anna, the daughter of the murdered *Commendatore*, made Julia's heart break. She endured the agonies of the young woman's emotional torture as if they were her own. During the opera, Julia mouthed the words of the libretto, which she knew almost from memory, sung by Anna when she finds her father's body:

"Mal qual mai s'offre, oh Dei, spettacolo funesto agli occhi miei!...Ah! l'assassino mel trucidò."

"But, oh God, what dreadful sight confronts my eyes!...Ah! The assassin has struck him down!"

These phrases alone were enough to bring tears to Julia's eyes, but the words that followed always evoked visions of her father expiring in her arms:

"Quel sangue...quella piaga...quel volto...tinto e coperto dei color di morte...Ei non respira più...fredde ha le membra."

"This blood...this wound...his face discolored with the pallor of death... he's not breathing anymore...his limbs are so cold..."

Julia thought these brilliant and evocative words flowing from the pen of Mozart's librettist Lorenzo Da Ponte genuinely portrayed the agony of every daughter who has lost a father, particularly if the loss was sudden and violent. Now that she was mourning the passing of Abel as well, Julia could not help being haunted by images of her mentor, his blood on her hands, being torn from her with as much brutality as Sol Kogan had been. It was as if she had lost her own father twice.

Now, overwrought and steeped in sorrow, she couldn't find the strength to budge from her spot. It was only after musicians and patrons had vacated the pit and the theater, that Julia managed to pack up her violin and make her way out of the comforting darkness of her orchestral womb.

The women's locker room was empty except for Katie, who had been waiting to walk home with Julia.

"What took you so long, Jul?"

Julia replied, a far-off look in her eyes. "I just needed to take my time. You know what that opera always does to me, especially now that Abel..."

Julia bit her lip to stem her pain but found comfort in Katie's supportive smile. It was then that Julia noticed an envelope taped to her locker door. Puzzled, Julia removed it, scanned its contents, and gave a little "humph" of surprise.

"It's from Larry. He wants me to come to the pit."

"What for?"

"Haven't got a clue." Julia thought for a moment. "He did seem a lot friendlier than usual when I saw him before the show—"

"O-o-h. And I thought there was no love lost between you two. Bet he's soft on you."

"I won't grace that with a response." Julia flashed Katie a mock warning look, opened her locker, and stuffed the envelope inside. "I'll be right back."

From the pit entrance, Julia scoured the dark, empty space. Larry was nowhere in sight. She climbed onto the podium and peeked over the pit rail into the audience. A protrusion from the ventilation hole in the pit wall caught her attention. Clambering down, she peered into the opening. Something was stuffed into it: a bludgeoned and bloodied body.

Matt.

* * *

Julia's screams echoing through the halls brought Katie racing into the pit, where she found Julia collapsed in shock on the floor next to the pit wall. Katie took one look at the grisly scene and averted her eyes. Choking back a wave of nausea, she instead focused on Julia.

Julia allowed Katie to pull her to her feet, just as a flock of security guards and stagehands arrived. Tony appeared and helped Katie escort Julia out of the pit and walk her to the locker room, where Julia crumpled onto a sofa in a distraught heap.

As she lay prostrate, Julia was not even aware that Katie and Tony had helped her there. She moaned, traumatized, while Katie applied an improvised compress of wet paper towels to her forehead. Julia was in such a state of shock she didn't try to push Katie's hand away as she normally would have done.

"How did I get here? Where's Charles?" Julia half-cried, half-groaned.

"Shh, Julia, it'll be okay," Katie whispered.

"Charles. I want Charles."

Katie arched her eyebrow at the name of the attractive understudy. "He'll be here soon. Just try to relax."

There was a soft knock at the door. Larry appeared, approached Katie, and spoke in a low whisper. "Poor kid. She found the body?"

Katie nodded.

Larry knelt by Julia, murmuring quietly. "Julia, can you get up?"

Julia groaned and shook her head.

"Katie," Larry said, "I need to go check out the murder scene. Anything I can do for her?"

"She's asked for Charles Tremaine. Could you find out if he's still in the opera house? He might be able to calm her down."

"I'll call upstairs."

Larry strode to the door, signaling Katie to follow him. Leaning over her, he whispered, "Her friend Richter's been arrested again. They're accusing him of this murder, too, on top of the other one."

Katie gasped. "Oh, no."

"Soon as he's out on bail, this has to happen. Unless he has a good alibi, it looks bad. Turns out he and Matt had a serious falling out recently." Larry shook his head. "Make sure Julia doesn't find out about Richter, not until she's in better shape. She doesn't need to know yet. But eventually, I'm going to have to ask her a few questions about the victim."

Katie nodded. Larry made his way out the door and down the hall toward the pit.

Another murder. This place is unbelievable.

* * *

Katie was dabbing Julia's forehead with the paper towels when Charles tiptoed in.

"How can I help?" he asked Katie.

"She just needs your support, Charles."

"Maybe a change of scene would do her some good." He leaned over Julia. "Julia, do you want me to take you to my apartment?"

Katie frowned. "I don't think that's a good idea."

"But she did ask for me, didn't she? Now I'm here to take care of her." He turned to Julia. "Do you want to come with me?"

Julia looked up at him with glazed eyes and managed a shaky nod.

"Are you sure, Jul?" Katie asked.

Again, Julia nodded. Katie unfastened the chain from around her neck and removed the delicate gold cross hanging from it. Then she unclasped the chain with Julia's locket, attached the cross to it, and reclasped it.

"She needs all the help she can get right now," Katie whispered to Charles. She turned to Julia. "It's for protection and strength. I know you're Jewish, but I don't think God will mind."

"That cross looks like it has magical powers," Charles said.

"It does," Katie said. "I have it on good authority."

Julia managed a weary smile and allowed Charles and Katie to help her up. She even let Charles hold tight to her waist as he led her to the door.

"Charles. Wait." Whispering into Charles's ear, Katie told him the terrible news Larry had confided to her about Sidney. "It's what the detective told me. Keep it under your hat."

Charles nodded. Then he gently guided Julia out the door.

"Take care of her," Katie said worriedly as she watched them leave.

* * *

In the secluded alley behind the Met loading dock, a face was obscured in shadow as a gloved hand punched a number on a burner phone. Only two words were spoken before the gloved hand clicked off.

"Condition corrected."

Chapter Twenty-Nine

Soglio in cittade uccidere, oppure nel mio tetto.
L'uomo di sera aspetto; una stoccata e muor
I kill my man in the town or under my own roof.
I wait for him at night; one thrust, and he's dead.
—Verdi, *Rigoletto*, Act I

J ulia collapsed on the sofa in Charles's living room. Her face was still tear-streaked, but she was a good deal calmer than she had been before they left the Met.

Charles gently laid a comforter over her and sat close by, gazing at her tortured face. "How do you feel? Can I do anything for you?"

She regarded him with grateful eyes. "No. But thank you. For being there for me."

"I promised you consolation, didn't I? I'm a man of my word."

A stubborn tear escaped from her eye and traveled down her cheek. "Matt was so sweet, so thoughtful. He didn't deserve this." Julia felt her eyelids, heavy with fatigue, wanting to shut. But haunting images forced them open. "Every time I close my eyes, I see him, just lying there."

Charles threaded his arms around her. She didn't pull away. "Shh, just rest now. There's nothing you can do."

She began to cry. He held her, comforting her, until her bitter sobs diminished. Suddenly she sat up, panicked. "Poor Sid, he'll be so upset. I've got to see him, to tell him—"

Charles gently lowered her back onto the sofa. "Julia..." He hesitated.

"Sid's back in jail."

"What? But he's been out for less than a day."

"They've accused him of killing Matt."

"No! They can't!" Julia's eyes widened in distress. "It makes no sense. Why would Sid—"

"It was a triangle." Charles's voice remained soft and steady. "I didn't want to tell you for fear of hurting you. But everyone backstage knew Sidney was jealous...because Abel threw him over for Matt."

"But Matt wasn't—"

"Gay? Yes, he was. It just so happened he couldn't resist you. No one can."

Julia broke down again.

"I'm so sorry, Julia." He leaned toward her and tried to put his arms around her.

She pushed him away. "No! Don't get close to me, something awful will happen to you. It's the story of my life. My father. Abel. Sid. Everyone I've ever cared about has disappeared from my life," she moaned. "You will, too. Oh, God, what am I going to do?"

"Lean on me. Trust me. I'm not going anywhere. *Lo giuro*—I swear it."

He clasped her tightly. She wrapped her arms around his neck, hanging on for dear life.

"Just let me take care of you." He planted tender kisses on her forehead.

Overwhelmed with emotion, Julia melted into him, finding solace in his arms. It felt wonderful, being in his powerful grasp, protected and cared for.

This can't be happening. No, no. I shouldn't allow myself this comfort.

But it only took a moment before her resistance dissolved. He was her rock, her strength, her safe haven in this tempest raging all around her, threatening her sanity. He was, truly, a man of his word.

* * *

In the pit, Larry conferred with the medical examiner as Matt's body, still in its original position, was being photographed. Larry's calm exterior belied his emotions. Julia's reaction to losing a second important person in her life within a matter of days had rattled him. Seeing Matt's remains stuffed into the crack in the pit wall gave him even more cause to feel anger toward the killer and immense sympathy toward the poor, naïve young violinist. It was hard to imagine what she must be going through.

"Anything?" Larry asked the M.E.

"Can't tell much, not until we get the body out of that crack."

"So, we have an appointment tomorrow morning?"

"You bring the espresso. And make it strong."

Larry frowned. Then he found his way to Patricia's office and calmly watched the general manager as she stood by the window, hunched over a cigarette.

"Tense, are we, Ms. Wells?"

Patricia took three hasty puffs and crushed out the cigarette with a nervous twist. "Wouldn't you be, with such hideous goings-on?"

As she drew another cigarette from her silver case, Larry shot her a disapproving glance. She returned it with a look of defiance.

"Yes, I'm breaking the law. Are you going to arrest me?"

Larry picked up the matching lighter from Patricia's desk and lit her cigarette. "On the contrary. As long as you don't cause anyone else physical harm."

"That's very benevolent of you."

Placing the lit stick in an ashtray, Patricia carefully polished the lighter with a soft cloth. Then she began puffing again, blowing the smoke out the window.

"And who do you think might clue me in to these 'hideous goings-on?'" Larry asked.

Patricia shot him a venomous look. "Why don't you talk to that little vixen, Julia? She's not as innocent as she seems."

"Come on, Ms. Wells, we both know Julia is no 'vixen.' Someone else is behind these murders. Who are you trying to protect?"

"I have no idea what you're talking about," snapped Patricia.

The abrupt jangle of Larry's cell phone—the "Anvil Chorus" from Verdi's *Il Trovatore*—disrupted their conversation. He picked up. "Yeah, Buddy. I'm on my way down. Come up and keep our manager company, okay?" Larry clicked off and turned to Patricia. "Don't try to go anywhere. There are cops all over the place."

"So I would imagine," she said. "Thank God, I feel all safe now."

Larry ignored her sarcastic tone and marched out of the office.

* * *

Patricia finished off the cigarette, exhaling forcefully, just as Buddy knocked. She gritted her teeth. "Come in."

"I'm afraid I have to ask you more questions, Ms. Wells."

"Oh? Am I a suspect now?"

"From now on, everyone is."

Chapter Thirty

Entrava ella, fragrante, mi cadea fra le braccia...e non ho amato mai tanto la vita!
Fragrant, she entered and fell into my arms...and never have I loved life so much!
—Puccini, *Tosca*, Act III

T he next morning, Larry and Buddy paid a visit to the Office of the Chief Medical Examiner on 26th Street in Manhattan. Since the case had escalated in importance, this latest murder was specified as significant enough to be handled by the city's top forensic specialist.

Larry hated to view the body of anyone he had known, even for a brief time.

No matter how many years of experience I might end up with, this is one part of the job that'll always leave a bad taste in my mouth.

The two detectives stood next to the M.E., who had Matt's body stretched out on a gurney. Larry tried to concentrate, but all he could think of was Julia's agonized face.

Two dead bodies in one week. The poor girl's suffered too much.

"Blunt metallic object to the head," the M.E. said. "Shape of the wound suggests a tool."

"Like...what kind?" Larry asked.

"Hard to tell. Looks like he put up a real fight, too. Torn fingernails. No fingerprints on the body, a very careful job."

"A tool?" Larry thought for a moment. "Maybe a...stagehand's wrench?"

"Possibly. I wouldn't rule it out. But it could be any other kind of blunt object. In any case, from the extreme head trauma, I'd say the person inflicting the wound was unusually strong."

Larry nodded, trying to decide what to do next. He and Buddy left the M.E. to his work and stepped outside.

"So, what now, boss? Richter's still the prime suspect, right?"

"Richter had motive, there's no doubt of that. It's a classic set of circumstances."

"Plus, the stagehand's murder happened within hours of Sidney's release."

"Right," Larry said. "Aside from the fact that Abel was about to throw over Sidney for Matt, the jealousy factor, Reynolds may have known something about Sidney that would implicate Richter in Trudeau's murder. Sidney wanted to make sure Matt was silenced before it got out."

"But if Reynolds knew something he could use to point the finger at Richter, wouldn't he have revealed it during his interview right after Trudeau's murder?"

"Not necessarily. It wouldn't be the first time someone lied by omission in a prelim, unless..."

"Unless what?"

"Unless Richter had something on Reynolds that he could hold over him."

"Like what, boss?"

"I don't know. I just have a hunch." Larry paused. Something just wasn't clicking. "Despite the overwhelming evidence against Richter, we can't rule out accomplices. Go search the stagehands' locker room again. I've got a date with *Tosca*."

"Meaning?"

"Meaning, it's time to look into possible conspiracies, Buddy boy."

Buddy eyed Larry. "You sure you want to bother? Richter's still gonna fry."

"Humor me."

Larry looked at the younger detective. He had Julia in mind. She was a good kid. He wanted to help her in some way if he could.

"You got it." With a mock salute, Buddy left.

This isn't going to be easy. With Giuseppe clueless about his attacker, we've got to be extra alert. And the stagehands won't be any help, either.

Larry was sure that all the Met's crewmembers looked out for each other. I.A.T.S.E., or the International Alliance of Theatrical and Stage Employees to those in the loop, was a powerful union, under the benevolent and far-reaching umbrella of the Teamsters. Everyone knew it was no fun messing with those guys.

Meanwhile, Larry was beginning to consider Julia's claim that the song Abel had written for her might well contain a clue to the conductor's murder. Larry was not educated in the nitty-gritty of music theory. He didn't even read music. But at the very least, he might cheer Julia up and distract her from her grief if he showed a bit of interest in her hypothesis. Plus, he still had to question her about Matt's murder. She was, after all, a witness.

* * *

Charles awakened Julia with a gentle kiss. Disoriented and still sleepy, she allowed his embrace, until the morning light illuminated his face. Then she sat bolt upright in the bed, drawing away from him.

What have I done?

In a moment of weakness, she had given in and let herself be seduced. Her vulnerability had caused her to let her guard down, to allow herself the consolation of the physical contact she had shunned for half her life.

What was I thinking? Just like Scarpia…he's nested inside my heart.

Charles pulled her back into his arms, holding her close.

"Good morning, my darling," he murmured.

Julia berated herself for what had happened the night before.

It was my fault, not his.

A ringing phone jarred her. Extricating herself, she fumbled in her purse for her cell phone.

"Don't answer it, Julia."

Ignoring his command, she swiped the screen. "Hello?"

"Julia, it's Larry."

Julia could hear urgency in his voice. "What's wrong?"

"I need you to come down to the Met right away. It's important."

"I already know about Sid's arrest."

"Oh? Somehow, I'm not surprised." Larry paused. "But no, there's a new twist involving him. Seems you've been holding out on me."

"What do you mean?" Julia sighed. She was tired. It had been a long night. "Okay, okay. I'll be right there."

Puzzled, and still groggy, Julia clicked off and started to rise, pulling the bedclothes around her. Sensing how Charles would react, she looked at him, girding herself.

"I have to go to the Met."

Charles tugged her back toward the bed. "Now? Is it that important?"

"There's a new development. About Sid."

He let go of her. "You've faced all your traumas so bravely, Julia. It's time you faced facts about Sidney."

Julia sensed Charles was about to tell her something she didn't want to hear. "What facts?"

"You're becoming an emotional wreck over him. He's taken advantage of your good will."

"How can you say that?" Julia asked, outraged. "He's my friend. My *loyal* friend."

"Your loyalty is admirable, Julia. But you can't go on fighting battles for him." Charles softened his tone. "Not if you want to give *us* a chance."

Warning bells went off in Julia's head.

"*Us?*"

The last thing she wanted was to become part of a relationship, a couple, if she felt the tug of attraction. But some overwhelming force drew her to him, and when he reached for her and pulled her down on the bed, clasping her to him, her resolve began to melt.

His voice soothed her, mesmerized her. "Stay another hour. The Met can wait."

"But...it sounded urgent."

Julia summoned up all her will power to untangle herself. This time, he didn't try to prevent her. She rose, scooping up her clothes, and dressed in haste in the bathroom.

When she returned to gather up her belongings, Charles continued to speak.

"If Abel had been about to throw over Sidney for Matt, it would have given Sidney motives for both murders. You've got to face that possibility."

"No! That can't be true! I refuse to listen to you!"

What if he's right?

"Charles, try to understand. I'm still reeling from…Matt's…" Julia's voice broke. "…from losing Matt. Now I've got to worry even more about Sid. I'm just…beside myself."

Charles reached out to her. "Then don't go, Julia."

Julia tore herself away. "I have to."

She left and did not turn back.

Chapter Thirty-One

Bello e fatale un giovane offriarsi al guardo mio...
se i labbri nostri tacquero dagliocchi il cor parlò.
Furtivo fra le tenebre sol ieri a me giungeva...
A fatally handsome young man met my gaze...
Though our lips were silent, our hearts spoke through our eyes.
Secretly in the darkness last night he came to see me...
—Verdi, *Rigoletto*, Act II

J ulia eyed the chaotic scene in the pit, cops stationed at each corner and crime techs sweeping the pit wall for fingerprints. She headed straight for Larry, who was inspecting the bloodstained floor. He looked up at her.

"Sorry, Julia, but I have to ask you some questions about Matt."

Julia's face darkened. "Oh. So that's what this is for?"

"Somewhat. How long did you know him?"

"Only since the beginning of pre-season rehearsals. About a month."

"And did you notice any conflicts between him and other company members?"

Julia thought for a moment. "Well, I've seen Patricia mouthing off at him, but she does that to everybody. And that guy Frank seemed to resent Matt. But Frank has it in for everyone."

"Did you see Matt the night he was murdered?"

"No." Julia shuddered. "I went looking for him but never found him."

"Did you know about Matt, Abel, and Sidney?"

"The love triangle between them? Yes. Charles told me."

"Did you know about...this?"

Larry held up a plastic evidence bag with a scrawled note showing through. Julia scanned it, recognized Abel's handwriting, and read aloud.

"'Sid, I'm sorry I had to bring Julia in on it. She's got to know the truth now. It's the only way. Please forgive me. Abel.'" Stunned, she drew in a sharp breath. "Where'd you get this?"

"Your boss Tony happened to recall that Sidney had a second locker. We found it there." He peered at her "So, what did Abel 'bring you in on?'"

"I...I have no clue."

"Think again. You told me about it in the record store."

Julia thought for a moment. "The song?"

"You've said it sounds strange, that Abel might have written it that way on purpose, because of some clue in it."

Julia bristled. "But I still haven't figured it out. I swear."

"Then it's about time you did."

"I can't, I only have the second page." She hesitated, reluctant to admit the truth. "I loaned the first page...to Charles."

"Then you'd better get it back, pronto."

The thought of going back to Charles made Julia squirm.

"You know, Larry, I never did find out why you left that note for me last night."

"Note? What note?" He frowned. "I didn't leave you a—"

They eyed each other for a second. Then Julia raced out of the pit toward the women's locker room, Larry following close behind her. Once there, Julia wrenched open her locker door. The contents were in disarray.

"Damn! Someone's been rifling through my things." She sifted through her locker and slammed the door in frustration. "The note's not there. I distinctly remember stuffing it in."

"Whoever wrote the note wanted you to find Matt's body," Larry said. "Probably to frighten you. Now I'm worried that you're being watched."

Sighing, Julia closed her locker and secured it. She and Larry headed out of the room and walked together as far as the pit.

"When you get the page back from Charles, bring it down to H.Q. I want to have a closer look at those weird notes," Larry said. "I'll be there if you need me. No note left unturned."

* * *

Julia dreaded the thought of having to seek out Charles. She navigated the crowded backstage wings, active with stagehands and other members preparing for rehearsal, and scanned the space. Spying Charles in a huddle with the stage manager, she walked toward them. Charles eyed her with unconcealed aloofness, and she shifted with discomfort. Nodding to the stage manager, Charles motioned Julia to a quiet corner.

"Did you want something, Julia?"

"I…" His cool manner undermined her courage. "I was wondering if…if you…had Abel's song with you?"

"Regretfully, I left it home. I'd pop back home and get it for you, but I'm needed onstage for today's rehearsal." Charles lowered his voice. "I'm replacing Giuseppe in Abel's tribute performance tomorrow night. He's still limping and not up to the stress of performing onstage."

"Charles, that's fantastic! Why didn't you tell me sooner?"

"I wanted it to keep it a secret, at least for now."

Julia looked around to see if anyone was looking. Then, throwing her arms around him, she gave him a hug. He embraced her for a long moment, and she reveled in it.

"I'll be in very intense rehearsing all day," he said. "Closed session away from the opera house. They won't even tell me where it's going to be."

Julia was impressed. "I'm so happy you're finally beginning to get the VIP treatment you so deserve."

"Then they're rushing me straight to the post-performance gala tonight. But after that, I'll swing by your place, and we can go over the song."

"I'd like that."

"Wonderful. Will you walk me to the stage?"

Heart fluttering with happiness, Julia followed Charles. Together they watched Frank supervise the stagehands. They were using a rope and pulley to haul a seventy-five-pound plaster face-shaped mask up to the proscenium fifty-four feet above.

Both Julia and Charles noticed Frank's glance in their direction.

"I still can't figure out why he has a grudge against me, Charles."

"I don't think he does. He's just gruff mannered. At heart, he's really a good guy."

Julia was doubtful. Charles pointed upward as a stagehand positioned atop the proscenium attached the mask and then came shimmying down. "That's for the new production of *'Butterfly'*. They're going to create a Japanese *'Noh'* play, with masks fastened to the proscenium."

"I'm impressed." Turning her eyes toward the floor, Julia spied a matchbook. She bent down to retrieve it. Thoughts of Matt made her eyes mist over.

They were interrupted by a cracking sound, then a groaning noise. Small plaster particles from above fell on Charles's shirt.

"Julia, watch out!"

Julia looked up, terror-stricken, as the mask broke loose from its anchoring and came crashing toward her. She was too petrified to scream—or to move. She just froze.

In a split-second, Charles grabbed her and yanked her out of the way. They both hit the floor as the mask landed inches from them, splintering into jagged shards.

Stagehands immediately swarmed the area. Frank cornered the stagehand who had attached the mask and began to shout at him.

The stage manager strode onto the scene. "Clear the stage, everyone!" he yelled.

Julia crouched down, terrified, struggling to catch her breath. She clutched Charles's arm as if it were the only thing saving her from falling off a cliff. He held her close.

"Oh my God, oh my God."

"Are you hurt, Julia?"

"No...just...very...shaken up."

"With brand-new sets under construction, accidents can happen," Charles said. "Take deep breaths, Julia. That's it."

She forced herself to obey, but his reassuring voice did nothing to soothe her.

She remembered one of her very first rehearsals, when a similar incident had taken place. A piece of scenery had come loose from the top of the proscenium. The very alert lead soprano saw it hurtling toward the stage and had enough presence of mind to shout a warning for everyone to scatter before it came crashing down; avoiding disaster, and perhaps even saving someone's life. Then there was the time when a poor unsuspecting chorister fell down an open elevator shaft—and died.

An opera house can be a dangerous place. But still...

Julia began to tremble.

"You poor thing, you're in shock," Charles said. "You can't rehearse in this condition. You'd best go home."

She was quick to protest. "But I can't miss rehearsal."

"Even your hard-nosed boss wouldn't expect you to play after what just happened," Charles said. "Though admittedly, if you'll forgive my selfishness, I'd like you to be in top form tonight."

In her battle-weary state, Charles's suggestion made perfect sense to Julia. But the thought of confronting her boss made her quake with anxiety.

"Tony will have a fit."

"I'll talk some sense into him."

"You will?"

She felt too traumatized to argue. Charles helped her up and led her through the onstage chaos toward the exit. Once out of the opera house, he walked her to Amsterdam Avenue, where he whistled for a taxi. Within seconds, a cab pulled up to the curb.

Charles helped Julia inside. "I'll try to catch a moment and call you later, okay?" He kissed her on the cheek.

Smiling bravely up at him, she leaned back into the seat as Charles closed the door. She caught a brief glimpse of his concerned expression as the cab zoomed away.

Chapter Thirty-Two

Entro il sen, dallo spavento, palpitar il cor mi sento.
Io non so che far, che dir.
I can feel in my heart, pounding with terror in my breast.
I don't know what to do, what to say.
—Mozart, *Don Giovanni*, Act I

J ulia took mincing steps as she climbed the outside stairs of her brownstone. The autumn temperature was nippier than it had been thus far, and she pulled her jacket closer around her.

She felt shaky, and she berated herself for being so fragile. The show was supposed to go on, no matter what. She could have—*should* have—stayed and done her work, even after her close call onstage. Where was her strength, her inner power?

My showing this morning was a disgrace to Abel's memory. He would not have been proud of me.

She turned the key to the outer door, entered the foyer, and climbed the stairs to her apartment, which was empty since Katie was still at the Met rehearsing.

Once inside, Julia curled up on the sofa. She hated missing any of her obligations at the Met so soon after her opening night, even if that had been a disaster. But she also knew Charles was right. She was much too shaken up to do justice to the rehearsal, and she needed to be in shape for the performance of *Rigoletto* that evening.

Rigoletto was not the most difficult opera to play, but it was one of her favorites. The scenes between the devoted father and his doomed daughter always gave Julia goose bumps. Unlike *Don Giovanni*, where a young woman mourns the loss of her father, *Rigoletto* told the tale of a father's anguish when he inadvertently causes the death of his beloved daughter, his only remaining family member. There was a certain tragic justice in that, Julia had often thought, a parallel to her own life. Her own brush with death earlier in the day brought this home.

Her ringing cell phone came as a welcome distraction from her thoughts. "Hello?"

"Is this Julia? Julia Kogan?"

"Yes. Who is this?"

"Herb Cafferty. Sidney Richter's attorney."

Julia became alert. "Oh, my God. Is everything…did something…is he okay?"

"He's okay. For now." Herb's booming voice rattled Julia's frayed nerves. "He wanted me to bring you up to date. About the grand jury today."

Julia gulped. "What…what happened?"

"Well, it doesn't look good." Herb's grim tone alarmed her. "D.A. always asks for the harshest possible sentence. But with this case being so high-profile…"

Julia swallowed hard. She knew, too well, that "harshest possible sentence" meant "Life."

"So that means he's hot to get a quick indictment in Sid's case and move it through the system," Herb continued. "When I pointed that out to the D.A., he said anyone who killed a beloved public figure in cold blood, not to mention in view of four thousand devoted fans, deserved to have the full wrath of God meted out to him."

"But Sid didn't do it."

"You know that, and I know that. But the D.A. thinks he's guilty."

Julia, feeling faint, remained silent.

"You still there, Julia?"

"Yes. I'm here."

Barely.

"Bottom line, after the final witness of the day testified, D.A. told the judge—he's a real *alte cocker*, if you know what I mean, old and bored—the State had shown probable cause. The judge agreed, so he handed down an indictment."

"Oh my God. What will happen next?"

"The trial." Herb paused. "I gotta go, Julia. Any questions, feel free to call. Your smart phone's got my number."

"Okay. Thank you."

Julia clicked off and sank into the sofa. The day kept getting worse. She still felt paralyzed with grief over Matt. Then there was the near miss onstage. Now this.

The downstairs buzzer jarred her from her brooding, however, and she reluctantly rose from her comfortable sofa. She pressed the intercom.

"Who is it?"

"Larry. Can I come up?"

Julia pressed the buzzer and opened the door, watching as Larry strode down the hall toward her. As she motioned him inside, she noticed his agitated demeanor.

"So, Julia, do you have the song? It's time we had a look at it."

"I…I couldn't get it. But as soon as—"

"'Soon as' is not soon enough."

Julia regarded him, annoyed. After what she had been through that morning, she didn't feel like being pushed.

"Look, I'm having a really bad day."

"I'm not surprised, between what occurred with Matt and what happened to you at the Met this morning."

"So you heard?"

"Yes, and it's under investigation. But I'm not so sure it was an accident."

"What?"

"First the note goes missing from your locker, then you barely escape being crushed to death. It's hard not to connect those incidents. That said…" There was urgency in Larry's voice. "I wanted to make sure to give you a heads up. Sid's case is super high profile. And believe me, I know this judge.

With the Grand Jury indictment, he'll want to show that he's not soft on violent crime. If anyone can put it on a fast track, he can."

Julia used the table by the door to steady herself. "Meaning?"

"Sidney'll plead not guilty in Felony Court, leaving no room for bargaining. The judge will lose no time ramming things into high gear with that hot-to-trot D.A. on his tail. Even with the usual delays, and Sidney's lawyer pushing for continuances, a trial date could be set quickly."

"Oh, my God."

Julia's feelings of hopelessness escalated. "Why do you even care, Larry?"

"Whatever the differences between us, I think you're a good kid trying to do the right thing. I'd like to help you out," Larry said. "That song is your only hope. You need to get hold of it, ASAP, get to the bottom of those weird notes and find out what they mean."

"But Charles has it. And he's unreachable for the rest of the day."

"When it comes to police business, no one is 'unreachable.'"

"No, really. He's coaching all day today for his big solo debut performance tomorrow night, in an undisclosed location."

"'Undisclosed location?' What is this, the Met Opera, or the International Monetary Fund?"

"It's what they do when someone is being replaced at the last minute for a specially important performance. But he'll be at the post-performance gala tonight."

"Fine. You can weasel it out of him there."

"Are you kidding? Lowly musicians aren't invited."

"But NYPD detectives are allowed anywhere. I think it's time Charles and I had a chat."

He reached over to give her a reassuring pat. She pulled back.

"You sit tight. I gotta go. You gonna be okay?"

"Other than stupendous boredom, I'm fine. What am I going to do with myself here, all alone?"

Larry looked around the room and caught sight of the shelf with the free weights on it.

"See those weights? Lift them," he said, and let himself out.

He's such a pain. But Katie was right. He is kind of cute.

Chapter Thirty-Three

Povsyudu radost otrazilas no ne v dushe moyei bolnoi
All around is happiness, but not in my stricken heart.
—Tchaikovsky, *Pique Dame*, Act I

Larry viewed the elite post-opera gala as a microcosm of the opera world, at least the Met's own version of it. From his post beside the entrance of the immense, sumptuously furnished high-ceilinged Belmont Room, he watched the elegantly dressed patrons interact with members of the board of directors. The privileged attendees sipped champagne, while a six-piece orchestra played in the background.

Charles would want them to be toasting him this evening. Fat chance.

Larry believed Patricia would see to it that all the attention was focused on her. From what he had perceived about Charles, Larry had no doubt the singer's every desire for attention, and longed-for praise, would be accorded to him during his curtain calls, and long after.

Larry glanced around the room and spied Patricia. She noticed him and headed his way. He tried to adopt his most cordial social manner as he admired her striking appearance: the burgundy-colored strapless ball gown and matching set of diamond tiara, necklace, and earrings that looked as if they had been borrowed from Her Majesty's Jewel House at the Tower of London.

"Swell gathering, Ms. Wells."

"Thank you, detective. Do enjoy yourself."

"Who are all these people, anyway?"

"Oh, patrons, benefactors, board members. The usual."

Patricia's impassive expression morphed into solicitousness when she spied Sophia Tallman, the elegant dowager and most important patroness of the Met, approach with Charles in her wake.

"Patricia, my dear, you've outdone yourself tonight," gushed the stately woman.

"My sentiments exactly," Charles said.

Larry recognized Charles's earnest attempt at echoing the dowager for the posturing it was, but he sensed Patricia was determined to convey only the utmost social refinement.

"Thank you both." Patricia gestured to Larry. "Mrs. Sophia Tallman, of the Tallman Foundation, may I introduce Detective Somers of the New York Police Department."

Larry attempted his most urbane tone. "How do you do?"

"And you know Charles Tremaine, our up-and-coming tenor," Patricia added.

"Yes, from the memorial service for Maestro Trudeau." Larry turned to Charles. "I'm a great fan of your Schubert art song recordings. You should do more."

Larry hoped his sincerity was not lost on Charles. The recording in question was brilliant but little known, and he thought he detected a bit of surprise in the tenor's reaction.

"Thank you. I'm just waiting for some luck—to make me a household name."

"Mrs. Tallman's foundation has made all of Abel's most brilliant productions possible, detective," Patricia said.

"You're too kind, Patricia."

Mrs. Tallman protested with such convincing modesty that Larry was unable to determine whether she was being genuine. But he easily could tell Charles was not about to be outclassed.

"And she's promised me a new production as well, haven't you, Sophia?"

"As I've already told you, Charles, I'll have to speak to my board about it."

Patricia's admonishing glance at Charles was not lost on Larry. "Detective

Somers is the one who's been investigating the shocking events here as of late, Sophia."

"We are all so distressed about Abel's death, Detective Somers."

"I'm doing my best to solve the case as quickly as possible, Ma'am. New York's finest."

This self-conscious dialogue was interrupted when Dorothy Muir swept grandly into the room. Statuesque, stunning, dressed to the nines, Larry thought her the absolute embodiment of "Diva." All eyes turned toward her as everyone in attendance began to applaud.

Larry watched as an overdressed matron dripping with jewels rushed over to the *prima donna*, grabbing the singer's hands in an intimate gesture.

"Dorothy, how nice to see you again."

The soprano regarded the effusive woman with a cold stare. "Likewise, *Miss* van Dam."

Patricia blanched, hurried over to Dorothy, and smiled an apology to Miss van Dam. Mrs. Tallman excused herself. Patricia took Dorothy by the arm and drew her toward Larry.

"Dorothy Muir, Detective Somers. He's investigating the...recent events."

Larry nodded at the diva. "I'm a great admirer of yours, Miss Muir."

Dorothy didn't offer her hand, so Larry didn't try to shake it. "Did that violinist do it?"

"I'm not at liberty to comment on that." Taken aback at her directness and slight sneer, he watched the singer lean over Patricia and whisper in her ear.

Patricia smiled politely and turned to Larry. "Would you excuse us, please?"

Larry nodded.

The general manager's honed her charm into an art form, no question.

As Patricia and Dorothy moved out of his earshot, Charles turned toward the detective. "Maybe by tomorrow, I'll be getting all the attention."

Larry was of two minds on the subject. On one hand, Charles was an accomplished tenor who had not yet had the opportunity to display his talent. On the other, Dorothy was a recognized diva with a worldwide following.

I imagine she gets her own way. In everything.

* * *

At that moment, the renowned soprano was exercising her customary right to make the general manager's life miserable.

"Why are you being so nice to that cop?"

"So he'll stay out of my way, of course. I've got an opera house to run, after all."

* * *

As the beautiful people of the opera world caroused without a care, Julia and Katie were sitting at the long, exquisite mahogany bar at Shun Lee West on 65th Street across from Lincoln Center, with the *après*-performance crowd.

Still spooked by the disastrous experience onstage that morning, Julia had begged Katie to spring her from house arrest and keep her company at the bar after the performance. Charles was otherwise engaged. Sidney was being held without visitor privileges and was not even allowed a phone call from the outside. And then there was the unrelenting image of Matt, which she just couldn't shake off. Julia needed moral support. She knew Katie would understand.

The fact Katie was a recovering alcoholic, and a card-carrying member of AA, didn't prevent Julia from prevailing on her that evening. Julia felt badly about roping Katie into a situation she generally tried to avoid, but she was right in guessing that Katie wouldn't have the heart to refuse if Pellegrino was obtainable.

Julia drained her first glass of Scotch in one long swallow and noticed Katie staring at her.

She should have no problem figuring out why I'm taking to the bottle.

In a few days' time, Julia had been subjected to an ordeal that had left her buckling under the strain. She admired Katie's efforts to steer the conversation away from Abel and Sidney. But she wasn't surprised when Katie voiced her concern over the near miss before rehearsal, and she was ready with a response.

"Scenery falls sometimes, especially in new productions," Julia said. "According to Charles."

"'According to Charles.' What's up with that? You're beginning to sound like his press agent."

Julia grimaced. "And you're starting to act like a mother hen."

"Hey, I only said it out of concern for you."

Julia instantly regretted her unkind remark. "I'm sorry, K. It's just that lately—"

"That's okay, Jul, I understand. I'm just worried about you."

"Sid's the one we should worry about. He's already been in that jail for three nights," Julia said. "And Matt..."

"There's nothing we can do for poor Matt," Katie said softly.

"Yes. I know." Julia bit her lip to keep her eyes from tearing up. "But still, K., you shouldn't be concerned about me. Between Charles and Larry, I've got plenty of protection."

"Speaking of Charles, what is going on between you two?"

"I'd love to tell you." Julia flashed Katie a sly smile. "But nature's calling."

After her uncharacteristic imbibing of two consecutive shots of whiskey, Julia was feeling all too relaxed and flubbed her first attempt to rise from the barstool. Smiling in embarrassment, she managed to slide from her perch on her second try and walked unsteadily toward the back of the bar, trying to move as normally as possible in her tipsy condition. Convinced that Katie would be anxious, Julia willed herself to walk a straight line. At least until she reached the restroom.

Chapter Thirty-Four

Di che fulgor, che musiche esulteran le soglie
With what magnificence and music, the ballroom shall resound.
—Verdi, *Un Ballo in Maschera*, Act III

L arry used his gumshoe stealth to approach Patricia and Dorothy without being noticed. He was not about to miss any of the juicy conversation between the two women. An exit from the star of the evening would not be welcomed, by Patricia or by the patrons. He couldn't help but feel admiration as he observed Patricia's controlled efforts to keep the temperamental diva's disposition in check.

"I've got to get out of here, Patricia. Now."

"But Dorothy, dearest, they're expecting—"

"I don't care what they're expecting. I've made my appearance." Dorothy grimaced at the room full of buoyant patrons who were becoming more boisterous by the minute. "Just look at these hypocritical Philistines! Makes me feel positively nauseated. Abel hardly cold, and—"

Patricia looked around, worried. "Shh, they'll hear you."

"Let them," spat Dorothy. "This ball is not happening, at least for me. I'm out of here."

"But what will I tell them?"

"Tell them anything. Tell them I'm...unwell."

Without waiting for a response from Patricia, Dorothy hastened toward the exit. Patricia managed to catch her by the arm, but Dorothy gave her a chilling "don't mess with me" look, shook her arm free and took off with a flurry of floor-length skirts.

Meanwhile, Larry, who had noticed the orchestra conductor waving in Patricia's direction, approached the general manager.

"Looks like you're on, Ms. Wells."

"Yes, thank you, detective." Larry saw no sign of the panic she must have felt at that moment. "Please excuse me."

Larry reached into his coat pocket, retrieved his memo book and pencil, and flashed her a bright smile. "Don't you worry. I'll just take notes in case there's a quiz later."

Patricia turned away, glided across the room with Mrs. Tallman, mounted the platform and waved delicately at the crowd. The room became hushed, all faces turned toward her.

"My dear friends, I'll be brief. We are all aware of the sadness that mars this momentous occasion, yet I feel sure Abel would not have wanted these festivities to be canceled. I'm certain his genius will live on, through the generosity of his greatest patrons." She cast a look in Mrs. Tallman's direction. "So let us all drink a toast to your continuing and renewed support of the greatest opera house in the Western Hemisphere, if not the world."

Larry watched Patricia as she raised her glass for a triumphant finish. Even he found her sincerity touching.

With Abel out of the way, she's the head honcho now. She can afford to be sincere.

"And to the memory of its guiding genius, whom we honor here tonight. Abel Trudeau."

In unison, the patrons echoed the general manager's tribute. "Abel Trudeau."

Patricia gestured to the conductor. He raised his baton, and the orchestra launched into the spirited waltz from the second act of *Die Fledermaus*. It was appropriate for the occasion: cheerful yet dignified. As the guests danced, Patricia watched, sipping champagne, and smiling.

Larry could see that she was savoring the moment, but he was intent on eyeing Charles, who was downing a tall glass of bubbly in one long gulp. "Thirsty, Mr. Tremaine?"

"These affairs always make me want to drink. Useless political pandering.

I'm so under-appreciated here," Charles grumbled. "Ever tried lobbying for something you want desperately, in a hopeless bureaucracy?"

Larry felt sympathy for the singer. "You've just described the NYPD, friend." He watched as the tenor grabbed another glass of champagne from a passing waiter and drank in deep swallows.

"But didn't Ms. Wells introduce you as up-and-coming?"

"For now, yes," Charles replied between gulps. "But that's today. With Abel gone, Patricia's taken the reins. She could toss in a wrench any time, throw her weight around at her own whim to show she's boss. You can never count chickens in this place."

Larry eyed Charles with curiosity.

What a strange guy, and what a weird world. People here are in a sort of limbo. One day you're on top, the next you're on Amsterdam Avenue.

"Though, to be fair," Charles added, "she did pay her dues."

Larry studied Patricia. He caught her eye and scribbled a few notes in his memo book.

"Paid her dues? How?"

"Beneath that self-important veneer lurks a disadvantaged girl from a Massachusetts mill town who'd never let anyone stand in her way. Not as a diva, and not now."

Larry thought back to his first encounter with Patricia in her office and the photos of her in costume with Dorothy. Meanwhile, Charles was imbibing another glass of champagne.

"Tallman's promised me a new production. Patricia could nix it at any time. Why? Because she can."

"Speaking of Maestro Trudeau," Larry began, "I've heard he wrote a song—"

But a fanfare from the orchestra interrupted him. All eyes turned toward the doorway, where Giuseppe the Stallion, still limping from his leg wound, was bravely making his grand entrance to admiring "bravos" from the crowd.

Larry couldn't see Charles's expression as the lesser tenor watched Giuseppe, but he imagined it probably was tinged with envy.

Charles turned back to Larry. "You were saying, detective?"

"Never mind, it can wait."

Julia was right. Helluva way to make a living.

* * *

Julia leaned over the sink in the ladies' room at the bar and threw water on her face, trying to regain her equilibrium. In the dim light, she thought at first the shadowy masked figure reflected in the mirror was a hallucination, a product of liquor-induced overindulgence. But when the person turned out to be real and seized her arm, Julia suddenly became alert and terrified.

Panicked, she reached her hands under the running faucet and pivoted around abruptly to spray water at the figure. Then, with a violent jerk, Julia pulled her arm free and raced toward the door.

Shaking off the water, the attacker went after Julia but slipped on a watery puddle and sprawled onto the floor. Julia ran to the door. When she had reached the hallway, she paused next to the ladies' room door, gulping for air, until she heard the door open. Twisting around, Julia gasped as she caught sight of the figure coming out.

Gotta escape. Gotta run!

But at that moment, the dizzying effects of the alcohol paralyzed her. Despite Herculean effort, she could not lift her legs. Cursing, she stood rooted to the spot.

What happened to my legs? How did I get so drunk?

At that moment, two women approached from the far end of the hallway on their way to the ladies' room. Their chatter frightened off Julia's assailant, who turned and darted through the fire exit. Heaving a sigh of relief, Julia caught her breath and panting, rushed back to Katie.

Katie gaped at her. "Jul, what happened? You look like you just saw a dead person."

Julia stammered between gasps for air. "S-someone was after me, trying to hurt me."

"After you? But why?"

"D-Don't know, K. But I'm…I'm scared."

* * *

After the Giuseppe-induced stir had wound down, Larry sidled closer to Charles.

"As I was saying, Mr. Tremaine—"

"Please. Call me Charles."

"That song, Charles, the one that the maestro gave to—" His jangling cell phone interrupted him. Grimacing, he yanked the phone from his pocket. "Somers here…She was…*what?*"

"What is it?" asked Charles.

"Emergency. Please excuse me…Charles."

Larry elbowed his way through the crowd toward the exit. Charles drained the last of his champagne and reached for another.

* * *

Larry tore across Broadway to Shun Lee, hastened inside, and found Katie hovering close to Julia. The flashing lights of two NYPD cruisers filtering through the window facing the street bathed Katie's face in a blue-red glow.

"Thanks for calling me, Katie."

"No problem."

Larry moved to the agitated Julia. Buddy, who had arrived in a cruiser and was already on the scene, joined Larry. Katie moved to the far end of the bar and ordered two cups of black coffee. Larry nodded his thanks to her and gestured to Buddy to interview the bartender. Then he leaned over Julia.

"Are you okay?"

Her voice trembled. "I…I…don't know."

"Did you get a look at the face? Male, female?"

"Couldn't…tell…mask."

He noticed she was slurring her speech. "Don't worry, we'll find this creep. Trust me."

Katie placed a cup of coffee in Julia's hand and started sipping her own.

Larry lowered his voice. "But you two are not safe going home. Is there another place you can crash?"

"I can stay at my mom's nursing home overnight," Katie said, "But they only allow immediate family as guests."

"You go there. Julia can stay at my place, and I can crash at Buddy's." He turned to his partner. "That okay, pal?"

"Sure, boss. Just please put a lid on the opera stuff."

"I'll try, but no guarantees." Larry turned back to Julia. "I'll put a police guard at the door tonight. And by the way," he added, "we're stopping at the hospital to do some tests. Someone could have slipped some drug, like Rohypnol, into your drink."

Katie gasped. "Oh, my God. Is that possible?"

"Unfortunately. It's a way of incapacitating an unsuspecting victim. If someone was going to attack her, she'd be unlikely to fight back if she was drugged."

Katie shook her head. "But how could someone just..."

Larry grimaced. "That's why Buddy here is interrogating the bartender. Shall we go?"

Katie nodded and retrieved Julia's violin next to the barstool. Signaling an officer stationed at the door to follow them, Larry led the two young women toward the exit and watched with admiration at Julia's attempt to carry herself in a dignified manner.

That poor kid. She just can't catch a break.

Chapter Thirty-Five

Ah, mi si aggela il core! Sino il rumor de' passi miei,
qui tutto m'empie di raccapriccio e di terrore!
Ah, but my heart freezes within me! Even the noise of my own steps
fills me with dread and fear!
—Verdi, *Un Ballo in Maschera*, Act II

To Julia, Larry's living room looked like the classic, hopelessly dull bachelor dwelling, with its brown-beige décor, uncontrolled clutter, sparse furnishings, and lack of "homey" *accoutrements*. The only upside was that it was on the first floor. She had overcome her fear of heights, at least temporarily, when she and Katie had found their fourth-floor walkup apartment on the Upper West Side. It was an opportunistic find, and they couldn't afford to pass it up. But Julia always felt more secure when she could look out a window and be on the same level as the street.

"Not the Plaza, but you'll be comfy here," Larry said.

"I'm glad you're on a low floor. Anything above street level spooks me. I've never gotten over nearly falling off the top deck of the Staten Island Ferry when I was two."

"You poor kid. No such worries here. Just make yourself at home."

Removing her shoes, Julia sank down onto the sofa, legs tucked up under her, and carefully placed her violin case on the floor next to her.

She noticed the plethora of vintage opera LPs and CDs in every possible edition, crammed into Larry's bookshelves in alphabetical order, and she couldn't take her eyes off the astounding wall display. All the collectors' editions of Domingo, Pavarotti, Te Kanawa, Bocelli. Vintage LPs of Bergonzi, Callas, di Stefano, Siepi. Mozart, Verdi, Puccini, Donizetti, Bellini. Historical performances of *Ernani, Madama Butterfly...*

"You weren't kidding when you said you were hooked on opera. Some of these are impossible to get now. Bergonzi's *Aida*, Siepi's *Figaro...*"

"My mom was Italian. We collected only the best recordings. First on LP, then on CD."

Larry grabbed the comforter folded over the back of the sofa and tucked it around Julia.

"Just try to relax, okay? Maybe listen to some music." Larry ambled to a shelf, studied the titles, and pulled out a CD. "How 'bout the Vickers *Otello*."

Julia thought *Otello* was the greatest opera ever written, the crowning achievement of Verdi's career. Of course, many opera aficionados considered his next and final opera, *Falstaff*, the zenith of the composer's lifework. But *Falstaff* was a comedy, and to Julia, dramas were always taken more seriously in the opera world. Thus, in her estimation, *Otello* remained the be-all and end-all of opera.

Something told her Larry felt the same. As they listened, she could see the dreamy look in his eyes, and it gave her a sense of being safe and cared for. The music from the first act love duet washed over them, its intimate, steamy quality wrapping them in its mantle of lush and passionate tenderness.

"No matter how many times I listen to it, I can never get tired of this opera."

"Me, neither." Larry turned to leave. "Well, I'm off. Make yourself comfy. If you need anything, Sammy is right outside the door. Or call me. I'll come check on you later."

"Detective..."

He turned back to her, smiling. "Please. You're sleeping at my place, you can call me Larry. Now you've seen my entire opera collection, I think it's permissible."

She grinned back. "Would you like me to play something for you on the violin?"

"Do you really feel like it? After what you've just been through?"

"I feel badly about not playing for you during that *Tosca* rehearsal. You've been so kind and generous. I could at least return the favor."

"You're just full of surprises, kid."

Julia's expression turned serious. "When Abel died, I...I tried to pour my heart out with my violin, but I couldn't. Playing for you now will make me feel better, believe me."

Before he could respond, Julia reached down for her violin case, opened it, and removed her violin. Larry reached over to turn off the stereo, but otherwise he didn't move from his spot. He listened as she rendered the poignant melodies of the "Meditation" from Massenet's opera *Thaïs* on her instrument. She played with a rapturous expression on her face, caressing every note and nuance, building phrase upon phrase, until the haunting melody soared into dizzying heights he had never believed attainable.

After the last note had faded away, she put down the violin. For once, he was at a loss for words. When he found his voice, it was full of emotion.

"That was wonderful."

"My father taught it to me." She lowered her head and returned the violin to its case.

"You definitely are concertmaster material, in my unbiased opinion."

"You really think so?" Despite his praise, she was still filled with doubt. "Abel did, too. But Sid says I'm far too sensitive to handle the pressure of being the lead violinist at the Met."

"*Sid* didn't see the tiger in you."

Julia's face darkened. "He...He'll be all right, won't he? I mean...if there were only some way I could speak to him..."

"I wish there were, kid. But he's the focus of a double murder investigation now. No contact allowed with the outside world."

She raised her face toward him. Their eyes met for a moment, sympathy flowing between them.

"You should get to bed. Here, let me help you..."

Julia pulled back from him, collapsed on the sofa and tugged the comforter tight around her body. "Thanks, but I'm fine right here."

"You sure?"

She nodded. He dimmed the lamp beside the sofa.

"Get some rest now. I'll check on you later."

"But I'm not sleepy. I've got too much to think about. There's Abel's song, and—"

"You're a stubborn one, Julia. And I really respect your determination. I just hope it doesn't get you into *real* trouble someday."

"I've heard that before," she murmured, as much to herself as to him, as her eyes fell shut.

With a quick but soft step, Larry left and closed the door without a sound.

* * *

Notwithstanding her efforts and Larry's orders, Julia tossed on the sofa in a fitful sleep until the wee hours. Then at three a.m., she heard the door open. She sat upright, panicked, until Larry peeked in.

"It's only me. I did say I'd check on you, didn't I?"

She sighed with relief. Closing the door behind him, Larry inspected her heavy-lidded, worn-out face. "Have you slept at all?"

"Does it look like I have?"

"Hey, I'm the detective here. You answer the questions, not ask them."

Julia was too tired to return his smile.

"Looks like some more music is in order," Larry said. "But forget opera." He pulled a CD from his jacket pocket and brandished it to her. "How about Elton John?"

"I'd rather listen to *La bohème*."

"Trust me, Elton John will do wonders."

He loaded the CD and clicked play. Julia grimaced, but as the music filtered through the room, she began to relax.

"This stuff's not half bad, Larry. And neither are you."

"That's a real compliment, coming from you."

"Don't let it go to your head." She locked her gaze, just for a moment, on his topaz-blue eyes. Then she leaned back and closed hers.

"Just FYI, Julia, I've been looking into your theory about Patricia. Nothing new yet. Right now, though, you need to sleep. Tomorrow you can attack the song with new eyes and ears."

Julia was too worn out to reply. Larry watched her drift off to sleep. Then he stole away.

Chapter Thirty-Six

L'on m'avait même dit de craindre pour ma vie;
mais je suis brave! Je n'ai pas voulu fuir!
I was even told to fear for my life;
but I'm not a coward, and I didn't want to run away!
—Bizet, *Carmen*, Act IV

S idney and his attorney occupied a table on the aisle opposite the district attorney in criminal court. All three rose as the judge strode in. He looked closely at Sidney and then addressed Sidney's attorney, without a trace of emotion. "Does the suspect's plea remain unchanged?"

Sidney, teeth clenched, flashed Herb a sober look and nodded.

"My client still pleads not guilty, Your Honor." Herb lowered his usually booming voice. "If I may point out, Your Honor, he was too ill to have committed murder at the time of—"

"Well, he looks healthy enough now." The Judge scowled at the lawyer. "You know the drill. Let's move this along, Counselor, there are too many hoops to jump through. We don't want to wait too long to set a trial date. This case is too hot."

"But Your Honor, I need time for discovery," Herb protested.

"You'll have plenty," the Judge snapped. "Better yet, see if you can get together on a plea agreement."

Sidney shook his head vehemently. He glared in defiance at the district attorney as the bailiff led him from the room. The D.A. leaned over to Herb.

"Let him glower away," he murmured. "It won't help."

* * *

Early afternoon light streamed into Larry's living room as Julia wakened and stretched her arms overhead. But she became alarmed when she glimpsed the clock.

Noon? How could I have slept so late?

Sitting up, she reached for her purse, pulled out her cell phone and dialed.

"Julia!" Charles exclaimed. "I've been frantic. Why haven't you called?"

She hesitated. "There was an incident last night, Charles. Someone... attacked me."

"Good God! Where are you?"

"I'm at the detective's apartment. He thought it wasn't safe for me to go home, so...I stayed here last night."

"But—"

"I'll explain later. Just come here. I need you. I'll text you the address. And bring Abel's song."

"Of course, my darling. I'll be right there."

* * *

By the time Charles arrived, Julia had been pacing back and forth for some time. Overwrought about her lack of communication with Sidney, she had looked online to find the number for The Tombs. It took some doing, but she was finally able to get through.

"Switchboard, may I help you?"

"Hello? Yes, I'm calling to check on a...detainee, Sidney Richter."

"I'll look him up. Please hold." There was a pause. "I'm sorry, but his information is not available at this time."

"Are you sure?"

"Yes, I'm sorry."

With a frustrated sigh, Julia clicked off. Her phone rang immediately. It was Larry.

"How're you doing today, kid?"

"I feel like I got hit by a truck."

"No surprise, since they found 'roofies' in your blood."

Julia was bewildered. "What?"

"Rohypnol, ten times more potent than Valium. Makes you look drunk, slurs your speech. Causes dizziness, loss of inhibitions, even loss of consciousness. Then it disrupts your sleep." He paused. "It's not legal in the U.S., but it is in other countries and is easily smuggled here. It's supposed to turn blue in clear liquid, but some generic versions don't have the blue dye, so you don't know it's there."

"I was...drugged?"

"Yep," Larry said. "Its effects usually start within thirty minutes and peak about two hours later. As little as one milligram can affect you for eight to twelve hours. Bartender says he didn't see anything suspicious. We're still looking into it."

Julia was speechless.

"You okay, kid?"

"Yes. But...why would someone do this?"

"That's what we're trying to find out. My theory is, someone wanted you out of the picture, at least temporarily. Sorry, but I gotta go. Check with you later."

She hung up, puzzled, her mind racing.

Someone drugged me? But who? And why?

After what seemed like hours, there was a faint knock at the door. Sammy, the police guard, peeked in. "This guy says you asked him here, Miss?"

Julia glimpsed Charles poised behind the guard and nodded. "Yes, I did. It's okay."

The guard stepped aside, let Charles pass, and closed the door. Charles dashed over to Julia and pulled her to him. After nearly a lifetime of shying away from physical contact, Charles's touch felt to her like the first drop of water after a week in the desert. The envelope he was carrying fluttered to the floor.

"Thank God you're safe!"

She clung to him. "Oh, Charles, it was horrible."

191

"Shh, darling, I'm here now."

They kissed. But instead of feeling invigorated, Julia felt worn out. She sat down on the sofa.

Oh, God, why did I sleep so late? Is that what drugs do?

"Tell me what happened, Julia."

Julia thought about telling him that she had been drugged but decided that deciphering the song was their first priority.

"I will, Charles. But first, we've got to look at the song."

"Of course." Charles picked up the envelope and placed it in her hands, eyeing her agitated face.

She opened the envelope and gazed at the music. "This...*this* is Sid's only chance!" She reached into the zipper compartment of her violin case and pulled out the second page.

The look of astonishment on Charles's face was unmistakable. "Where did you find that?"

"It's not important. Just sing it with me, Charles."

Julia gazed at the first page, hummed a note, and took a deep breath. Then, in a tentative voice, she began to sing. Charles joined in, but when they came to the odd-sounding notes at the bottom of the page, they both stopped.

"It's no use, Charles. They're just as wrong as ever."

"Let's try the second page."

The music on the next page was just as puzzling.

Julia shook her head. "I think Abel planted those notes for a reason."

"What possible reason could he have had?"

"He said if anything ever happened to him, I would find answers in the song," Julia said. "When he was mentoring me, he always told me to look beyond the notes. That's what I'm trying to do now. Beyond these notes there's a clue, an explanation. I'm sure of it."

"Have you tried transposing it to another clef? It might sound completely different."

She gasped. "Of course! Why didn't I think of that? I'm no good at transposition, though, without a piano."

"We could go to the Met. I can't stay with you, but I can escort you there."

CHAPTER THIRTY-SIX

Charles checked his watch. "If we're going, we should leave now."

"But how will we get past 'Sammy the gatekeeper?'"

"Not a problem." He flashed a reassuring smile. "Just watch me."

Sammy looked up as Charles opened the door and approached with Julia by his side. When Julia explained she wanted to go to the Met to practice, the guard hesitated. But Charles assured Sammy he was going to accompany Julia safely there and asked him to call Larry for permission.

After he had spoken to Larry, Sammy addressed Julia. "As long as your friend stays with you, Detective Somers says it's okay to go. He'll be waiting at the women's locker room."

"Thank you, Officer."

Charles winked at Julia. Taking her by the arm, he shepherded her down the hall.

Julia clutched both music and violin under her other arm. For the first time since her terrifying encounter at the bar the night before, she felt safe.

Chapter Thirty-Seven

Il passo è periglioso, può nascer qualche imbroglio.
The step we take is dangerous, I fear it might provoke an entanglement.
—Mozart, *Don Giovanni*, Act I

P atricia heard through the opera house grapevine that Julia had acted with great courage during a potentially fatal encounter the previous night. She herself wondered if she could have gotten safely out of such a scrape, though she considered herself clever enough to squeeze out of difficulty. After all, she was Patricia. Nonetheless, she admired the young woman's pluck.

Perhaps Julia isn't such a pain in the ass after all.

In fact, Patricia had to admit Julia was just the sort of female whom she generally found attractive. Those coal-black, smoky eyes, luscious sweetheart lips, slender curvaceous body, and magnificent *derrière* made Patricia salivate.

She stopped herself from fantasizing about Julia, though, when she thought about Dorothy, with whom she had been having a long-standing love affair. The Junoesque diva was a stark contrast to the youthful violinist: more mature and likely more experienced in bed, though Patricia imagined Julia to be every bit as hot-blooded as Dorothy was, musically and otherwise.

Undoubtedly, passion lurked underneath the young musician's reserved exterior. At least the girl was reputed to play the violin with that kind of dynamism and intensity. Not that it mattered. Julia was probably as straight as they come, at least in her present undeveloped state. But in a few years, once the girl had ripened and evolved a bit...

Well, who knows?

Patricia remembered the strained meeting in her office shortly after Abel was murdered. Yes, indeed, the girl had shown spunk, despite her controlled speech and mannerisms. She had comported herself with great dignity. Patricia admired that.

In any case, she was beginning to rethink her harsh treatment of Julia, and her own behavior as well. Abel was dead, and now that cute stagehand Matt, too. The whole drug thing was getting out of hand, and despite Sidney's being detained indefinitely the temptation would always be there. Maybe it was time to end her forays into the drug underworld. Permanently. Even with Geraldo locked up, there was always going to be a reliable source for the white powder—"happy dust," they called it, in *Porgy and Bess.*

Now she had to move to the catacombs of the theater and deal with the descending hordes of patrons and company members who would soon be gathering for Abel's tribute performance. It was a splendid occasion, and she intended to shine. As she browsed through her cache of jewels to find the perfect pair of earrings, her mind began to wander again.

Too bad Matt got caught in the crossfire of the entire mess.

She missed his handsome, macho presence. He was, without doubt, her type, as far as men were concerned. If only he hadn't spied her walking hand in hand with Dorothy one golden afternoon in Central Park, she might not have had to contemplate firing him.

Of course, that's all moot. Now that he's dead.

She turned her thoughts to Frank, Matt's replacement. With his surly attitude and looks to match, he was not going to be as submissive as Matt. But she was never one to shirk from a challenge. And as far as that was concerned, Charles was proving to be a stronger force than she had reckoned. She had noted the body language between him and Julia, and it occurred to her that Charles might have found his way into the violinist's affections. Patricia was surprised to find herself very slightly envious.

How interesting. Well, there's no doubt he has taste.

* * *

Patricia smiled at Julia and Charles as they made their way through the Security checkpoint. Julia looked at Patricia with surprise. Then she returned the smile, wondering what the friendly pretense was all about.

Did I just see Patricia smile at me? Maybe I'm hallucinating. After-effects of the drugs?

Whatever the reason, Julia was not about to ignore any sign of cordiality from the general manager. Such things were all too rare.

After Julia had followed Charles through the gate, he reached for her hand and led her through a door toward the rear of the security area. They reached a quiet hallway, devoid of people, where Julia rarely ventured. She felt intimidated by these lush trappings of opera glamour reserved for a well-heeled clientele: subtle lighting; plush love seats made for comfortable lounging between acts; glass cases displaying historical opera lore, perched on pedestals; vintage paintings of opera greats and distinguished-looking former Met dignitaries and luminaries on the walls. It was all daunting to her, but she noticed that Charles seemed quite at home in this atmosphere.

When he had determined they were alone, Charles leaned over Julia, pulled her to him, and kissed her. Anxious about being seen, she was afraid to respond at first, but she could not resist.

After a long moment, Charles let go of her, held her face close to his, and murmured. "I can't tell you what it means to me, knowing you'll be there, playing for me tonight." He sang a snippet from *Tosca* in a soft voice. *"L'ardente amante mia...il mio solo pensiero...sei tu!* My ardent lover...my only thought is of you!"

Her heart pounding, Julia held his gaze until she heard a hallway door open. She gave Charles one last elated hug.

"I'll be with you on every single note." She turned to go. "And...*Bocca al lupo*."

To Julia, "In the mouth of the wolf" sounded better than *merde*.

* * *

196

As Julia took off down the hall, Charles watched her, flushing with pleasure. Being on the Met stage in front of an audience at long last undoubtedly would feel like being in the jaws of the wolf.

But it's also going to feel like being at the top of the world. Of that, there's no doubt.

* * *

Julia suddenly remembered they had planned to look for a piano, but she was reluctant to go after Charles when his all-important debut was foremost in his mind. It didn't matter. She could always find a piano herself in one of the practice rooms on Orchestra Level.

Or maybe I'll get lucky and figure out the song without a piano. It can happen. Right?

* * *

Larry was waiting in front of the women's locker room door when he spied Julia striding down the hall.

He glanced at the wall clock above their heads: five-thirty p.m. Julia held up a sheet of music. "I'm going to work on this thing the rest of the day and evening if need be. I'll change into my concert clothes first. If I can't find any clues by the last intermission, I'll jump off the parapet with Tosca."

"I somehow doubt it," Larry said. "By the way, I followed up on your hunch about Patricia. Turns out she has airtight alibis for every incident that's taken place."

Julia frowned. "Then, if not Patricia, who?"

"Patience, Julia. In this business, things are rarely revealed as quickly as you might like. And p.s.," he added, "no fingerprints on the chess pieces. It's not surprising a perp would wipe everything clean. But cheer up. Buddy and I'll be on the lookout for anyone suspicious."

"This is all my fault."

"How do you figure that?"

"It's the playbook of my life. When I was ten, my dad was killed trying to save my life. I came to the Met, and now Abel and Matt are both dead. And Sid, who's like a brother to me, is on trial for murder."

"You're too hard on yourself, Julia. Trust me, none of it is your fault. Want my advice?"

"Do I have any choice?"

"Nope. I have twenty years on you, so listen up. Stop blaming yourself. Learn to trust your instincts. Take ownership of your life. No one else can do it for you. Got that?"

Despite misgivings, she nodded.

"Good girl. I'll be around. Give a yell or beep me if you find anything. I'll make sure there's a guard placed outside your practice room."

"This is Sid's fourth night locked up, Larry. Can't you do something?"

"Nope." Larry gestured at the music. "Only you can."

He signaled a police officer waiting at the other end of the hallway and hurried away.

* * *

After changing into the black velvet pants and blouse she kept in her locker, Julia searched among the practice rooms along the hallway for a room with a piano. Since those were occupied, she settled for a piano-less room and went inside. The officer followed her and stood guard outside.

The cramped, sterile cubicle had gray walls, and a concrete floor, with a table and a black metal music stand as its sole furnishings. Julia stood in front of the music stand, opened the music, and began to play the song. She tried it in every possible key and transposition, varying the notes, trying to make sense of them. Every so often, she gave up out of frustration and played some Bach or Mozart or noodled at the Sibelius Concerto. Before she knew it, it was seven-thirty p.m. and time to get ready for the pit.

Exhausted, Julia laid her violin in the open case on the table.

How could Abel have composed such a baffling piece? And then given it to me to decipher?

Julia stared at the music, idly fidgeting with Abel's violin pin, which, as always, was fastened to her blouse. Suddenly, the pin broke apart and, before she could catch it, fell to the floor. Julia cried out in dismay.

The precious object shattered into unrecognizable shards. Julia bent over to retrieve the pieces, tears welling up in her eyes. But she was astonished to find among the fragments a minuscule plastic square. She stared at it, puzzled. Then she stood up and opened the door.

"Larry!"

Within seconds, Larry and Buddy appeared.

"What is it?" Larry asked. "What happened?"

"My violin pin broke, and I found this." She thrust the plastic square at Larry.

"Haven't you ever seen a flash card from a digital camera?" he asked.

"Me? Those are for left-brained people."

Buddy gave Larry an incredulous look. "Is this girl for real?"

Julia ignored his sarcasm. "Besides, when do I have time to take pictures? I always wondered how Abel found time for it, though. I guess he needed a hobby to divert his attention from work-related stress. He was always bugging me to become interested in digital pho—"

"Why didn't you tell me that before?" Larry demanded. "Buddy, get this to H.Q. and have it uploaded ASAP."

"On it before you can say, '*Coraggio.*'"

Larry stared at his partner. "What?"

"I thought I'd surprise you by learning some opera talk."

Before Larry could react, Buddy grabbed the flash card and hurried off. Julia, meanwhile, gathered the remnants of the pin and regarded them with sadness.

"Take heart, kid," Larry said. "That card is an important piece of the puzzle. The pin, well, that can be fixed. Just give me the pieces."

Julia reluctantly relinquished the remains of her beloved pin.

"You've got two intermissions to find the clues in the song. Consider it part of your detective training. I'm putting my faith in your musical smarts. Now that we're a team, don't disappoint me." He held open the door.

"As cops go, you're not so bad," she said, and with music and violin, headed for the pit.

Chapter Thirty-Eight

Ah di quegli occhi vittoriosi veder la fiamma illanguidir
con spasimo d'amor Fra le mie braccia...
Ah, to see the flame of those imperious eyes grow faint and
languid with passion in my arms...
—Puccini, *Tosca*, Act I

When Julia arrived in the pit, she noticed Katie eyeing the gold cross nestled at Julia's throat.

"I'm glad to see you're still wearing my protective amulet," Katie said. "You never know when vampires are going to attack."

Julia was glad for a bit of Katie's wry humor to distract her. "I'm happy to know you have faith in my ability to take care of myself."

"I have it on good authority you're going to find whatever you're looking for in Abel's song tonight," Katie said. "Speaking of which, how's Charlie?"

Julia ignored Katie's innuendo, opened the music on the stand, and gazed at the title: *Tosca*, by Giacomo Puccini. Now, involved with the leading man, the opera had taken on a whole new meaning. She just wasn't sure what that meaning was. Yet.

Julia glanced at the bug mashed into the top of the page. Someone had drawn an arrow pointing to it and labeled it "Mario," after the tenor lead in that evening's opera. She smiled with nostalgia, remembering the person responsible.

"There's the mosquito Sid squashed at the Parks concert, K. Remember?"

Katie grinned and nodded but didn't comment. Julia appreciated that.

Right now she just needed a friendly ear when it came to the subject of Sidney. She and Katie had both sat with him enough times during the outdoor concerts the Met played every summer in the parks in and around New York City to know how bored and antsy he became.

Sidney didn't consider sitting on a stage behind a row of solo singers in searing heat and relentless humidity to be a lot of fun, and as a result, he fidgeted nonstop. In his non-playing moments, he alternated looking out into the audience seated on the lawn for interesting faces with searching the sky for low-flying airplanes—or flattening any errant insects unfortunate enough to cross his path.

"He always complained about the bugs dive-bombing us in the great outdoors…"

Julia's voice trailed off. She didn't want to dissolve into tears. Instead, she decided to practice a passage in the music. But when she reached over to turn the page, she didn't notice the paper clip attached to the top corner and caught her finger on the sharp metal edge. The finger began to bleed, and she sucked on it, murmuring under her breath.

The last thing I need is something else to keep me from playing the violin.

But the finger was beginning to hurt, and her muttering became more vocal.

"Ouch! The librarians know they're not supposed to put paper clips in the music. What were they thinking? Damn!" Julia saw Katie cringe. "Oh, sorry, K. I'm swearing an awful lot these days. Not that you're all that virtuous."

"Maybe, but cursing is discouraged in my church group."

"I know. I'll try to be more careful."

Then Julia glimpsed the typewritten note attached to the clip.

"MIND YOUR OWN BUSINESS. OR NEXT TIME YOU'LL BE SQUASHED LIKE A BUG."

Julia gasped. Katie regarded Julia's shocked expression. "What is it, Jul?"

"Nothing," Julia replied with little conviction. "I…I'll be right back."

Not wanting to alarm Katie, Julia grabbed the note and raced out of the pit. She approached the officer stationed at the pit entrance and told him what had occurred. Together they went in search of Larry. When they found the detective in the wings, Julia showed him the note.

"Where did you find this?"

"It was attached to my music."

"Any idea where it came from?"

Julia shook her head.

Larry placed the note in a plastic evidence bag. "I'll send it down to the station for analysis right away. Maybe the lab can get some prints off it."

Larry nodded to the officer, who escorted Julia back to the pit and resumed his position at the door. Still shaken by the less than veiled threat, Julia re-entered the pit, sat down, took out her violin and put on a brave face for Katie.

Katie studied Julia's grim expression. "I've never seen you leave the pit so close to curtain time. It's bizarre, even for you. What's going on?"

"I'll explain later, K."

"But—"

At that moment, the concertmaster stepped onto the podium, halting any further discussion. The first oboist gave the "A" for the orchestra, and Julia and Katie tuned along with the other musicians. But sensing Katie's burning stare, Julia felt obligated to make idle chitchat while she struggled with her cantankerous violin pegs.

"I spent all afternoon on Abel's song. Still can't make sense of it."

"You'll figure it out, I know you will. Abel had faith in you."

"But time's running out for Sid."

Julia was forced into silence, as the audience became hushed for the conductor's entrance. By the time he reached the podium, Julia's brow was still furrowed with anxiety.

Katie held her bow close to Julia's. "To Sidney."

They clicked the bottoms of their bows together. Julia returned Katie's encouraging smile. "Sidney. And hope."

The conductor raised his baton to give the upbeat, and the musicians blasted their way through the dramatic, high-octane opening bars of *Tosca*. Julia willed herself to concentrate, but when Charles made his first entrance she allowed her eyes to stray to the stage. As a result, she missed a note. In response to Katie's mock chastising look, Julia smiled sheepishly, went back to her music, and made an extra effort to concentrate.

But Julia could not hide her overall distress from Katie, who saw the distracted look on Julia's face out of the corner of her eye. Despite Charles's impressive singing, Julia sat motionless as she played, not even mouthing the words of her favorite passages as she usually did.

* * *

Larry, meanwhile, had found a niche in the wings in view of the stage, which replicated an enormous Baroque Roman church. He had never been so close to the mammoth sets, even when he had watched *Tosca* rehearsals from the first row of orchestra seats. Other than that, he had only seen the sets from a sky-scraping perch in the Family Circle or in HD in a theatre.

He gazed in wonder at the church of Sant'Andrea della Valle, its lofty ceilings, huge pillars, and magnificent artwork reproduced in gorgeous detail, which he imagined must have duplicated the real one in Rome. He tried to envision himself as the painter Cavaradossi, balanced precariously on that towering ladder toward the back of the stage.

That thing is high enough to give anyone a serious case of vertigo.

Thoughts of vertigo reminded him of Julia. He made a mental note to ask her details about her childhood trauma on the Staten Island Ferry. Then he turned his gaze back to the monitor, which showed the conductor and the musicians in the pit, and made sure Julia was there. Once he established her presence, Larry diverted his attention to the action onstage.

He thought back to the rehearsal he had attended, when he had asked Julia to play for him, and remembered her arrogant reaction. At the time, he thought she was a snob, but realized now she had been responding to the pressures of her situation.

She's really a nice girl at heart.

He reflected on the exquisite *Thaïs* excerpt she had played for him in his apartment and smiled to himself.

Guess I'll have to sing for her at some point. How the heck am I going to manage that?

Charles's first entrance brought Larry back to attention, as the tenor's appearance elicited a fit of enthusiastic audience applause. Larry listened as Charles sang his exchange with the Sacristan, admiring the star singer's self-confident air.

Got to admit the guy has stage presence out the wazoo.

The performance went smoothly through the first two acts. When Charles and several other singers, Dorothy included, returned to the wings from their Act Two curtain calls, Larry couldn't help staring at them. He wasn't surprised that Dorothy ignored his presence. But Charles's friendly smile of acknowledgment made Larry feel like he was "in the loop," or at least on its fringes.

Larry eyed the tenor's blood-red stage makeup. "Very lifelike, Charles. If I didn't know any better, I'd say you were tortured for real in that last act."

"What a way to make a living, right?"

"For sure," Larry said. "The great diva Beverly Sills knew what she was talking about."

Charles grinned and made his way to the exit. Larry smiled to himself. This nonchalant little "what a way to make a living" quote was about to become permanently engraved in his personal lexicon of quips.

Coming from a rising star in his hour of glory, that's very cool.

Before he became involved in all the hubbub at the Met, Larry had no idea how integral the individual personalities were to the workings of the theater. In tandem with the adversity he had witnessed behind the "golden curtain," he also had become privy to an insider's view of the place he had worshipped since he was a child. He blessed his luck in being chosen for this assignment.

How many people experience that during a lifetime?

But Larry knew his happy moment was only temporary when he saw a breathless Buddy, iPad in hand, headed straight toward him.

Buddy opened the device, fired it up, and held it out to Larry. "I downloaded these at H.Q., boss. Results from the flashcard you sent over."

Larry studied the screen, quickly scrolling through reproductions of photos and newspaper articles, dating back to past decades. Once he had gone about halfway through, he eyed Buddy, puzzled. "What does a drowning at a music camp decades ago have to do with anything?"

"Read on, boss."

Larry continued and whistled in surprise. "This is unbelievable."

"Yep. Read it out loud."

Grabbing Buddy by the arm, Larry led him to a far corner of the hallway outside the entrance to the wings. He waited for the always-beleaguered stage manager to pass by before he read aloud from the iPad.

"July, Nineteen Eighty-Two: Trudeau Brothers, Abel and Carl, brilliant young pianist-singer duo, perform at prestigious Upstate Willowstream Music Camp under guidance of renowned music pedagogue Haim Ghent...'"

Larry turned to Buddy in disbelief. "Wait a minute. 'Trudeau...brothers?'"

With a sober nod, Buddy motioned to Larry to continue.

"'August, Nineteen Eighty-Two: Mysterious Death of Camper at Summer Music Festival Goes Unsolved.'"

Larry peered at a photo of a stocky young Asian boy. His mouth dropped in astonishment.

"Don't stop there, boss."

Larry read on. "'After a detailed inquest, the County Coroner's Office has ruled the drowning of nine-year-old camper Patrick Wu, a vocal student at Willowstream Music Camp, an accident. The sole witness, camper and vocal student Carl Trudeau...' Wait. What?"

"It gets better," Buddy said. "Keep going."

"'...Vocal student Carl Trudeau told Police that Wu ignored camp rules prohibiting swimming without supervision and went by himself to the lake. Carl noticed Patrick missing and arrived just as the boy went under. Carl's twelve-year-old brother, camper Abel Trudeau...'" Larry was stunned. "Abel's brother was a singer?"

* * *

The two boys frolicked in the crystal-clear lake water, splashing each other playfully. The slender one, Carl, mischievously pushed the stout one, Patrick, under the water. When Patrick came up for air, both boys giggled.

Then Carl shoved Patrick under again, but this time he held Patrick down. Patrick surfaced, laughing, and they grinned impishly at each other. But when Carl shoved Patrick under again and intensified his grip, Patrick struggled, barely managing to come up for air—and regarded Carl with horror.

Carl plunged Patrick under once more and held him there. When Patrick disappeared for the last time, Carl paddled to shore and leapt onto the sand, his expression evilly triumphant. He started to sprint toward camp when an older boy confronted him.

"My God, Carl, what have you done?"

Carl stared at the boy in alarm. "Swear you'll never tell, Abel."

"Why would you do this to Patrick?"

"They gave him the singing role I wanted. The one *I* deserved."

"And for that you'd...*drown him?*"

"If you tell, Abel, you're an accomplice. You didn't call for help."

"No, no, I'm not!" Abel was panicked. "I got here just in time to see you hold him under!"

"It's your word against mine, Abel."

Smiling deviously, Carl broke into a run. Too terrified to move, Abel just watched him go.

* * *

"'Renowned music pedagogue Haim Ghent.' Is this guy still alive, Buddy?"

"He's old but still going strong," Buddy said. "And waiting for you at the Ansonia."

Chapter Thirty-Nine

Ore di morte e di vendetta...ormai t'affretta! Incancellabile il fato ha scritto:
l'impresa compier deve il delitto poichè col sangue s'inagurò
Hours of death and of vengeance...come swiftly now! Immutable fate
has writ:
the enterprise by crime must end, since with blood it was begun.
—Verdi, *Macbeth*, Act I

Having witnessed his spectacular showing in the first act, Julia felt overjoyed for Charles. She couldn't wait to see him afterwards and lavish some well-deserved praise on him. During the second act, she diverted herself from troubled thoughts of Sidney by speculating on just what she would say to Charles.

Meanwhile, I've still got to get through Acts Two and Three.

During the first intermission, Julia was too exhausted to do anything but crumple onto the sofa in the ladies' locker room. She needed some time to chill out before discussing the details about the threatening note and figured Katie would understand. By the time Act Two ended, however, Julia felt Katie would want an explanation.

Onstage, Dorothy, as Tosca, was placing a crucifix on the chest of the character of Scarpia—played by the ubiquitous Roberto—who was lying prostrate on the floor, and whom she had just assassinated. She uttered her final line of the act in solemn tones.

"*E avanti a lui tremava tutta Roma.*" And before him, all Rome trembled.

At that moment, it dawned on Julia that the parallel between this stage drama and the events that had occurred since Abel's murder was astonishing. At the Met, Abel had been the power behind the throne, at least from a musical perspective. Patricia had tried to usurp Abel's authority and made every pretense of dominating their operatic world.

But Julia knew the opera house revolved around music, and in this sense, Abel was the undisputed ruler—at least until his murder. In *Tosca*, the fiery diva reigned over the villainous police chief Scarpia for only a brief part of the action, just as Patricia was doing.

She must be involved in Abel's murder somehow.

Then, with a shudder, Julia returned to reality.

Dear God, what was I thinking? None of this makes any sense. I've got to hold on to what's real.

One way to do that was to focus on the tangible elements in her life.

Like helping Sid. Or appreciating Katie's friendship more. Or...Charles?

Act Two ended with roaring applause. By this time, Julia's anxiety about finding the secret she was convinced lay within the notes of Abel's song was at full tilt. Balancing violin and bow in one hand and the song in the other, she headed for the exit, where she was greeted with, "Act Three of *Tosca* in twenty-five minutes, ladies and gentlemen," from the P.A. system.

Katie caught up with Julia at the pit entrance. "Are you sure you want to spend the intermission practicing?"

Julia fixed Katie with a determined look. "I've got to give the song one more go. If I'm going to find answers, it's now or never. Otherwise, there's no way I'll ever get through the damned last act of *Tosca*."

"There you go, swearing again. We've got to have a heart-to-heart once the present insanity is all over and done with," Katie declared. "Anyway, it's just a short intermission, Jul. You won't have much time."

"It doesn't matter, K. Now that I've unearthed that...whatever it was, hidden in the violin pin, I'm going for every note in Abel's song, big time."

Julia acknowledged the officer standing guard at the pit entrance. He accompanied both women into the hallway. She informed the officer of her plan to sequester herself in a practice room during the intermission. He escorted Katie as far as the women's locker room and followed Julia to the practice room, where she had labored before the performance.

"I'll be right outside, Miss Kogan." The officer smiled at her, adding, "You must be pretty devoted to your music to want to practice while everyone else is swigging coffee in the cafeteria."

Julia returned his smile, stepped inside the room, and closed the door.

* * *

The grand piano took up most of the space in the small parlor of Dr. Haim Ghent's Upper West Side apartment in the Ansonia, an historical landmark on 73rd Street, just off Broadway. Larry had heard the eighteen-story Beaux Arts building was the last bastion of New York's former musical and artistic glory, housing famous musicians of all generations whose names evoked renown. Now converted to condos, most of the rent-controlled tenants had moved out. Haim Ghent was one exception.

In the case of Dr. Ghent, a benevolent relic of a man, the notoriety involved was from times long past. That's what Larry gathered, as he gazed at the ancient photographs covering the walls: Dr. Ghent at various ages, with Pablo Casals, Arturo Toscanini, Jascha Heifetz, and other luminaries of the music world who had long since passed away. The old professor himself was a rarity, an artifact, one last remaining vestige of a golden generation of performers who could never quite be replaced.

Dr. Ghent squinted with difficulty as he perused the screen of Larry's iPad. Larry understood the old man was of an age where a small computer screen reproduction of newsprint must be a real bear to read, but it was all he could do to remain patient. He needed to find out something, anything, to fill in the gap in his existing chain of information—and soon. That missing link was preventing him from solving two murders, and possibly avoiding a future one. And he hated to be so far away from Julia when she could be in danger. He finally moved things along by increasing the screen to its largest size.

"Ah, yes, the Trudeau Brothers, I remember them well." Having at last made out the troublesome print on the page through bifocals, Dr. Ghent smiled in triumph. "They were prodigiously gifted, and in constant intense competition with one another."

"What else do you recall about them, sir?"

Larry could detect regret in the professor's voice. "Carl was always in his older brother's shadow, poor child, looking for an outlet for his frustration. He was perpetually jealous of Abel, always trying to match his brother's achievements, as if he had to prove by his one-upmanship that he could be as good as, or even superior to, Abel."

"And did Carl ever overcome that gap between them?"

"I'm afraid not. It was an insurmountable task to outshine his brother. Abel was several years older, and always more adept at capturing people's attention." Dr. Ghent shook his head. "Blessed as he was with his lovely voice, Carl could never come close to Abel's success."

"What do you know about that camper's mysterious death?"

"Ah, yes. Unfortunate incident. Carl was the sole witness. The poor boy drowned. It was deemed an accident, but frankly, I was never quite convinced..." His voice trailed off.

Larry could see Ghent was struggling to remember an ancient place and time.

"Could you elaborate, sir?"

"According to Carl's version of the story, he saw the boy drowning and jumped in after him but was too late to save him. The coroner found a skull contusion but determined the boy must have hit his head on the rocks at the bottom of the lake. At least, that was what was ruled at the inquest." Dr. Ghent regarded Larry with a faint smile. "Interestingly, the boy and Carl were both up for the lead role in the camp musical..."

Dr. Ghent paused. Larry assumed the professor had difficulty focusing his mind on such a long-ago occurrence.

"In any case, because of the powerful P.R. machine behind the distinguished Trudeau family, they were able to keep the entire affair as quiet as possible, though not entirely out of the media."

"Professor, do you remember the names of any of the other campers that year?"

"It was so very long ago. But I might remember the most talented ones. Let's see…"

It seemed an eternity to Larry while the professor pondered. As the minutes ticked by, Larry prayed Dr. Ghent's failing memory could dredge up a few more facts.

"Yes, I remember now." The old man flashed a pleased smile. "Other than Abel and Carl, there were…ah, hmm…Yes. Sidney Richter and Matt…what was his name? Reynolds. They were inseparable, those four. Thick as thieves, but as different as night and day."

Larry stared, open-mouthed, at the professor. After he had recovered from his astonishment, he said, "No one else seems to know Trudeau even had a brother, Dr. Ghent. How is that possible?"

"Ah. That was difficult. After the, ah…incident, Carl was sent away to boarding school in Europe, and stayed there to pursue a singing career. Changed his name. Gained quite a reputation for himself, I'm told."

"Did he ever come back?"

"Not to my knowledge. But then, I've been retired and 'out of the loop,' as they say."

"If he did come back, would anyone know who he was?"

"After so many years? I doubt anyone would recognize him. Except, perhaps, the maestro himself."

"Thank you, Professor, you've been very helpful." Larry flipped his notebook shut and peered at Dr. Ghent. "By the way, do you know what Carl changed his name to?"

The professor deliberated for a long moment. "It was something like… excuse me, a 'senior moment'…"

He paused, as Larry waited breathlessly.

"Ah, I remember now. It was Charles. Charles Tremaine."

Chapter Forty

Ma v'ha fra loro il tradito; più d'uno forse
But among them there is a traitor; more than one perhaps.
—Verdi, *Un Ballo in Maschera*, Act I

J ulia watched the wall clock out of the corner of her eye as she played. She repeated notes, tried playing every other note, and played the notes out of sequence repeatedly.

Wrong. Still wrong.

Finally, out of desperation, she turned the music upside down and tried once more. This time, a coherent melody emerged. But it stopped at the bottom of the page. She groaned.

Oh, no, not again.

Then, with a sudden flash of recognition, she turned the second page upside down as well. The melody continued and resolved in a familiar-sounding tune. Flabbergasted, she stopped and sang it to herself, adding the Italian words she knew belonged with it, from the first act of *Tosca*:

"'*Va, Tosca, nel tuo cuor s'annida Scarpia!*'" Then she translated it into English. The words fit exactly. "Go, Tosca, Scarpia is nesting inside your heart...' But who did Abel mean...and why did he...?"

Glancing at the former bottoms, now the tops, of the pages, where Abel had scribbled his last-minute changes, she took a closer look. The notes appeared different upside down. She paused, conjuring up the image of Abel saying to her, "Remember, always think *beyond* the notes," and realized this could be an opportunity to utilize his advice.

C...B-flat...no, B-natural...

Julia closed her eyes, trying to recapture what Abel had taught her about translating musical notes into letters. She recalled that, in some foreign languages, the letters converted to non-musical ones. In this case, "B natural" in English became "H" in German.

"Yes! That must be it." She leaned in closer and carefully inspected the notes, playing them, and slowly repeating them out loud. The picture started to become clearer.

C...H...A...?

Then she gasped and turned ghostly pale, staring at her music in disbelief.

"Oh, no! It can't be! *'Nel tuo cuor s'annida Scarpia*. Scarpia is nesting inside your heart.' Oh my God, that's what Charles said to me the night we—"

An announcement from the P.A. system jolted her. She jumped, startled.

"Five minutes, ladies and gentlemen. Orchestra to the pit, please."

Heaving an anxious sigh, Julia headed for the door, violin in hand. She was torn between her duty to the Met and her pressing need to reveal her new discovery to Larry.

There just isn't time right now. I'll have to wait until after the opera. Damn.

Throwing open the door, Julia glanced around. With everyone in the pit, the hallway was empty. The officer was nowhere in sight, and Julia paused, puzzled. But when she heard sounds of the orchestra tuning up, she panicked.

I'd better hustle if I don't want to miss the beginning of Act Three.

She was just about to break into a run when she felt an arm grab her from behind. Annoyed, she stopped and started to turn around.

"Larry, will you ever stop sneaking up on me—?"

But it wasn't Larry who was standing behind her.

* * *

Larry rose abruptly from Dr. Ghent's sofa. He had heard enough.

"Dr. Ghent, I can't tell you how valuable this has been. Thank you so much."

214

Nodding his thanks, Larry departed in haste. It was time to get back to the Met and do some very aggressive questioning, even if it meant disrupting a performance in progress.

I need to find out more about Charles. Immediately.

After his hasty departure from the Ansonia, Larry cursed to himself as he shoved his way through the throngs of people clogging the streets. The crowds pouring out from Lincoln Center were always a bitch to navigate. But on weekends, when the theatergoers surged from multiple venues at the same time as the after-dinner hordes, the chaos resulted in gridlock.

He had abandoned his police cruiser at the traffic-choked corner of Broadway and 72nd when he realized he would not make it to the Met unless he hoofed his way there. Walking down any of these congested streets beat driving, but with this mob, going on foot was proving to be a slow process.

Since operas lasted longer than any other type of performance, the Met multitudes were always the last to exit the theater. Larry thanked his lucky stars *Tosca* was still going on when the Philharmonic, the Koch Theater, and Vivian Beaumont were already dark. Otherwise, negotiating the journey down Broadway would have been more like jockeying for space in front of the Saks Fifth Avenue window displays at Christmastime.

As it was, he knew every moment was precious. He checked his watch. Rather than wait for the light to change at 70th Street, he jaywalked across, simultaneously whipping out his cell phone and calling Buddy, who was at the Met, keeping an eye on things.

"Where the hell have you been?"

Larry had no time. "Get up to the stage and make sure Tremaine doesn't go anywhere."

"Where else is he gonna go, boss?"

Larry yelled through the din of traffic and wall-to-wall pedestrians as he pushed his way through the clogged intersection. "I don't have time to explain, just do it."

"One more thing, boss."

"What is it?" Larry strained to hear Buddy through the phone.

"I did some more research and found out the latest. The Wu kid's family's reopened the case. They say it wasn't an accident. That it was murder. No statute of limitations. I think Tremaine came back to the Met and tried to blackmail Trudeau into giving him leading roles, threatening that if the truth finally came out, he would claim Trudeau was an accomplice in the murder. But Trudeau didn't cave, so Tremaine had him killed. The guy's a total psychopath."

"And running loose at the Met." Larry echoed.

Without another word, Buddy clicked off and rushed up to the stage. Larry put on the afterburners.

* * *

Before Julia could turn around fully, she felt something wedged in her back. Something cold and hard, like metal. She pivoted abruptly and found herself facing Frank, wielding a pistol.

Frank wasted no time reacting to her shock. He pointed with his Beretta at her violin.

"Leave it inside the room."

Without a word, Julia stepped back into the room, hesitating for a moment.

"You heard me," he growled, waving the gun. "Hurry it up, I haven't got all night."

Julia placed her violin and bow on the table, closed the door, and came back outside. Frank roughly turned her around and, jamming the gun into her back, thrust her forward, down the hall toward the back stairway. Once they had turned the corner, Julia spied the unconscious officer, prostrate on the floor. She shuddered in terror.

"Is...is he...?"

Frank forced her to step over the body and move on. "No. But that don't mean it won't happen to you."

Without waiting for her response, Frank shoved Julia through the maze of dim hallways and back stairways into unfamiliar territory. She thought of Tony, probably cursing her for not being there, with no clue as to her whereabouts. The sounds of the orchestra playing the Prelude to Act Three of *Tosca* filtering through the P.A. system kept her from losing her grip. The idyllic shepherd's song, accompanied by the innocent cowbell ringing in the background, wafted through the hallways of the opera house, followed by the tolling of a thousand church bells awakening the Eternal City of Rome from its pre-dawn slumber.

Julia strained to listen to the reassuring sounds of the music, which became more distant with each nudge of Frank's revolver, as they wound their way to the most hidden recesses of the opera house. After a few minutes, she had trouble hearing the rich resonance of the four cellos accompanying the dialogue between Charles and the jailer, or the plaintive tones of the clarinet's introduction to Charles's aria, *E lucevan le stelle.* "And the stars were shining..."

Charles. Finding his name in Abel's song had rocked her world.

What did it mean? Why did Abel take such pains to write Charles's name into his song, then encrypt it to be practically undecipherable? And then give it to me?

Julia feared she might never find out the answer to this conundrum. She strained to hear the music, but it faded further into the background as her fright escalated into sheer terror.

* * *

Patricia stood poised over the gleaming stainless-steel toilet in her private executive bathroom. Everything in this lavatory had been custom ordered in stainless steel, from the washbasin to the tiles on the wall. It seemed much cleaner, more sanitary somehow.

She took a long look at her silver vial filled with the precious white powder and rolled it sensuously between her long fingers.

I had to give this up someday, after all. It's as inevitable as giving up a married lover.

Now was as good a time as any to take care of her little "problem." But she had no idea how she was going to get along without the cocaine.

More sex, I imagine, with more "admirers."

She had no lack of them. Perhaps a nice young boy-toy. That might help her forget the comforting rush of the drug seeping into every pore of her body, satisfying a need she thought must have dated from her early childhood. Those fine white particles were the only remedy for the pain: the shame of growing up in a sordid lower-class neighborhood, the wrong side of the tracks in a western Massachusetts mill town. Those memories stayed with her, plaguing her.

Emptying the contents of the vial into the toilet, she watched the grains flush away and disappear. Then she reached her index finger into the vial to extract the last few particles and placed them delicately on her tongue. As she felt the final granules disintegrate, she sighed a regretful farewell.

"Ah...how I will miss you all."

* * *

As Frank led her up darkened back stairways and down secluded hallways with the gun jabbed in her back, Julia quaked with fear. She had never realized how extensive the mazes of isolated back corridors and passageways snaking through the Metropolitan Opera House were. They reminded her of the tunnels leading into *Aida*'s Egyptian pyramids. The vastness of it all...

How will anyone find me? Only a stagehand could make their way through this labyrinth.

Most frightening of all, she had no idea where she was. But she knew she had to maintain whatever composure she possessed to keep her wits about her. Her very survival depended on it.

"Where are you taking me?"

Frank didn't respond.

"They've got cops all over the opera house, you know."

He poked the gun more forcefully into Julia's back and snarled. "Where we're going, they'll never find you. Now move."

Julia stumbled up steep stairs as Frank pushed her along; through a door and over a catwalk with a sheer drop of fifty feet below them, through another door into yet another darkened hallway. She strained to hear the opera sounds coming over the P.A. system, and barely detected the passion between Charles and Dorothy Muir as they sang to each other onstage.

Gradually the music and singing faded into the background until they became inaudible, cutting her off from everything connecting her to her world.

Chapter Forty-One

L'effroi me pénètre
I'm filled with terror.
—Offenbach, *Les Contes d'Hoffman*, Act III

Julia got the answer to her question when she and Frank ended up in front of a door marked "Roof: Caution." Kicking the door open, he shoved her outside. She stumbled out and, overcome with vertigo, blinked at the glittering lights of Lincoln Plaza, nine dizzying stories below.

Frank trained his gun on her. "I tol' ya' they'd never find ya'."

Trying to mask her fear, Julia faced him defiantly. "Oh yes, they will. And you'll be caught red-handed."

Frank sneered. "Too late for you, chickie. Much too late."

Is he going to shoot me? Or something worse...?

Julia tried to think of some way to buy time, to forestall the inevitable.

If I can hold him off, someone will come. I've got to believe that.

She pretended bravado. "I'm missing the third act finale, you know."

"Don't worry, you'll get your finale all right. Your last."

Her stomach sank. His mad expression terrified her.

"Now you mention it, good things come in threes. First Trudeau, then Reynolds—"

Julia gasped. "Abel...and Matt? It was *you*?" She stared at him in disbelief. "I know you were jealous of Matt, but murder? For a job?"

"Are you kiddin' me? It's the best one in the house. The head stagehand has more power than the general manager. I'm on top of the world in that job." Frank smirked. "And I deserve it, too. Reynolds didn't. He was always lording it over me, the bastard."

"But...Abel?"

"That s.o.b.? He was the one who appointed Matt, just because he liked him in bed. God, I hated that Trudeau."

"Enough to kill him? Oh, my God." Agonized, she choked back a sob. "But how—?"

"You can thank the US Army. Their sniper training is the best. Shooting him was easy. So was planting the evidence against Richter and polluting his coffee so he'd have to leave the pit just before the murder. Too bad that orderly in The Tombs didn't use enough poison to kill him. And wasting Reynolds? Easy. But I had to make sure that greaser Geraldo didn't put too much roofie in your drink. That'd deprive me of the pleasure of your company."

"Oh my God. *You* had me drugged?" Julia's voice was now a throaty whisper.

Frank's satisfied smirk spooked Julia even further. "As I was sayin', I hated them both, Trudeau, and Reynolds. They deserved to die. Compared to you, they were easy. You're a feisty piece of ass."

"But why *me*? What have I ever done to you?"

"'*Me*?'" He snorted. "Whaddya' think? Payback. You had to come along, snooping around, sticking your nose where you have no business."

He began to drag her toward the roof's edge. She resisted, kicking, panting from the effort.

He tightened his grip. "See what I mean? Feisty."

As they reached the brink, she averted her eyes from the dizzying height.

"Nothing personal. I was just following orders. We would 'a done the same to any busybody who got in our way."

Her confusion was now complete. "*We?*"

* * *

The third act of *Tosca* was progressing at its normal pace. It was time for the mock fusillade. In the wings, the stage manager spoke into his microphone.

"Firing squad to wings, stage right."

An array of supers in firing squad costumes filtered in and took their positions at the entrance to the stage with military precision. The stage director had coached them to stand in readiness for the dramatic shooting to follow, no matter how impassioned the exchange between the two protagonists. The squad kept their eyes glued to Dorothy and Charles, who were singing their last farewells onstage before Cavaradossi's final ascent to his doom on the flanks of the Castel Sant'Angelo.

"*Tiene a mente: al primo colpo, giù...E cadi bene,*" Tosca reminded Mario. "Keep in mind: at the first shot, down...And fall properly."

"*Come la Tosca in teatro...*like Tosca on the stage."

To his jest, she replied, "*Non ridere.* Mustn't laugh."

The stage manager approached the prop master. "You've checked all the rifles—and the bullets?" he asked through clenched teeth.

The prop master nodded. He had personally double- and triple-checked every weapon to make sure they were filled with blanks. Since Giuseppe's "accidental" shooting onstage, the prop master had been warned repeatedly to be exceptionally sure of the company members' safety when it came to firearms. It was enough to make anyone contemplate early retirement, especially someone who had been in his position for as long as he had been.

Dorothy crouched at Stage Right as the firing squad took aim at Charles and fired. He fell to the floor, just as Tosca had asked him to do.

She exclaimed in triumph. "*Lá! Muori! Ecco un artista!* There! Die! What an actor!"

The dramatic tension of the third act *dénouement* continued to rise. Dorothy crept to Charles's side, singing to his prostrate form in hushed, urgent tones, casting furtive glances at the firing squad.

"*Mario, non ti muovere...*You mustn't move yet."

The squadron walked off scene just as Buddy reached the wings at stage left. He stopped short of the stage, readying himself to detain Charles as soon as the curtain fell. He couldn't wait to find out what Larry had learned from the elderly musician he had interviewed, something that pointed to

Tremaine as a source of information for the investigation. Maybe Larry even liked Charles for a perp.

But whatever the reason for Larry's orders to apprehend the guy, there was no escape for Charles, nowhere he could go but into Buddy's custody.

There was only one problem. The guy lying on the floor wasn't Charles.

Chapter Forty-Two

Quegli è il carnefice...!
He is the murderer...!
—Mozart, *Don Giovanni*, Act I

F rank gave Julia a cryptic smile. "Yeah. *'WE.'* Me and my partner wanted the same thing. Power."

"Good work, partner."

Julia's eyes widened with shock when she turned and saw a tall, costumed figure step out onto the roof.

Charles.

The tenor smiled, first at Frank, then at Julia. "You're wondering why I'm not onstage for the climax, aren't you, Julia? How thoughtful. Right, Frankie?"

Frank nodded, tightening his hold on the Beretta.

"I had a super take my place," Charles continued. "I was more than willing to give up my curtain calls, if it meant I could have the privilege to personally get rid of you."

Julia was incredulous. "Get rid of me! But why?"

Charles smiled. "As an artist, Julia, you of all people should understand my humiliation, my bitterness, at seeing my brother Abel get *all* the kudos through the years."

Julia was overwhelmed with confusion. "Your...brother?

He allowed a moment to let the disclosure sink in. "I changed my name after Abel sank my career. Frankly, I didn't want to share his name, after all the leading roles he'd promised and not delivered." He sneered. "Leading roles? That conniving liar."

Julia regarded Charles in horror as he approached her and Frank. "But what does that have to do with me?"

"Abel chose you over me for his protégée, while he made *me* suffer as an understudy. I just couldn't live with that."

He turned toward Frank. "Give me the gun, Frankie. Your work is done here."

Julia could see that Frank was reluctant to relinquish the weapon. But she was not expecting what happened next. Without a moment's hesitation, Charles fired at Frank, one clean shot aimed straight at the heart. Frank collapsed to the ground in a lifeless heap.

Gaping in disbelief, Julia uttered a sharp cry and was overcome by nausea. *Two important people in my life, murdered. And now, this?*

Julia summoned up her last remaining shred of calm. "Charles, I do understand your feelings of frustration about Abel, but...*murder?*"

Charles raised his eyebrows.

"Just think about it, Julia. From the time we were kids, Abel did everything he could to assure I would remain in his shadow. He garnered all our parents' attention. Then, as adults, all the public's adulation, and all of Mrs. Tallman's money. It was always Abel...Abel...*ABEL.*"

Frantic, Julia tried to think.

By now Larry must know I'm missing. Somehow, he has to figure out where I am, if not now, then within a few minutes. If I'm going to survive, I've got to keep Charles talking.

Fortunately for her, as Julia could see, Charles was in a garrulous mood. "My greatest desire was to see Abel pay. And he did. In front of four thousand of his most adoring fans, thanks to Frank's military training. One shot to the back of the head was all it took."

As surely as the revelation from Sharpless in Act Two of *Madama Butterfly* had punched Cio-Cio San in the gut, Charles's shocker about Abel's murder clobbered Julia like a baseball bat.

Frank shot Abel on orders...from Charles?

Julia was reeling, but she knew her minutes were ticking away. She willed herself to recover from the blow. "But you still made it to the top."

Charles's face turned a furious red. He began to tremble. "No thanks to Abel. He would have done *anything* to keep me off the stage!"

Oh my God, what if the gun goes off, just from the fallout of his anger?

She tried a different tack, softening her voice and summoning up her last shreds of composure. "That night…the one we spent together…"

"Ah, yes, paradise, my darling." He shivered.

"I let you into my heart, Charles. I thought you cared."

"I did. I cared about Abel, too. Just as Cain cared about *his* brother. But…"

He stepped closer to Julia. She cringed.

"Abel knew his days were numbered. After I stole the song, with my name encrypted in it, from Patricia's interoffice mail, he went and gave the only other copy to you. Bastard. I knew then it was just a matter of time until you figured it out and took it to the police to save Sidney's neck."

Julia knew she couldn't deny his claim. She saw his face glow with a surge of what she guessed were feelings of gratification or resentment—or both.

"It was stupid of me not to have destroyed that piece of rubbish when I had the chance. I don't know why I didn't. Perhaps I had a soft spot for you after all."

He pinned her arms behind her back, making her wince. She kept her mouth tightly shut to keep from crying out.

I'm not going to give him the satisfaction of knowing I'm in pain.

"But enough about me. It's time we turned our attention to you, Julia."

Without missing a beat, Charles grabbed Julia by the shoulders and inched her toward the edge. She resisted with all the strength she had acquired from years of holding up a violin for hours on end—and from lifting the dumbbells she kept on her bookshelf.

"Charles, stop!"

"Ah, the girl has spirit, she tries to thwart me." He gave an appreciative little laugh. "'*Ha più forte sapore la conquista violenta*…How much better the taste of a violent conquest.'"

Julia shuddered at his reference to Scarpia's speech, extolling the virtues of taking love by force. Suddenly she understood Charles's identification with the villainous character from Puccini's *Tosca*. Like Scarpia, Charles had a taste for beautiful women. And, like Scarpia, he also happened to be a ruthless, cold-hearted killer.

Breathing heavily, Julia struggled to extricate herself from his ever-tightening grip. "Think, Charles! You won't get away with this."

"Oh, but I will." He smiled. "When the police interview me, I'll tell them I knew Frank had it in for you. The conflicts between you two were well documented. Everyone knew about it. Frank even confided to me he might do you harm."

Julia gasped. "Is that really true?"

"Actually, it is." Charles laughed. "I looked down at the pit during the firing squad scene and saw you were missing. In the melee after the shots were fired onstage, I slipped offstage, ordered a super to take my place and rushed up to the roof. But it was too late to save you. Frank and I struggled for the gun. It went off…"

"No one will believe that!"

"Of course, they will. I'm the star."

"You're insane!"

"Am I? No more so than my dear brother Abel writing my name into a song he knew would outlive him. All performers are insane, you know, one way or another. Who was it that said the music world has the largest number of sociopaths?"

Charles viciously grabbed her shoulder, wrenched her around to face the drop-off, and leaned heavily on her. The lights of Lincoln Center radiated below them, their brilliant glow blinding Julia as her vertigo intensified. She made a Herculean effort to keep her balance.

"What a shame. A pretty, talented girl like you, murdered at the beginning of a stellar career."

Julia strained to keep her footing. Charles turned her around to face him and forced a kiss on her lips. Then he turned her back again and positioned himself.

"Jump, Julia. This is your final performance."

Chapter Forty-Three

Dieu me préserve de ton conseil, misérable assassin!
God save me from your advice, you wretched murderer!...
Il serait dommage en vérité de laisser à la mort une si belle proie...
It would indeed be a shame to hand such a pretty victim over to death...
À la mort qui t'attend je saurai, pauvre enfant, t'arracher, je l'éspère.
From the death that waits for you, you poor child, I hope I shall know how to save you.
—Offenbach, *Les Contes d'Hoffman*, Act III

Lincoln Plaza was quiet, empty of theater-going patrons. The evening's Philharmonic and New York City Ballet performances were long over, and the spaces surrounding the fountain stood at the ready to receive the post-*Tosca* crowd from the Met.

Winded from his sprint down Broadway, Larry darted past the fountain and the street violinist at his usual place, toward the glass revolving doors to the opera house. But before he could reach the entrance, the violinist grabbed Larry's elbow and pointed up to the roof, where Larry could make out the forms of Julia and Charles.

"Jesus!"

Larry dashed into the lobby and screamed at the nearest security guard.

"Get me to the roof! Pronto!"

* * *

228

Discovering that her lover was dead, Tosca/Dorothy became hysterical. A platoon of supers dressed as armed guards charged toward her. She thrust back the leader and made a run for the steep stairs of the parapet.

Larry hurriedly followed the security guard through hallways, up stairways, through one door after another, across catwalks perched precariously above forty- or fifty-foot drops—all in the pursuit of Julia. Larry couldn't believe how complex the opera house landscape was, a veritable network of passageways, back alley-type paths evoking images of Babylon or a futuristic mini-metropolis.

Still, they had not yet reached the roof. And time was running out.

* * *

On the rooftop, Julia could see Charles was basking in his moment of glory.

"Witnessing your demise will be just as pleasurable as seeing Frank blow away my brother," he boasted. "Poor child. If you hadn't antagonized Frank, he wouldn't have pushed you off."

"But he didn't push me!"

Charles ignored her outburst. He turned her to face him, taking a step back for one last admiring glance.

"Let me look at you once more." He sighed. "So naïve, so ingenuous."

Gazing at her, Charles caught a glimpse of Katie's gold cross, nestled at Julia's throat. He laughed. "Ah, the magical cross! How touching. But it won't do anything for you now, Julia. Even God can't save you." With a malevolent smile, he reached over to pluck the necklace from Julia's throat. "You don't mind if I take it as a souvenir?"

Julia clutched the cross. "*Non toccarmi, demonio, vile Scarpia!* Don't dare touch me, you vile—'"

Charles smirked. "How well you've learned your libretto. And how you flatter me, comparing me to that most admirable of villains. I've been waiting for that all my life."

He paused, brushing her neck with his lips. She shuddered in response. Then he drew himself up, shouting. "*Tosca—finalmente mia!*"

Julia recognized the ecstatic expression, the faraway look in Charles's eyes, as the fervor of a performer. She could see that for a split second, he was distracted. It was long enough for her to seize her opportunity. With a sudden jerk, she jammed her elbow into Charles's stomach. He stumbled, losing his footing. Using every shred of her strength, Julia thrust her body at him.

Onstage, Dorothy shrieked her final line as she leapt off the parapet. "*O, Scarpia, avanti a Dio!*" Oh, Scarpia, before God!

At that precise moment, Charles Trudeau plunged to the plaza of Lincoln Center, his body smashing to the pavement.

* * *

Julia looked down from her precarious position on the roof's edge, gasping for breath, as Dorothy/Tosca's last line echoed through her brain.

"Oh, Scarpia, before God!"

The cry, loud and clear, pulsated throughout Julia's mind as if Dorothy's onstage shriek had carried from the theater through the hallways and up the stairways to the soaring heights of the roof.

Julia was still in shock when Larry burst through the door and rushed to her.

"Julia, thank God!"

"Frank and Charles!" Julia sobbed. "They're dead. They killed—"

She clung to him, trembling, sobbing in terror and relief. But when the shock of her near-death encounter with Charles wore off, she pulled back from Larry.

"Where were you? What took you so long?" she asked, her expression suddenly childlike.

"I'm sorry. I had no idea how tough it would be to find my way up here. Are you okay?"

Julia wavered for a moment. "I am now."

She threw her arms around him, hugging him tightly, fully expecting him to be astonished at her spontaneous show of affection. But she was surprised at his readiness to return the gesture, even more so at how comfortable she felt being held by him. He squeezed her so hard she thought he would cut off her oxygen supply, but she didn't care. She just allowed herself to feel cared for.

* * *

Lincoln Plaza was crowded with onlookers. The opera patrons who were just exiting the Met, unaware of what had transpired outdoors, came upon a scene surpassing the one they had just witnessed on the stage. Security guards and NYPD officers were forced to hold them back, along with the bystanders who gathered from the street.

Larry and Buddy discussed the evening's shocking events with two detectives and a police officer from the Twentieth Precinct. Julia stood between them, feeling stunned and drained. She watched, shaken, as paramedics loaded a stretcher carrying Charles's covered body into a waiting ambulance and placed Frank's body in another.

As the E.M.S. vans drove away across the Plaza, lights flashing, Julia felt a slight chill and shivered. Larry took off his jacket and placed it around her shoulders.

"How about a nice, hot cup of tea and *La bohème*—the Carreras recording?" he asked, gazing at her catatonic face.

"Sure, but…" She managed a weary smile. "I'm also open to Elton John."

Larry draped his arm across her shoulders. Julia, glad to entrust herself to him, did not pull away. As they walked off together, he began to sing in a tentative voice.

"'*Dammi il braccio, mia piccina.* Give me your arm, my little one.'"

"Ah, so you're finally singing in public."

He stopped singing and removed his arm. "Not 'in public.' Just with you."

She grinned. "You have quite a nice voice, after all."

"So? Are you going to respond?"

She gave him her arm and joined in, melding Mimì's voice with Rodolfo's.

"'*Obbedisco, Signor.* I obey, sir.'"

Their singing dissolved into the voices of the two lovers pledging their mutual adoration at the end of Act I of Puccini's iconic love story. Julia was surprised at how easy it was, how comfortable for them to harmonize together. She wondered why Larry, whose voice sounded so mellifluous, had kept it to himself for so long. She was overjoyed that he had chosen to share this intimate aspect of his being with her, and she sang along with enthusiasm.

We're just like Mimì and Rodolfo. Well, not quite, but almost. We're not poor artists, but we do have a lot in common, after all.

Rehearsals for *La bohème* were about to start. Evidently, they both had studied the libretto.

Epilogue

È avanti a lui tremava tutta Roma!
And before him, all Rome trembled!
—Puccini, *Tosca*, Act II

The lights in Lincoln Plaza sparkled. Julia ambled past the fountain toward the Met's front entrance and stopped to listen to the street violinist's performance. Smiling her appreciation as he finished his cadenza, Julia reached into her own violin case, pulled out her cherished libretto of *Tosca*, and placed it in his instrument case. He acknowledged her gift with a deep bow. Blushing, she nodded to him and followed the crowds through the revolving doors.

At the switchboard inside the stage door, the security guard greeted Julia with a friendly grin. She reached for her ID, but he waved it aside and ushered her through the gate.

Julia made her way downstairs to Pit Level and went to sign the attendance sheet. Noticing a small "heart symbol" scrawled next to her name, she looked up to see Sidney, close by her side, beaming at her. She gave his arm an affectionate squeeze.

"Thank God, you finally made it, Sid."

"But for the grace of Julia."

"You're not out of the woods yet. You still have to pass probation."

"With my 'little sister' by my side, it'll be a piece of cherry strudel."

As they bantered, Tony appeared and pointed to his watch with a sour expression. Julia and Sidney both groaned. Then Tony grinned at them and walked away, waving his baton at the empty air. Julia and Sidney looked at each other and burst out laughing.

Julia wandered into the women's locker room to find Katie seated on a bench, a sly smile on her face, pointing at a small box taped to Julia's locker. Opening the box, Julia found her violin pin, repaired to perfection, along with a handwritten note.

Katie looked at her, expectant. "Well? My breath is baiting."

Julia read aloud. "'Here's to your real, much overdue debut performance. From Larry.'"

"I once had a fling with a cop. Very hot." Katie grinned. "You could do worse."

"Want me to set you up with one of his friends?"

"Hell, yes."

Without missing a beat, Julia fastened the pin to her blouse and hoisted the strap of her violin case onto her shoulder. She and Katie sauntered toward the door.

Once seated in the pit, Julia tuned her violin, working her brand-new pegs without a problem. Then, when Sidney sat beside her, she pretended to struggle with them.

"What the hell. I just got you brand-new ones."

"I know, Sid. I was just messing with you."

"You'll be the death of me yet, girl."

Sidney nodded in the direction of the pit rail. Julia looked up toward the first row of orchestra seats to see Larry leaning over the rail, beaming at her.

"Better be careful, Larry. It's a long way down."

"You should know."

Julia smiled back at him and pointed to her pin, smiling. He retreated to his seat.

The lights dimmed, and the crystal chandeliers rose to the ceiling, heralding yet another enthralling operatic tour-de-force.

Outside, overlooking all of Lincoln Center, the immense, brilliantly colored Chagall murals stood witness to the greatness of the Metropolitan Opera House.

* * *

Questo è il fin di chi fa mal!
E de' perfidi La morte all' vita è sempre ugual!
This is the fate of those who do wrong!
Evildoers always come to an equally evil end!
—Mozart, *Don Giovanni*, Act II Finale

A Note from the Author

In my 21 years as a violinist at the Metropolitan Opera in New York, I witnessed deadly accidents, suicides, onstage fatalities, and any number of nefarious goings-on behind the scenes. In fact, the level of drama backstage far surpassed what was revealed to the audience onstage. It occurred to me that both opera lovers and mystery novel aficionados might be fascinated by an insider's view of the dark sides of individuals who made the opera house tick: their egos, rivalries, and startling behavior. What I discovered was that the potential for murder and mayhem at an opera house is virtually limitless, and that it's always "dark and stormy" at the Metropolitan Opera. My writer's wicked imagination conjured up scenarios of life imitating art, and the next thing I knew I was solving a whodunit that took place in the world of opera. I tossed my unsuspecting young violinist protagonist into the fray, and voilà: the "Opera Mystery" was born.

Acknowledgements

I would like to thank the following colleagues, both writing and operatic, for their support and inspiration:

Writers James Ziskin and Aaron Paul Lazar for their appreciation of my writing.

International opera stars Richard Stilwell, Lawrence Brownlee and Erin Morley for their inspirational artistry in this unique art form

Met Opera colleagues Mary Ann Archer, Heather Kelley Vella, and Elena Barere, for updating me on the current atmosphere at the opera house.

My writing colleagues at the Puget Sound chapter of Sisters in Crime for their advice and support, and to Mark Wittow of Washington Lawyers for the Arts for his exceptional counsel.

And finally, a shout out to Level Best Books and to my "Besties" for their support. A special thanks to Harriette Sackler, my "Primary" at LLB, for her patience and her belief in my work, and to my extraordinary editor, Shawn Reilly Simmons, for her invaluable help in making the manuscript shine.

About the Author

Formerly a Metropolitan Opera Orchestra violinist for 21 years, Erica Miner now enjoys a multi-faceted career as an award-winning author, lecturer, screenwriter, and arts journalist. Erica's debut novel, *Travels with my Lovers*, won the Fiction Prize in the Direct from the Author Book Awards, and her screenplays have won awards in the Santa Fe, WinFemme and Writer's Digest competitions.

Erica's passion for "Bringing Murder and Music together" is embodied in her 3-part "Opera Mystery" novel series, now being re-published by Level Best Books, starting with *Aria for Murder* at New York's Metropolitan Opera. Drawing on Erica's own real-life experiences working at the Met with Maestro Leonard Bernstein and other superstars of the music world, Erica's young violinist sleuth, Julia Kogan, investigates high-profile murder and mayhem behind the Met's "Golden Curtain." The series continues with the second and third novels taking place at the Santa Fe and San Francisco Opera.

Now based in the Pacific Northwest, Erica also is a top speaker and lecturer. In the music world, she has presented pre-concert lectures for the Seattle Symphony at Benaroya Hall; Osher Lifelong Learning Institute at the University of California San Diego and the University of Washington; the Creative Retirement Institute at Edmonds College in the greater Seattle area; and Wagner Societies in Boston, New York, the Bay Area, Los Angeles, San Diego, North Carolina, and New South Wales (Sydney, Australia). As a writer, Erica has given workshops for Sisters in Crime; Los Angles Creative

Writing Conference; EPIC Group Writers; Write on the Sound; Fields End Writer's Community; Savvy Authors; and numerous libraries on the west coast.

SOCIAL MEDIA HANDLES:
    https://www.facebook.com/erica.miner1
    https://twitter.com/EmwrtrErica
    https://www.instagram.com/emwriter3/

AUTHOR WEBSITE:
    https://www.ericaminer.com

Also by Erica Miner

Murder in the Pit

Death by Opera

Staged for Murder

Travels with my Lovers

FourEver Friends

CPSIA information can be obtained
at www.ICGtesting.com
Printed in the USA
JSHW041920181022
31825JS00001B/71